Great Bones

By
Lynn Ames

GREAT BONES
© 2018 BY LYNN AMES

ISBN: 978-1-936429-14-1

OTHER AVAILABLE FORMATS

eBOOK EDITION
ISBN: 978-1-936429-15-8

PUBLISHED BY
PHOENIX RISING PRESS
PHOENIX, ARIZONA
www.phoenixrisingpress.com

CREDITS
EXECUTIVE EDITOR: ELIZABETH SIMS
AUTHOR PHOTO: JUDY FRANCESCONI
COVER DESIGN: TREEHOUSE STUDIO

Dedication

To my amazing little sister of choice, Ann McMan, who always keeps me on my toes and pushes me to be the very best I can be. This one's for you.

Laughter truly is the best medicine. I love you, Thumper.

In memory of my Grandma Goldie. I can see your twinkling, mischievous blue eyes sparkling as you read over my shoulder. I hope you recognize your spirit in Goldie's adventures, lovingly imagined in these pages. This so would've been you. I love you so much, Grandma. All these years and I still miss you every day.

Acknowledgments

Great Bones has been a long time in the making. Twenty months, to be exact.

It all began on a warm summer day, with a challenge from my dear friend, Ann McMan.

"Get outside your comfort zone," she said. "Write a romantic comedy," she said. "You'll be great at it."

I thought perhaps she'd gone daft from creating one-too-many perfect book covers, but she persisted and insisted that I should do this thing. We workshopped ideas, potential plots, and characters. From that discussion was born the great bones for *Great Bones*. Thank you, Thumper, for the shove in the back and for the fabulous and fabulously fun cover.

Great Bones is my thirteenth book. I work hard at my craft. With each endeavor, I strive to be a better writer than I've ever been before. No one has taught me more about craft than my long-time editor, Linda Lorenzo, who retired just before I finished writing this book. Linda was not just my editor, but a gifted teacher. Linda? Your lessons continue to resonate, helping me to be the best I can be. You have my eternal gratitude for all your hard work. Enjoy your well-earned retirement.

The relationship between an author and editor is paramount. A good book, in the hands of a skilled editor, becomes a great book. A great book becomes even better. My gratitude to editor-extraordinaire, Elizabeth Sims, for stepping into the breach and helping me make *Great Bones* the very best work I've ever done.

My thanks to my team of "first readers" for offering invaluable feedback during the writing process, and to my e-book/website guru, Toni Whitaker, for helping me to make my books available in multiple formats and through multiple avenues, for all of you to enjoy.

Finally, to my extraordinary wife, Cheryl Pletcher, whose love and support carried me through this project—darling, you teach me every day the true meaning of unconditional love. Thank you for laughing with me and loving me. You make all things possible.

*Source for statistics on greeting cards: www.greetingcard.org.

CHAPTER ONE

Rachel Wallach stared at the painting on the wall behind the soft brown leather chair where her therapist sat. It was an abstract, and she found herself wondering if the picture and the placement were intentional. Perhaps the idea was to keep the patient off balance.

"You're staring at the painting again, Rachel."

"I am?"

"You know you are."

"Did you put it there to psych out your patients? You know, to make them wonder…"

"Wonder what?"

"Wonder what they're supposed to see in the image. You know, like in bad movies where the shrink draws conclusions about serial killers based on what they see in an ink blot."

"What do you see in the painting, Rachel?" The therapist's tone was warm and mellifluous, and the skin around her eyes crinkled as she smiled.

"Now you're just playing with me." Rachel picked at a cuticle. She was fond of Malinda. Like Rachel, she was in her mid-thirties, a professional woman, a straight shooter, and, most importantly, she was patient with Rachel's foibles.

"Yep, I am. So, let's pick up where we last left off. As I recall, I asked you a question: What do you see when you look in the mirror? You said you wanted time to contemplate your answer, and that you'd get back to me at our next session."

Rachel sighed and fished in her pocket. She pulled out a crumpled, folded sheet of lined paper and smoothed it on her khaki-clad knee. She cleared her throat and kept her eyes down.

"How I see myself," she read. "Lank brunette hair, an annoying widow's peak, a square jaw, too-high cheekbones, plain brown eyes, a-once-fit-body-now-gone-too-soft…" She chanced a glance at the therapist, then averted her eyes again. "Do I have to go on?"

"No. I get the idea."

"Why was I taking inventory?"

"Because what you see is not what the world sees." The therapist said gently.

Rachel shifted uncomfortably in the buttery leather chair as a silence lingered.

"What if you took the same attributes and described them like this instead?" Malinda finally asked. "Lush, thick brown hair, a distinctive widow's peak, long seen as a sign of beauty, a strong jaw, well-defined cheekbones, intelligent brown eyes, a lithe, capable, curvaceous body…"

"You'd be describing some fantasy woman, not me," Rachel mumbled.

"Says you. Let me ask you another question. Why do you think you described only physical attributes?"

"You asked me what I saw when I looked in a mir—" Rachel wagged a finger. "That was tricky."

"No. That was purposeful. What about the big-hearted woman who read a story about a shortage of blankets and pillows at the local homeless shelter, bought twenty of each online, and had them delivered anonymously the next day?"

"What does that have to do with anything?" Rachel asked.

"Why do you suppose you didn't see that woman in the mirror? That was you, wasn't it?"

"Yes." Rachel pulled at a loose thread on her sleeve. "But those aren't tangible attributes."

"Does that make them any less real?"

"I don't see those in the mirror."

"Maybe you should look a little more closely."

"No, thanks."

Malinda sat forward, hands clasped, elbows resting on her knees. "This is going to seem like a non sequitur, but I assure you it's not. Rachel, you and I have known each other a long time. I remember when you made the decision to go freelance and work from home. Do you remember that?"

"Of course I do. It was a great career move. Working for myself, creating romantic greeting card sentiments for multiple companies, gave me more flexibility and freedom."

"It gave you an out—a way to isolate yourself further—to disappear into your own little world. And that's just what you've done."

"I…" Rachel began, then closed her mouth.

"You what?"

Rachel shrugged. "I'm successful at what I do."

"Yes, you certainly are. But you spend far too much time alone. You need to get back out into the world. You need to integrate the person who writes such beautiful, heartfelt sentiments and gives away anonymous gifts to strangers with the Rachel Wallach who lives in the real world."

Rachel frowned. What was her ex's parting shot? *You're brilliant, but you don't know how to tie your own shoelace. Get your head out of the clouds and get a clue. You're socially inept, devoid of common sense, and terminally awkward. You don't know how to function on a practical level, and you have no idea how to interact with people.*

"When's the last time you went on a date?"

"A date?" Rachel's eyes opened wide with fear.

"Yes. You know, when you meet someone you're attracted to, or might be attracted to—"

"I know what a date is." Rachel tried to quell the panic bubbling up inside. She was no good at dating. Everything her ex had said about her was true.

"Should I repeat the question?" the therapist asked.

"No."

"Rachel," Malinda said softly, "there's no shame or crime in being shy, introverted, and sensitive. You're bright and caring, compassionate and kind. You just need to find the right match for you. You can do this. Let go of your anxiety. Remember to take deep breaths in and let them out slowly."

Rachel rolled her eyes.

"I can't help you if you won't help yourself." Malinda sat back. "Time's up. Do you still have the affirmations I gave you?"

"Yes."

"Good. Keep repeating them. Before the next time I see you, I want you to do two other things for me."

Oh, boy.

"First, I want you to get out of the house and do something ordinary. Go to the store and interact with a stranger. It will do you good. Second, I want you to go on at least one date."

"I… It's going to be a busy time. I've got three sentiments due next week."

"Come on, Rachel. Surely you can find the time to do something fun. Pick an activity you like to do and ask someone to do it with you."

"Like what?"

"What brings you joy? What brought you joy as a child?"

Rachel pursed her lips. "I loved to ride my bike. I could ride forever."

"Good! Invite someone who likes to bike ride to go for a ride with you. It's not that hard. You might like it." Malinda stood. "I'll see you in a couple of weeks."

∾∾

"Be cool. Don't blow it. Blend in." Rachel leaned back and twisted to the side to get a better view of the elderly woman in the housecoat perusing the "Romantic Sentiments" spinner. She recognized that skulking around in the greeting card section of the East Greenbush, New York Target store wasn't exactly what the therapist meant by interaction, but…

She wrapped her fingers around the nearby plastic-and-metal end cap to better balance herself, and gasped as she felt the flimsy metal support break free.

"Oh, my God!" She fell as if in slow motion, the grimy tile rising to meet her left shoulder, elbow, and hip. The metal support strip clattered to the ground next to her, echoing loudly in her ear, only making things worse.

"Dear? Are you all right?" The elderly woman rushed to Rachel's side and stood over her, giving Rachel an up-close-and-personal view of her Tweety Bird slippers with duct tape holding the soles together.

"I'm fine." Rachel scrambled to her feet, her face flushed and hot. She brushed herself off and straightened her blouse, trying to recapture some semblance of dignity. She shoved at the metal support piece with her shoe, trying to hide it under the shelving.

The woman clucked her tongue at the broken rack. "These things are so poorly constructed nowadays."

Rachel met the woman's gaze for the first time. Her eyes were an arresting shade of blue, crystal clear, and kind—so very kind. She reminded Rachel of her Grandma Goldie. Belatedly, she noticed the card the woman was clutching. Her heart thumped happily.

"That's one of my favorites."

"I'm sorry. What?"

Rachel pointed to the card, closed her eyes, and recited the verse from heart, shouting to be heard over the tin tones of the dronelike voice on the public-address system announcing a sale on tampons in aisle fourteen.

"When I awake to see your eyes gazing at me, and your smile welcoming me to the day, the years melt away and we are young again. *I* am young again, and more in love with you than ever. Thank you for being my one and only."

When Rachel finished, she opened her eyes.

The woman sniffled, removed a Kleenex from her left sleeve, and noisily blew her nose.

Rachel's heart sank. "I'm so sorry. I didn't mean to upset you."

"It's not your fault, dear. That was a beautiful sentiment. It's just..." Tears spilled over and the woman used the tissue to stanch the flow. "My Herbert died a few months ago. He loved to surprise me with romantic greeting cards. I miss him so." She moved closer to Rachel and whispered conspiratorially, "Sometimes I come here just to imagine which card he would've bought me next." She paused. "He definitely would've gone for this one."

Rachel swallowed around the lump in her throat.

"Say... How did you know what was in the card?"

Rachel, having barely recovered from the first round of embarrassment, blushed once again to the roots of her hair. What should she say? *Because I wrote it?* She'd never been caught before. There was no precedent for this emergency.

Suddenly, loud music burst forth from Rachel's back pocket.

The elderly woman jumped back and put a hand to her heart. "Goodness, is that the theme from that awful shark movie? What was it? 'Teeth'?"

"'Jaws,'" Rachel supplied.

"That film gave me nightmares for a year."

"Me too." *Which is kind of the point*, Rachel thought. "I'm sorry, I have to take this. If I don't, she'll just keep calling back."

"Don't worry, dear. Nice to meet you."

"Nice to meet you too." Rachel smiled at the woman.

"Who are you talking to?" The voice on the other end of the phone demanded.

"Hello, Mother."

"Is that another new girlfriend? What's this one's name?"

Rachel sighed. "No, Mother. That was just a nice little old lady I met in the store."

"Well, you shouldn't talk to strangers. It's not safe."

"Yes, Mother. Is there something you wanted?"

"I wanted to know if you're coming to Shabbat dinner?"

Rachel rolled her eyes. "I come every Friday, don't I?"

"Well, a mother likes to be sure, you know. I have to decide how much chicken to make and whether I need one challah or two."

Rachel switched hands and put the phone to her other ear as she picked up a tin of Altoids at the checkout counter, paid for them, exited the store, and stepped out into the bright August sunshine. She pocketed the mints, donned her shades, looked both ways, and crossed at the crosswalk. "Do what you've been doing every Friday for the past however many years."

"Did Mrs. Fischer get hold of you?"

Rachel used the key fob to unlock her car door. "For the last time, Mother, I have a job. A job I love. I don't need or want Mrs. Fischer's resume-building services." She slid into the driver's seat and gripped the steering wheel with her free hand, praying for patience.

"What you do *isn't* a real job. Sitting around, making up slogans for old men who can't figure out how to apologize to their wives."

Rachel silently counted to ten. "They're not slogans, they're sentiments. And demographic surveys and focus groups clearly show that women purchase a full eighty percent of all greeting cards. Seven out of ten card buyers say that buying greeting cards is vitally important to them. Annual retail sales for greeting cards run between seven and eight billion dollars."

"Don't be rude."

"What you mean is, don't confuse you with the facts."

"If you're going to insult me like this—"

"Mother, I'm not having this conversation with you. I can't talk on the phone and drive. I'll see you Friday. 'Bye." Rachel leaned her head against the steering wheel...and jumped when the horn sounded. "Perfect." She pulled out of the parking lot. Could this day get any worse?

Goldie Horowitz stuck her head out the door of her one-bedroom apartment in the staff-supervised section of the Shady Acres Assisted Living Community and looked in both directions. She checked her purse for her car keys. She knew it was a risk. She'd already violated the terms of her agreement and gotten caught once using the car. Getting caught a second time likely would get her tossed out on her ear.

She hated being cooped up. Heck, half the reason she'd suggested leaving her car in the parking lot for her granddaughter to use was so she could take it out for a spin when she got tired of the old folks. Nobody knew she kept a spare set of keys, and she intended to keep it that way. She checked the hallway one more time. The coast was clear.

If she hurried, she could catch the one o'clock showing of "Grandma," starring Lily Tomlin, at the cheap theater. She liked Tomlin. She was especially fond of her character, Edith Ann, from the old TV show "Laugh-In." As quickly as her feet would carry her, she bustled down the corridor.

"Mrs. Horowitz!"

Damn. Goldie pretended not to hear.

"Mrs. Horowitz!" The aide tapped Goldie on the shoulder from behind.

Goldie turned around and feigned surprise.

"Where are you going?" The aide yelled and gestured simultaneously. "Did you sign out? Is someone here to pick you up? You know your family took your car keys. You're not allowed to drive anymore."

Goldie blinked as if she was trying to make out what the young man was saying. "Hello, Evan. Beautiful day, isn't it?"

"It is, Mrs. Horowitz. Were you going somewhere?" Evan pointed to Goldie's purse.

"What? Oh, you like my purse? Why, thank you. You have excellent taste. My granddaughter bought it for me." Goldie winked. "She stops by to see me every Friday. She's a good girl."

"She is, Mrs. Horowitz."

"Now don't go getting any ideas, young man." Goldie playfully wagged her finger at Evan. "You're not Rachel's type, if you know what I mean." She winked. She motioned him closer and stage-whispered, "She likes girls."

Evan made a choking sound.

"You shouldn't be so surprised. Even good-looking girls who wear lipstick like my Rachel can be lesbians, you know."

"Of course." Evan looked down at his watch. "Look at the time. I've got to go check on Mr. Bernstein and make sure he's taken his pills."

Goldie blinked as if she wasn't sure what Evan said.

"You need to put in your hearing aids, Mrs. Horowitz," he screamed.

"You have a nice day too, Evan." Goldie lifted her hand in a half wave. When he turned the corner, she checked her own watch. If she hustled, she could still sneak out, make the movie, and be back before dinnertime.

Rachel swallowed the last bite of the Neapolitan ice cream bar she'd bought from the food concession and stared out the window of the southbound Amtrak train at the beauty of the Hudson River on a late summer's day. She imagined she was on one of those cute little sailboats with the love of her life, cruising downriver. She could hear the robins singing in the trees on the shoreline.

"Keep dreaming, Wallach." She cringed as she thought about last Saturday night's disastrous date. Everything had been going so well... Right up until the moment when Rachel helpfully opened the car door at the same time Natalie bent over to retrieve the shiny quarter on the curb outside the restaurant. Three hours in the emergency room, one mild concussion, and a dozen stitches later, they parted ways without so much as a handshake.

Well, at least her therapist couldn't say she wasn't trying. And she'd gotten to dinner. That was a marginal improvement over the previous three dates, none of which had progressed beyond a cup of coffee.

Rachel sighed. She threw away the ice cream wrapper and stick, picked up her pen, and refocused on the yellow legal pad in front of her.

"When I look into your eyes, I see my past, my present, and my future. You make my world complete. Happy anniversary to the great love of my life."

She cocked her head and considered what she'd written. It wasn't horrible. But it didn't exactly have great bones, either. That's what her editor would say. Every greeting card sentiment needed to pop—beginning with the perfect foundation.

"It's a start, anyway," Rachel mumbled. She yawned and her eyelids drooped. If she closed her eyes now, she could get in a quick power nap before Penn Station. There, she would catch the shuttle to Grand Central Station and transfer to the commuter train to New Rochelle, where her Grandma Goldie would be waiting for her weekly visit. "I just need ten minutes..."

The conductor woke her as he passed by. "Penn Station! Last stop. Penn Station. Make sure to check around your seat for your belongings."

Rachel stretched and wiped the back of her hand across her mouth. Apparently, she'd been catching flies again, her mouth no doubt agape as she drooled and quite possibly snored. "All traits certain to land you the woman of your dreams," she mumbled to herself.

The train slowed and stopped. Rachel slipped the writing pad into her briefcase. Her fingers brushed against the carefully wrapped rectangular box inside. She hoped Grandma Goldie would love her new iPad. Rachel planned to teach her how to buy movies and ebooks and how to video chat. She worried about her cherished grandmother. Surely the move to that sterile old-folks environment must be taking a toll on her.

In truth, these Friday treks south to her parents' house in Scarsdale to honor the Sabbath had nothing to do with being a dutiful daughter, and everything to do with having an opportunity to visit with her favorite grandmother along the way. Rachel checked her watch. If the shuttle to Grand Central showed up quickly enough, she could catch the 3:35 and have a little extra time with Goldie before dinner.

∾∿

"Bubbeleh, you look so tired. Are you sure you're getting enough sleep? Is that nasty editor of yours being too hard on you again? Do you want me to go over there and give her what-for and how-come?"

Goldie patted the bed and motioned for Rachel to sit next to her. Her favorite granddaughter looked gaunt, with dark circles under her eyes. Her shoulders were rounded as if in defeat. This wouldn't do at all.

"I'm fine, Grandma."

Goldie worked hard not to wince as Rachel shouted in her ear. It was her own fault, she knew. Whatever had possessed her to feign deafness and memory issues, she couldn't imagine.

Ahh, who was she kidding? Of course she knew why. Anybody who spent more than five minutes with her overbearing, pain-in-the-tush daughter knew why. True, Goldie admitted to herself, she might have picked more convenient afflictions to warrant moving out of the in-law apartment behind her daughter and overmatched son-in-law's house. But it was too late for that now and there was no use crying over spilled milk.

"Yeah, well, you don't look so fine to me." Goldie affectionately pinched Rachel's cheek.

"I brought something for you." Rachel fished in her briefcase and pulled out a purple polka-dotted package tied with a pretty pink bow.

"That's nice, but you know I don't need anything."

"I know, but I wanted to get this for you." Rachel presented her with the box.

Goldie set it aside. She didn't like the idea of her granddaughter spending hard-earned money on trinkets for her. It should be the other way around—she should be buying for Rachel.

"Aren't you even going to open it?"

"Later, darling. Right now it's time for the show."

"What show?"

"It's suppertime in this joint. You can keep me company before you have to deal with your mother. Let's go make fun of the old folks."

Goldie's heart swelled with affection as Rachel stood and held her hands out for Goldie to take. She was so thoughtful, this girl—so unlike her mother. Where had she gone wrong with Deborah? "I didn't. Morris spoiled her. That was the trouble. If only he'd listened to me..."

"What's that, Grandma?"

"Hmm?" She hadn't realized she'd spoken out loud.

"You were saying something."

"Was I?" Goldie waved dismissively. "Never mind that. I'll bet you five dollars that pork chops are on the menu tonight." This was an ongoing joke between them.

Rachel squeezed Goldie's hand. "Why, Grandma. I'm shocked. Shocked, I tell you. A respectable, kosher facility like this serving pork on the Sabbath? I'll take that bet and double it."

"Save your money so you can break me out of this joint and take me to the ocean on vacation."

The dining room was bustling. Wheelchairs and walkers lined the walls, staff scurried back and forth carrying plates of food to the residents from the kitchen, and the loud buzz of conversation sounded like the hum of thousands of bees.

Goldie paused just inside the glass double doors. There wasn't an empty table in sight.

"Gold-e-lah. Could it be? Is that you?"

Goldie squinted at the matronly woman waddling toward them with a walker, one arm waving and the walker weaving unsteadily. No, it couldn't be. "Ida? Ida Pinsky?"

"Yep. Believe it or not, I'm still alive and kicking. God willing, I'll be here a while longer."

17

"How did you end up here?"

"Meh. You know how it is, Gold-e-lah. One day you're useful and trundling along, the next you're yesterday's news and life has passed you by. But, I don't complain. After all, I'm still here and I've got all my marbles."

"Thank God," Goldie said.

"Who's this beautiful young woman?" Ida nodded in Rachel's direction.

"This?" Goldie beamed at Rachel. "This is—"

"Oy! Look at the time!" Ida pointed to the oversized clock on the dining hall wall. "I'm going to be late for water aerobics!" She patted Goldie on the arm. "Good to see you, darling. We'll catch up soon."

Before Goldie could answer, Ida was out the door.

✦✦

"Hurry up! It's almost sundown. You know we have to get the Shabbat candles lit before sunset. Where have you been?"

Rachel prayed for patience. "I got here as soon as I could, Mother. It's nice to see you too." She gave her mother the obligatory peck on the cheek.

"Squirt." Rachel's older brother, Paul, punched her lightly in the arm. "I see you dressed for the occasion." He tugged on the sleeves of his custom-made dress shirt, the diamonds in his cufflinks winking in the light from the setting sun streaming in through the open blinds.

Rachel caught herself as she self-consciously glanced down at her khakis and Eddie Bauer non-wrinkle button-front shirt. "Paul." She crossed her arms.

"Hello, Rachel." Her sister-in-law, Tiffany, gave her an air kiss.

Rachel's eyes watered. Her nose twitched. *Here it comes.* She closed her eyes. *Don't do it. Hold it. Don't do it...* Ahhh... Ahhh... Ahhh chooooo! That darned cloying perfume got her every time.

Rachel refocused on her sister-in-law. Was it possible that Tiffany had had even more Botox? Pretty soon her lips were going to precede her through the door.

18

"Hi, honey." Rachel's father gave her a warm hug.

"Hi, Daddy."

"Rach." Rachel's sister nodded coolly in her direction.

Rachel lifted her chin in return greeting. As usual, Erin looked flawless—self-assured and in control. And why wouldn't she be? Rachel felt the familiar blanket of insecurity creep over her.

Erin was everything she was not—confident, accomplished, beautiful—the most sought-after eligible doctor in the tri-state area. She had more suitors than the government had lawsuits against it, and she presided over a thriving plastic surgery practice that boasted a coterie of A-list actors and actresses.

I am successful. I am accomplished. I am enough. Rachel silently repeated the mantra Malinda insisted she carry on a piece of paper in her wallet, even though she had long ago memorized the phrases.

"Let's go, everybody. It's almost sundown." Deborah Wallach scurried around the kitchen, her apron stretched tightly over her belly. Her practical low heels clicked with purpose on the worn hardwood floor. "Here, take these." She shoved two white tapers at Rachel along with a book of matches from the Chinese restaurant down the block.

Rachel carried the candles into the dining room and placed them on the sideboard. She turned just as her mother thrust the pewter tray with the challah bread at her. Dutifully, Rachel reached into the top drawer of the sideboard and withdrew a white linen napkin. She used it to cover the loaf of bread and set the tray in the middle of dining room table.

Paul was busy pouring the wine into fine crystal goblets. As usual, Tiffany pretended to find something fascinating to look at on the wall.

"God forbid you should ruin your manicure doing manual labor like preparing the Sabbath table," Rachel grumbled under her breath. She blew a puff of air up in an effort to move an errant strand of hair out of her eyes. As usual, she was in dire need of a haircut.

"Places everyone!" Rachel's mother bellowed. "Richard!"

"I'm right here, dear. No need to shout." He winked at Rachel behind his wife's back.

The family gathered in a semicircle behind Deborah as she fumbled with the matchbook.

Rachel rolled her eyes. "Mother, you know it's not against the law to use a lighter, or at least a box of wooden matches, right?"

Her mother shot her a withering glare. "Our foremothers didn't use lighters or wooden matches," she snapped.

"They didn't use paper matches, either," Rachel said behind her hand.

After wasting three matches, Deborah finally was able to get one to flare. She lit the pair of tapers, set the spent match in a small silver dish, extended her hands over the candles, drew them toward her three times in a circular motion, then covered her eyes.

In her most dramatic voice, she intoned the blessing of the candles:

"Baruch a-ta A-do-nay Elo-hei-nu me-lech ha-o-lam a-sher ki-di-sha-nu bi-mitz-vo-tav vi-tzi-va-noo li-had-leek ner shel Sha-bat. Blessed are you, Lord our God, King of the universe, who has sanctified us with His commandments, and commanded us to kindle the light of the Holy Shabbat."

"Good Shabbes everyone," Deborah said.

They seated themselves, Richard at one end, Deborah at the other, Paul and Tiffany on one side of the oblong table, Erin and Rachel on the other. Richard blessed the wine, Paul blessed the challah and sliced it, and Deborah commanded, "Eat slowly, everyone. This meal took me all day to make."

Over the clattering of the dishes, Deborah smiled at Paul and patted him affectionately on the hand. "So, what's this talk I hear about the stock market taking a nose dive? Do your father and I need to worry?"

"Absolutely not. I closed three multimillion-dollar trades in an hour today. The market's rock solid."

"Paul bought me a new necklace to celebrate. See?" Tiffany leaned forward so that the sapphire-and-diamond pendant swung freely from the delicate gold chain.

"It's beautiful," Deborah said. "See, Richard? Our son knows how to reward a woman properly."

"Mm-hmm."

"And you, Erin darling? Treat anyone exciting this week?"

"Mother, you know I can't divulge who my patients are."

"I know that. But you could at least give us a hint. It wouldn't kill you to throw us a bone."

Erin expertly dissected the chicken leg and thigh on her plate. "Okay. And this is all I'm going to say: His butt has launched a thousand female fantasies."

"Oh." Deborah put her fork down and rested her chin on her palm. "If I guess it, will you confirm?"

"Mother..."

"Well, you can't just leave it at that."

"I can and I did. Change the topic."

"What about you, Rach?" Paul asked. "Saving the world one saccharine sentiment at a time?"

Rachel's nostrils flared. She pushed the pile of peas around her plate. "As it happens, I picked up a contract with a new boutique greeting card company that looks promising."

When no one else said anything, Richard said, "Good for you, sweetheart. Pass the bread, please."

Rachel sighed. *I am successful. I am accomplished. I am enough. I am successful. I am accomplished. I am enough.*

CHAPTER TWO

Rachel stood with her hands on her hips in front of the mirror. This was a bad idea. A very, very bad idea. A blind date based on what was likely a false online-dating profile? Heck, she couldn't even have a good dating experience with someone she already sort of knew. And a twelve-mile bicycle ride? Oy!

She tugged at the too-tight spandex shorts. She grabbed the crotch pad in the front and back and pulled down, and then turned sideways to view the effect. The wedgie persisted.

"I bet these monstrosities were designed by the same idiot who invented panty hose and high heels," she muttered. "Smart money says it was a man. No woman in her right mind would think these were flattering."

A car horn blared in the driveway and Rachel jumped. She put her hand to her heart and checked her watch. "Early? Who in the world arrives early to a first date?"

Rachel took one last look in the mirror, tucked her moisture-wicking shirt in, thought better of it, and pulled it out again. She grabbed her newly filled water bottle off the kitchen counter on her way out the door.

The late-summer sun's rays temporarily blinded her, preventing her from seeing her date's face as she sat behind the steering wheel.

Rachel grumbled, "That's probably intentional because she's hiding the fact that her face doesn't match her profile. Besides, what kind of person doesn't at least get out of the car to introduce herself the first time she meets someone?" Rachel shook off the sinking feeling that this was going to be a disastrous day. She rehearsed lines on her way down the front steps.

"Hi, how are you? Yes, I know these shorts make me look like a sausage busting out of its casing. I hope you'll overlook that and withhold judgment until you get to know me." *Brilliant. Apologize upfront for your shortcomings. That's attractive.*

Rachel reached the bottom step and gave a small wave in the direction of the Subaru as her would-be date finally emerged. Remarkably, her appearance did match her online profile. She was long, lean, and leggy, obviously fit, and dressed in the type of bike shorts racers wore. They showed off her muscular thighs.

Maybe this won't be so bad, after all. Just then, out of the corner of her eye, Rachel spied a blonde streak barreling directly toward her. Panic welled up in her chest. Her heart pounded and she screamed, "Freud!"

Rachel waved her hands in the air ineffectually as a huge, fluffy golden retriever/Siberian husky mix began weaving in and out of her legs. When he tired of that, he jumped up on Rachel, a paw on either shoulder, and licked her face. "Get him off me! Get him off me!"

"There, there, handsome man. Don't mind the hysterical woman," Rachel's date said. "Come here."

Rachel watched in horror as her date rubbed the dog and allowed him to slobber on her leg at will.

Rachel's elderly next-door neighbor, Mr. Crawford, toddled over. "Hiya, Rachel. I'm sorry about that. You know how this guy is. He's drawn to the ones who are afraid of him."

"You're afraid of dogs?"

Rachel bristled at the disapprobation on her date's face. "I'm not scared."

"Really? Because you just screamed like a girl."

"I am a girl, in case you didn't notice."

The dog's head swiveled from Rachel to her date and back again. He panted and wagged his tail.

Mr. Crawford took off his sweat-stained ball cap and scratched his head. "C'mon, Freud. I think we'd best leave this to the girls to sort out." He whistled, and the dog heeled as he walked away. "See you later, Rachel...and your friend."

Rachel wanted to sink into a hole. The entire ordeal was mortifying. And now she was supposed to spend the day with this woman?

"Let's start over, shall we?" Her date held out her hand. "Hi. I'm Stephanie. You must be Rachel."

"I am." Reluctantly, Rachel shook the slightly slobber-coated outstretched hand. "For the record, my only exposure to dogs was being chased down and bitten by a standard poodle when I was five. I had an impression of a bite mark on my arm for weeks and I had to get rabies shots. I had nightmares for months. We never had animals in our house."

"You don't know what you were missing. Animals are about unconditional love, unlike humans," she added, with a shudder.

I will not make snap judgments, I will not make snap judgments, I will not make snap judgments. Just because the woman doesn't believe humans are capable of unconditional love doesn't mean she's incapable of opening her heart to it.

"Let's get rolling," Stephanie said. She stalked over to where Rachel's old ten-speed bicycle was leaning against the garage, grabbed it, and secured it to her bike rack.

Despite mounting misgivings about this date, especially Stephanie's apparent lack of empathy for her, Rachel got in the Subaru. She pressed her back into the welcoming support of the passenger seat. She squeezed her shoulder blades together in an effort to release the tension that had taken up residence in the center of her spine the moment Freud made his ill-timed dive between her legs.

Stephanie slid into the driver's seat and backed out of the driveway without another word.

After fifteen too-quiet minutes, Rachel chanced a glance at her date's profile. Her jaw muscles were jogging back and forth like athletes doing wind sprints. Rachel idly wondered if Stephanie had her endodontist on speed dial. She searched for something, anything, to say to break the ice.

"So, do you bike often?" *Lame, Rach. Totally, embarrassingly lame.*

"I belong to a women's collective. Three days a week we tend our communal organic garden. The other four days, we cycle.

Every other week, we take Saturday off. It's why I had time to fit you in today."

"That sounds very...regimented." Rachel winced at her word choice. "And by that I mean, that takes a lot of dedication. I admire that kind of commitment." *Oh, my God. Did I just use the "C" word? On a first date? Oy!* Maybe the floorboards would open up and she could just fall through. But Subarus were too well built for any hope of that.

In the awkward silence that ensued, Rachel counted the number of bugs bouncing off the windshield. Ten minutes later, they pulled into a parking lot accessing the Mohawk Hudson Bike Trail.

"We're here," Stephanie announced.

No kidding. Rachel unbuckled her seatbelt and, with as much grace as she could muster, scrambled out of the bucket seat. By the time she reached the back of the vehicle, Stephanie had unfastened both bikes from the rack. Rachel's steel-frame bike looked positively ancient next to Stephanie's state-of-the-art, carbon-fiber bike.

"I hope you brought your own water," Stephanie said. "I didn't bring any extra."

"I did." Rachel held up the plastic bottle she'd dug out of her childhood sleep-away camp trunk. She took a swig of water and nearly spit it out on the ground. *Eww. Eww. Eww.* It tasted like the bottom of Lake Sebago. She calculated in her head. The last time she'd swum in that lake had been...too long ago to count on her fingers. Fabulous. Why hadn't she rinsed out the darned bottle?

"This trail is rated for novices." Stephanie was sizing her up. "You should be all right."

Rachel opened her mouth to object—to tell her she worked out three times a week—and then decided it wasn't worth the effort. Stephanie held her bike out to her. She took it and swung her leg over the seat, grateful that she cleared it without incident. "Lead the way."

∾∿

Rachel squinted. She could make out Stephanie's royal purple bike jersey faintly, in the distance. She pedaled harder, grunting as her front tire bounced over yet another melon-sized stone on the rough path. Her spine had already suffered so many shocks she was sure this ride would make her two inches shorter.

"Stop isolating yourself," Grandma Goldie and Malinda had said. "As a little girl, you loved riding your bike. Find a girl who likes to ride bikes."

"Well, here I am following your advice. And all it's getting me is a sore ass and an acute need for a chiropractor."

Rachel's teeth knocked together as if to emphasize the point. She rounded a bend in the trail. That's when she heard a sharp pop and the telltale hiss of air. "A puncture? Seriously? You've got to be kidding me!"

She managed to brake the bike to a safe stop as the front tire went dead flat, perfectly matching Rachel's mood. She dismounted and stared at the bike in disgust. Her date was nowhere in sight. Briefly, she contemplated calling or texting Stephanie's cell phone.

"Surely when she realizes I'm not behind her anymore she'll double back and check on me." Rachel calculated that they'd ridden approximately six miles, meaning they were just about halfway back to the car. Rachel hoisted the bike onto her shoulder and walked.

Two hours later, neither the parking lot nor her date were anywhere in sight. Sweat dripped into Rachel's eyes and down between her breasts. She groaned and lowered the bike down off her shoulder. Rest. She just needed a few minutes of rest. She tipped up her bottle and drank the last of the vile water.

Her phone, nestled in a holster on her hip, buzzed. She grabbed it up and scanned the text on the screen.

"Where in the blazes are you?"

Rachel typed. "NOW you want to know? I've been missing for hours, and NOW you want to know where I am????" She closed her eyes, composed herself, and held her finger down on the words. When the pop-up box appeared, she clicked on "Select All," and "Cut."

"I had a flat tire two hours ago. I've been carrying my bike ever since."

She watched the telltale three dots appear. Stephanie was typing. *Thank God, she'll come back and help me out.* Her shoulder was so raw where the bike frame rubbed against it, she half expected a mountain lion to appear to claim the fresh meat.

"Well, that blows. Get a move on or we'll be late for our dinner reservation."

Rachel read the text twice. Surely there must be missing sentences, like the part where Stephanie said, "Oh, my God. Stay there, I'll come get you." She waited. Nope. No more three dots. She waited some more. Her incredulity turned to irritation, and then anger. She shoved the phone back into the holster, shifted the bike to the other, only-half-raw shoulder, and trudged onward.

An hour later, she limped off the trail and onto the pavement. She stumbled forward, dropped to her knees, and let the bike slide off her shoulder and to the ground.

"Why didn't you have a tire repair kit with you?"

Rachel blinked and shook the sweat out of her eyes. Stephanie was standing over her, cool as could be and looking peeved. Rachel considered and rejected a dozen sarcastic retorts. Instead, she pushed herself to her feet and brushed the gravel from her hands.

"I guess I wasn't expecting to have a flat tire." There, that was neutral, practical, and honest.

Stephanie glanced at her watch. "If we hurry, we'll still have time to shower and make the reservation."

Rachel opened her mouth to tell Stephanie what she could do with the dinner reservation. But she was hungry. As if to emphasize the point, her stomach growled.

Stephanie hoisted the bike onto the rack and motioned for Rachel to get in the car. "I'll drop you at your place, go shower, and come back and get you. Can you be ready within an hour?"

"From now? Or from when you drop me off?"

"Now."

"I suppose." Her body wanted to object. Heck, every part of her being wanted to object. This encounter was going farther south than a snowbird migration. Still, she was hungry. Surely the date couldn't get any worse than this...

℞℞

"She took me to an Indian restaurant, Grandma. An Indian restaurant!" Rachel made a face like she'd just tasted a mouthful of gefilte fish. "She never even asked me whether I liked Indian food. It was the worst meal I've ever eaten."

Goldie wanted to lighten the mood. She wanted to see her beautiful Rachel smile again. Not to mention that the decibel at which her granddaughter was screaming the story was making her ears practically bleed. "I bet it wasn't worse than that time you ate that tube of Nivea cream. Or that time your mother accidentally made the turkey gravy with baby powder instead of flour."

"Grandma! I'm being serious here. This was the worst date in the history of worst dates! I will never, *ever* use a dating service again."

"Okay. Genug. Enough, already. We'll cross that evil girl, whatever-her-name-is, off the list. She's not good enough for you anyway."

Rachel put her head on Goldie's shoulder. "I should just give up, Grandma. I try and try, but I just don't think the right woman is out there for me."

Goldie wrapped her arms around Rachel and rocked her. "Nonsense. The right girl is out there, you just haven't found her yet."

"I don't think I ever will."

"Hush. Of course you will. Any girl with half a brain would be lucky to have you."

"I love you, Grandma, but I'm just a disaster waiting to happen on dates. I've got to go. I'll be late, and you know how Mother is."

"Oy, do I know how your mother is." Goldie pulled back and kissed Rachel on the cheek. "Will I see you next week?"

"Have I ever missed a Friday?"

"Not so far."

"I'll see you next week, Grandma. I love you."

"I love you, too, bubbeleh."

Rachel paused at the door to Goldie's tiny bedroom and waved before disappearing out of sight.

Goldie sat on the edge of the bed, waiting for the sound of the apartment door closing. "One-Mississippi, two-Mississippi, three-Mississippi, four-Mississippi... When she'd counted to ten, she rose, shuffled over to the door leading to the hallway, and peeked around the corner. Not a soul in sight. Not even that eagle-eyed pain-in-the-tush, Evan. Good. In truth, Goldie admitted, he was a nice young man—good-looking too. He had good teeth, a full head of black hair, muscles, and a sincere smile. But his timing always was problematic for her escapades.

"Room 1492. The year Columbus discovered America." Goldie consulted the oversized facility map on the back of her door. Of course Ida's room would have to be clear on the other side of the building. Well, no distance was too far when the happiness of her granddaughter was at stake.

"Hi, Saul... What? No, I don't want to see your cummerbund from your high school prom." Goldie shook her head and continued down the hall. Old men. She was glad her Morris, God rest his soul, hadn't outlived his mind.

"Aha." After what seemed like miles, Goldie finally found Ida's place. She knocked on the door.

"Come!"

"Ida? Are you decent?"

"Gold-e-lah? It depends on your definition. Come on in."

Goldie stepped inside and glanced around. Ida's place was identical to hers. She passed through the tiny kitchenette and into the living room. Ida's sofa was against the wall under the bank of windows, just like hers. Ida even had a red velvet lift chair in the space where Goldie's recliner sat. That's where Ida was sitting. The place smelled of chocolate and air fresheners. "So, are you settling in?"

"Eh. I'm doing, you know what I mean?"

Goldie nodded. She remained standing in the center of the living room.

"It's not the old neighborhood, that's for sure. And the food? Oy. Don't get me started. Still, I wake up on the right side of the dirt. Life is good. Speaking of which... Did you know they make t-shirts that say that now? 'Life is good?' Can you imagine? I hear it's a multimillion-dollar business. Gold-e-lah, if we'd known all we needed to do was put three words on a piece of cotton, we'd have hit it rich!"

Goldie watched for her opening. Surely Ida would run out of air and have to take a breath soon so she could get a word in edgewise.

30

"Anyway… I'm sure that's not why you're here." Ida pointed to the sofa. "Come. Sit and tell me what brings you to my neck of the woods."

Finally! "Are you still a yenta?" Goldie sat on the end of the sofa nearest her friend.

"Goldie Horowitz! You should be ashamed of yourself. I, my dear, am a shadchan. Why do you suppose those nebbishes who wrote 'Fiddler on the Roof' got such an important detail wrong? Everybody knows a yenta is a busybody. A shadchan…" Ida puffed out her chest. "A shadchan is a matchmaker."

"So, Ida. Are you still in the business?"

"Me? Nah. Are you kidding? Nowadays these kids go on the radio…"

"The computer. You mean they go on the computer."

"Yeah, yeah. That box thing that sits like a paperweight on their desks." Ida stared off into space.

"You were saying?" Goldie prompted.

"What? Oh, yeah. Nowadays these youngsters find their own dates. They do a lousy job of it too. Have you seen the Jerry Springer show? Oy. The number of divorces. In our day, you got married and you stayed married."

"Ida?"

"Anyway, the damned radio…"

"Computer."

"Put us out of business."

"That's a shame."

"Why are you asking?"

"It's my granddaughter-the-lesbian."

"Your granddaughter is an actress?"

Goldie paused. "No. Not a THESPIAN. A l-e-s-b-i-a-n!" she shouted.

"Your granddaughter's a lesbian? Shh. Who are you telling?"

"Oy." Goldie slapped her palm to her forehead. "It's not the way it used to be. You should try to keep up with current events, you know that? Anyway, she's got terrible girl troubles and I'm determined to see her happy and settled before I kick the bucket. But she's already told me she'd never resort to a computer dating service again. Thinks they're a waste of time. She had a bad experience."

Ida tapped her finger against her temple. "I don't know, Gold-e-lah. Girls looking for love matches with other girls?"

Goldie's back stiffened. "Love is love, Ida. There's nothing wrong with my Rachel. She just happens to prefer other women to men. Truth be told, she's probably the smartest of the bunch."

Ida held up a hand defensively. "Slow down. No one's casting aspersions here. I just meant that I don't have any experience..."

Goldie waited patiently. She'd seen that expression on her friend's face many times. She was sorting through the challenge.

Finally, Ida's eyes lit up. "You know, I *did* train my granddaughter in the old ways. She's young and hip. I'm sure she's dealt with this sort of thing before. She runs some fancy-schmancy dot-come matchmaking service. Why they named it after some woman named Dorothy I have no idea—"

"Dot com," Goldie interrupted. "Like on the computer. There was no Dorothy."

"Whatever, Gold-e-lah. The point is, she still knows how to do things old-school. I could talk to her about it."

"We'd have to be sneaky about it. My granddaughter wouldn't like us unterschtupping."

"Discreet is my granddaughter's middle name. Your Rachel will never know we had anything to do with it."

"Your granddaughter could never let on what she was doing. She'd have to find a way to send dates without letting my granddaughter know where they came from."

"That wouldn't be a problem. My Julia is very clever."

"I can pay her."

"It's a deal. She's coming to visit on Tuesday. I'll introduce you."

CHAPTER THREE

Rachel stared at the computer screen. The blinking cursor mocked her. In fact, it had been mocking her for the past three hours. "It's a simple thing. Three lines. Four max. You've just found your true love. The one. How do you feel?" She drummed her fingers on the keyboard. "How the hell would I know?"

She laid her head on the desk. Her shoulders screamed as the cotton fabric of her shirt brushed against her still-inflamed skin. "Ouch."

Her pop-up alert chimed. She lifted her head to read it. Hi. This is yourbestdate.com. We see that you accepted a date with Stephanie, whose profile you saved. We're just checking to see how your date went? Would you like to send feedback to her?

Rachel blew a raspberry at the screen. "How's that for feedback?" She grabbed the mouse with more force than was necessary and navigated to the dating company's website. She positioned the mouse over the "delete profile" button only for a second before clicking on it.

Are you sure?

"I am more positive than you can ever imagine." Then, for good measure, she went to the "My Account" page and deleted her account.

Are you sure? Once you delete this account, it cannot be reopened.

"Oh, I am so sure." Once it was done, Rachel felt unaccountably lighter. She toggled back to her Word document.

"I never imagined in my lifetime I would find THE one. In you, I fulfilled all of my heart's desires. You are the answer to every dream I ever had and every prayer I ever whispered. In you, I found my one, true love."

Rachel rolled back her chair and reread the words. It would need some revision, but it was a good start.

◈◈

"Knock, knock."

Goldie looked up from her game of solitaire to see Ida standing in her doorway. Next to her was a tall, lanky drink of water, stylishly dressed in black slacks and a gray sleeveless sweater.

"Goldie Horowitz, this is my beautiful granddaughter, Julia Spielman." Ida beamed with pride and nudged the woman forward.

"It's a pleasure to meet you, Mrs. Horowitz." Julia held out her hand.

Goldie pushed aside the snack table on which she'd been playing the card game, leveraged herself out of her La-Z-Boy, and took the proffered hand. "Oh, you have a firm grip. Good for you. That says a lot about a person."

"Mrs. Horowitz—"

"Goldie, please. Mrs. Horowitz was my mother."

"Goldie."

Julia smiled and Goldie was happy to see that it reached her eyes. You could tell a lot about a person from her smile. And her eyes. Goldie peered into Julia's eyes. The sunlight streaming in through the half-opened blinds made it easier for Goldie to see. Julia's eyes were hazel, and warm. Good.

"Gold-e-lah? You okay?"

Goldie blinked. It wasn't polite to stare. Had she been staring? Probably. Eh. She was an old lady. Everybody expected old people to do odd things. "You were saying?"

Julia smiled indulgently. "I was about to say that my grandmother tells me you're a very special friend of hers. Any friend of my grandma is a friend of mine."

"Your grandmother and I have known each other ever since we were little girls. We played together, went to school together as children, and came from the same neighborhood."

"Wow. That's a lot of history."

34

Goldie decided to dive right in. "Speaking of history, your grandmother was known far and wide for her matchmaking skills. She tells me the apple doesn't fall far from the tree. Is that true?"

"I'm telling you, Gold-e-lah. This girl knows from the old ways. Don't you, bubbeleh?" Ida squeezed Julia's hand.

"Don't exaggerate, Grandma."

"Who's exaggerating?"

"Anyway, I'm sure you don't want to hear about that, Mrs. Hor…Goldie."

"Actually, that's exactly what I want to talk to you about." Goldie motioned for Ida and Julia to sit on the sofa.

"Goldie has a granddaughter." Ida lowered her voice to a conspiratorial whisper. "She's one of…*those*."

"What your grandmother is telling you is that my Rachel is a lesbian." Goldie held Julia's gaze. "That's not a problem for you, is it?"

Julia swallowed hard. Her eyebrows rose and she blanched. "Of course not. But I don't see what that has to do—"

"Goldie says her granddaughter has girl trouble. She wants you to find her a match. A *girl* match."

Goldie thought Julia looked about to bolt. "Do you have something against lesbians?" she asked.

"Me? N-no," Julia sputtered.

"Ida tells me you run some fancy dating service. My Rachel had a very bad experience with one of those. I hope it wasn't yours."

"I-I'm sure it wasn't."

"I was telling Goldie, here, that you wouldn't need any fershtinkiner radio—"

"Computer," Goldie and Julia said simultaneously.

Ida dismissed the correction with a wave of her hand. "The point is, you don't need any fancy-schmancy machine to make a perfect match."

"Grandma, the internet is a staple of my business. That's how I find prospects."

Goldie frowned. Rachel wouldn't like that. Not one little bit. "Could you use the computer in the background? My granddaughter wouldn't have to go on the computer, right? Only you?"

"I suppose." Julia sounded dubious.

"Rachel couldn't know that you were helping her find love. She would have to think these women found her on their own. Can you do that?"

Julia pursed her lips.

"I would pay you, of course." Maybe this was about money? "What's the going rate for these things?"

Julia shook her head. "It isn't that. I'm just not sure this is ethically correct."

"What could be wrong with helping a beautiful young woman find her perfect match?" Goldie asked practically.

"She's not a knowing, willing participant."

"Nonsense," Ida said. "Of course she is. She's a big girl. If she says 'yes' to a date, then she's consenting. You'd just be giving her a little nudge."

Julia seemed reluctant.

"What if I presented her with a hypothetical situation?" Goldie jumped in.

"What do you mean?"

"What if I asked her, in general, if she would say 'yes' to a date with a woman who appeared out of nowhere, if it was the right woman?"

"I don't know…"

"It's settled," Ida said.

Julia opened her mouth to object.

"Uh-uh," Ida cautioned. "Gold-e-lah here is one of my oldest, dearest friends. If she comes to me for help and we can help her, then we'll do it. Let's get started." Ida winked at Goldie. "I've seen this girl. She's got great bone structure. Nice, high cheekbones, soulful brown eyes… Gold-e-lah, show Julia some pictures and tell her about your Rachel. Where does she live? What are her hobbies? What does she do for a living?"

Rachel's favorite Hallmark store was conveniently located just around the corner from Shady Acres. If she hurried, she could get there in time to check out the layout for her latest release with the new boutique greeting card company. It was such a coup for them to secure a rollout at the grand dame of card stores. She was proud of her work on these cards, and for once her editor had been complimentary. That was a rarity for Claudette, who demanded the best Rachel had to give and seldom doled out compliments. Rachel hoped this female-owned start-up company would succeed.

Her internet station cycled to Beyoncé's "Single Ladies," and she cranked the volume in her ear buds. As she waited for the light to change, she busted a few dance moves.

A second later, she got a funny feeling on the back of her neck. She stopped dancing and looked around. She only spotted a few pedestrians, none of whom seemed to be paying her any particular mind. The light changed and she bopped across the street and into the store. It was well lit, with widely spaced aisles, excellent signage, and a good selection of cards. Traffic was heavy, with dozens of women and couples cruising the aisles.

As she turned the corner, she counted six women browsing the "romantic sentiments" section. Her heart swelled with joy. She tilted her head and ducked in order to see the cover of the card the well-dressed woman in the fuchsia blouse and A-line skirt was reading. Was it? Yes! Her latest creation.

The woman's head jerked up and her eyebrows knitted in consternation. Rachel quickly turned away and pretended to peruse the sympathy cards. She hated getting caught. She held her breath until the woman returned her attention to the card. Rachel practically did a fist pump when the customer fished in the slot for the corresponding envelope and made her way to the checkout counter. Rachel counted to twenty after the woman exited the store, and then followed suit. She skipped back across the street, fumbled in her bag for the keys to Goldie's car, and whistled a happy tune. Not even the prospect of suffering through another Sabbath meal with her family could dampen her good humor.

Julia bided her time browsing the kitschy knick-knacks until she was sure Rachel was gone. She shrugged off the discomfort of spying on Goldie's granddaughter. It wasn't spying, per se. After all, Goldie had hired her out of love for Rachel. Julia's job was to help secure this woman's happily ever after. What was so wrong about that? And what were the chances that Rachel would live in Chatham, less than an hour from Julia's office?

"You're justifying questionable behavior and you know it," the professional in Julia screamed. That was another thing. Why had she gone along with Grandma Ida when she had insisted that Julia omit the fact that the dating site was a just a sideline, and that her true vocation was a jury consultant who spent her days analyzing human behavior?

"If you tell Goldie that, she'll worry that you'll find something wrong with her granddaughter—that you'll size her up and determine she's meshugenah."

Julia pursed her lips. There were so many things wrong with this situation she couldn't count them on two hands. She never should have agreed to take the job. Still, she was here... She strode over to the card she'd seen the woman in pink pick up and flipped it open. She read the sentiment inside and tears welled in her eyes. It was beautiful, romantic, and heartfelt. At the bottom of the card, in mass-produced script, was Rachel's name.

"How can a woman so obviously filled with love have so much trouble finding it for herself?" Julia tapped the card against her chin, put the card back, and walked away. It was none of her business. And that was the problem—she'd said "yes."

She simply would go back and tell Goldie and Ida that she wanted no part of this. Julia got all the way to the door before her resolve faltered. What if she could make a positive difference in Rachel's life? Wasn't that what had driven her to get multiple degrees in psychology in the first place? And why she'd started her dating company, *Lez Find Love*?

Julia trudged back to the "romantic sentiments" aisle and picked up the card one more time. She reread Rachel's words. Then, on a whim, she turned the card over to see the name of the company that produced it.

Forty-five minutes later, she'd examined every card in the section. She brought the dozen cards written by Rachel to the counter, paid an astronomical sum for them, and left the store. As expensive as greeting cards were, she hoped that the writers at least saw a hefty percentage of the profits. At least she could claim the purchases as a tax deduction. After all, this qualified as client research, right?

Julia reached her car, opened the door, and tossed the paper bag full of cards onto the passenger seat. It landed with a thud, and she sighed. "Twelve cards, Jules? Twelve?" In her mind's eye, she glimpsed a snapshot of Goldie's kind face. She was so sweet, and so earnest in her desire to see her granddaughter happy. Julia saw no indication that Goldie had any issue with Rachel's sexuality. To the contrary, she seemed genuinely proud of Rachel's lesbianism, as if it was a badge of honor. Would Grandma Ida feel the same if she knew?

"Don't you dare tell your grandmother. You'll break her heart. It's enough that you've broken ours." Julia's mother had spat on the ground in disgust after discovering Julia and her college roommate in a compromising position during a surprise visit to their campus dorm room.

Julia cleared her throat, straightened up in the driver's seat, and started the car. These many years later, it still stung. Oh, her parents hadn't cut her off entirely. That would've reflected too badly on them. Instead, they maintained an air of polite civility toward her, and Julia maintained a superficial, fragile peace with them. Never had she so much as brought a woman home to their house. And never again had she given away her heart.

A wave of sadness flooded over her, and Julia did her best to shake it off. Her relationship with her folks was what it was. It made her treasure the pride Ida showed in her that much more. She had no desire to jeopardize that closeness by revealing her sexuality. There was no reason to chance it.

Julia started the car and pulled out of the parking lot. If she helped Goldie, it would bring Ida such joy. Who was she to deny her elderly grandmother one last match?

Rachel gazed blankly out the kitchen window, her hands buried in soap suds. Another dinner alone. Another night reading a book in which other women found true love in the space of two hundred fifty pages.

The sound of a siren in the near distance caught her attention. Her eyes widened as the sound grew closer and flashing lights became visible. An ambulance? Out here?

The ambulance screamed to a halt in Mr. Crawford's driveway, and a lump formed in Rachel's throat. She ran outside, the dishes and her troubles instantly forgotten.

A pair of EMTs jumped out of the ambulance and raced toward her neighbor's house.

"What's going on?"

"Not now, miss."

"Please, step aside."

Rachel hopped out of the way as one of the two burly men retrieved a gurney and took it inside Mr. Crawford's house. In seconds, she was standing alone in the darkness. It was several minutes later when they came back out.

There on the gurney was Mr. Crawford, his face pale, his hair soaked with sweat. His eyes lit on Rachel.

"Rachel." He grabbed her arm. His speech was slurred.

"What happened, Mr. Crawford?"

"Miss, we need you to get out of the way."

The EMT was hanging an IV on a portable pole.

"Just a second, young man." Mr. Crawford croaked out the words. "Rachel. I need you. Please. Freud is alone in the house. I have no one. I need you to look after him."

Rachel felt the heat in her face as she deciphered his words. Panic raced through her. "Mr. Crawford, I can't—"

"I need you, Rachel. I know you won't let me down."

"That's it, miss. We need to go. Now!"

The EMTs practically shoved her out of the way as they loaded Mr. Crawford into the back of the ambulance. And then they were gone, leaving Rachel, stunned and alone in the fading twilight.

She had no idea how much time passed before she heard the howling from inside the house. Freud. Oh, dear God. What was she supposed to do?

Tentatively, Rachel poked her head inside Mr. Crawford's still-unlocked front door. Although she could hear him, there was no visual sign of the dog, so she crept inside. *So far, so good.* As gently and quietly as she could, Rachel closed the door behind her. Momentarily, she leaned her forehead against the cool wood and breathed deeply. *I can do this.*

She spun around, and squealed at the two large, iridescent blue eyes blinking at her. "G-good doggie." She held her hands out in front of her as if to ward off the zombie apocalypse.

Freud sat ramrod straight, his bushy tail wagging in a circular pattern on the floor. He barked, and Rachel flinched and clutched her chest.

"Don't do that." She took two steps to the side. If she made a break for it, she might be able to dash past the beast and reach the living room to turn off the blaring television. *Mr. Crawford must be almost as hard of hearing as Grandma Goldie.*

Freud scooted his butt to the side so that he blocked Rachel's path and sat staring at her.

"Look, I need to get over there." Rachel pointed in the direction of the living room. "If you would just go away like a good doggie, I'd appreciate it."

Freud cocked his head inquisitively. His underbite made it look as though he was smirking at her. He didn't budge.

"I'm serious, here." Rachel shifted from foot to foot. "I have to get over there." She gestured once again in the direction of the television. "Shoo." She waved as if to sweep the dog away.

Freud blinked and pounded his tail on the hardwood floor. *Bam-bam-bam.* The sound was loud enough to compete with Alex Trebek and Jeopardy.

"Stop it."

Blink, blink.

"I mean it." Rachel realized that she was whining. She decided to try a different approach. "How about if you just let me go turn the sound down? Do you have a favorite show? I could turn it on for you."

Blink, blink.

She put a hand on her hip. "Look. If you let me do this, I'll get out of your hair." Under her breath, she added, "All nine hundred pounds of it."

Blink blink.

"That's it. No more Ms. Nice Guy." Rachel took one step forward. Freud barked. "Agh!" Rachel retreated so that her back was pressed against the door. "Okay. I take that for a 'no.'"

When her heart settled back down, she assessed her options. She couldn't very well stand here all night, pinned into a corner by this intractable he-wolf. Besides, she had to pee.

"How about this? I'll just go back over to my house, and you can go about your business, whatever that is." Rachel reached behind her back and fumbled for the doorknob. She didn't want to take her eyes off the dog. Heaven only knew what he might do. Three attempts later, she finally felt the latch give way. She pointed a finger. "Don't move."

Blink, blink.

Rachel turned on her heel, yanked the door open, slid through, and slammed the door shut behind her. Safely on the other side, she closed her eyes and breathed a sigh of relief. As she congratulated herself on getting out alive, she heard the plaintive howling from within. What in the world could Mr. Crawford have been thinking, putting her in charge of this beast?

CHAPTER FOUR

Rachel paced in her great room. She had no way of knowing when Mr. Crawford might be back. She knew from conversations with him over the years that he had no family. His wife died long ago and they'd never had children. He had no living siblings. There was no one to call in the event of an emergency.

Even from this distance, she still could hear Freud howling like something out of a werewolf movie. "Think, Rach. Think, think, think." She took three steps toward the kitchen, pivoted, and took another three steps back toward the sliding glass doors that led from the great room to the backyard. "Nothing." She threw her hands up in the air in a gesture of helplessness. "I've got nothing."

Finally, desperate to stop the incessant wailing, she snatched up her iPad, clicked open the Safari app, and waited for the Google homepage to open. *Google knows everything.* She typed, "How do I get a dog to do what I want him to do?"

Her eyes scanned the page. About 121,000,000 results. (1.01 seconds). *Great.* She read the first entry. How to get your dog to come (with pictures). Well, she certainly wasn't interested in getting the dog to come any closer. The next entry caught her eye. How to get your dog to listen to you. She read the teaser paragraph. So, where do you start if your dog doesn't obey – either in specific situations or in all...

Rachel scoffed and muttered, "First of all, he isn't my dog." Still, she clicked on the link since it seemed a logical place to start. Half an hour and a bag of barbeque potato chips later, Rachel still felt totally at sea. It was time for Plan B. Who did she know that had dogs? She was a lesbian. Surely, she must know dozens of women who owned the miscreants and could help her out.

She scrolled through her contacts. *Madison*... She didn't have a dog, but she worked as a vet tech. Rachel opened the contact. Just as she was about to touch the call button, she pulled her finger away. They'd gone out. Once. The night had ended with an awkward first kiss during which Madison's hair somehow got ensnared in the catch of Rachel's bracelet. When Rachel pulled away, Madison's hair extension was hanging from her wrist. No, she couldn't call Madison.

Molly. She could call Molly. No, that probably wasn't a good idea, either. Molly was still mad at her because Rachel wouldn't write her a personal sentiment to help her woo her girlfriend back after Molly cheated on her.

Rachel continued to scroll through the "M's." When she'd exhausted those, she moved on to the "N's." Nancy, Nanette, Nicole... She discounted every one of the contacts for one reason or another.

Finally, her eyes alighted on Sabrina. They'd never dated, Sabrina was happily married, and she and her wife fostered some big breed of dog Rachel couldn't pronounce. It was perfect. She powered on her Bluetooth and placed the call.

"Hi, Sabrina. It's Rachel. I've got a dog problem and I'm wondering if you could help me out."

"You've got a dog problem? You, Rachel-I-jump-up-on-a-couch-if-a-dog-comes-into-the-room-Wallach has a dog problem? Honey, what you've got isn't a dog problem, it's a dog phobia."

Rachel rolled her eyes. "Thanks for that. But this is serious."

"I was being serious."

Rachel explained her predicament, even including her attempt to get past Freud to turn off the television, and the fact that the beast was still in there, howling.

"You left him in there? Alone?"

"Of course he's alone. I told you, Mr. Crawford got taken away in an ambulance."

"Oh, my God. That poor baby."

"That poor baby? What about me?"

"What about you? That sweet boy just watched his owner be carted off. He's frightened out of his mind. He doesn't understand what's happening."

Rachel frowned. It hadn't occurred to her that the dog might be scared. How had that thought not entered her mind? *Because you don't know the first thing about dogs.* Rachel felt horrible. Ignorance was no excuse for lack of empathy. "What am I supposed to do?"

"First, go in there and hug him."

Rachel shuddered and her teeth chattered. "H-hug him? You want me to put my arms around the dog?"

"Yes. Animals are people too."

Rachel tried to envision herself opening her arms and... And that beast would bowl her over and...

"Earth to Rachel? I can hear you hyperventilating. Listen. You are one of the warmest, kindest, most compassionate people I know. Just use those same skills with the puppy."

"What if he knocks me over? What if he gets territorial and he thinks I'm an intruder? Dogs do that, right?"

"You told me you already went in there once. Did he attack you or show any signs of being aggressive?"

Rachel considered her encounter with Freud. "Well, he barked at me. Twice."

"Did he growl?"

"No."

"Okay, then. He's not being territorial. He's talking to you."

"And he banged his tail on the floor so hard it practically shook the house."

Sabrina laughed.

"Why are you laughing?"

"He was sitting at the time, right?"

"Yes."

"Right. He was wagging his tail. The floor got in his way."

"You don't know that." Rachel hated how she was sounding: defensive, clueless.

"What kind of dog did you say this was?"

"A big one."

"That's not a breed."

Rachel scrunched her nose up in thought. "Mr. Crawford said he was some kind of mix. Mostly golden retriever, but he's got the weirdest, most terrifying blue eyes."

"Like a Siberian Husky?"

"I have no idea."

"Google is your friend, Rach. At any rate, if that dog has any golden retriever in him, he's probably the friendliest dog in the world. He'd be far more likely to let you in and show you to the valuables than he would be to bite you or hurt you."

"Easy for you to say."

"Rachel Wallach. You need to get over your bad old self, walk over there, and show that puppy some love. When was the last time he went potty?"

Rachel's eyes grew wide. Walk Freud? As in, put him on a leash and willingly walk out the door with him? She'd have to do that? "I have no idea."

"And the last time he ate?"

"How should I know?"

"Did you check his bowl?" Sabrina asked.

Rachel's cheeks reddened at her friend's condescending tone. "Don't make it sound as though I'm some sort of criminal. I'm not. I'm just afraid and I've never had to do this before."

"I'm sorry, Rach. I simply cannot imagine that anyone doesn't at least know the basics. Listen, I'm too far away to get there tonight. But I can stay on the line and talk you through it, if you want."

"No." Rachel straightened her shoulders. "I'll figure it out."

"Okay, if you're sure. If he doesn't have any food in his bowl, search the kitchen cupboards, the pantry if there is one, or the garage. Those are the most likely places to keep the dog food. If all else fails, cook him some boneless chicken breast. That'll work."

You want me to cook for the dog? I don't even cook that for myself. Rachel decided not to share that. "Roger that. Thanks for the help."

"I'm here if you need me. And remember to fill his water bowl."

"Right. Fill the water bowl. Got it."

"And if he hasn't eaten, make sure you take him out directly afterward. He'll probably have to poop. And you'll have to pick it up."

Eww. "Got it. See you around, Sabrina."

"Good luck, Rach. Remember, dogs are people too."

Rachel disconnected the call. It was time to put on her big girl pants and face the beast.

∽⊱⋙

Athletic girls, intellectual girls, girls that were commitment-phobic, girls that wanted to settle down… Julia chewed her lip as she scrolled through her detailed database of clients. What type of woman would capture Rachel Wallach's heart?

She considered what she knew about Rachel from Goldie, what she had observed of her in the Hallmark store, and the collection of greeting cards that were splayed across her kitchen island, and created a profile for her.

Rachel clearly had a romantic, sensitive side. She was attractive…very attractive, Julia amended. According to Goldie, she was an introvert. She was highly educated, with a bachelor's degree in English from Princeton and a master's from Yale. She had no pets, lived alone in a house she purchased with her own money, preferred suburban living to cities, and drove a sensible car. It was a good start.

Julia plugged Rachel's attributes into the search algorithm she'd created to cross-match clients. Immediately, three possible matches popped up on the screen. Julia selected the first option, opened a new email and typed:

Hi, JoAnn. I think I may have found the perfect match for you. If you are interested, give me a call and I'll fill you in on the details.

Julia paused, her cursor hovering over the "send" button. How on earth was she going to explain that prospective dates would have to approach Rachel on their own, and that Rachel had never submitted a profile? This was a conundrum.

Julia grabbed up a pen and doodled on a nearby pad of paper. She imagined how a conversation would go with a client she wanted to send in Rachel's direction.

"So, here's the thing. I have no idea at any given point where this woman will be, but I'll lurk in the shadows, and when I see that she's going to be stationary for any length of time, I'll text you and you can casually show up."

Julia let out a sound of disgust. "Yeah, that's not the least bit creepy and unethical, is it?"

No, that wasn't the answer. But she'd agreed that Rachel would never know that her dates were pre-arranged. Julia briefly considered putting multiple clients together in a social environment, but that meant that they'd compare notes about Julia's services, and that would make Rachel suspicious. No, a party or other social gathering was out too. "You've put yourself in a pickle this time, Spielman."

Julia doodled some more, then ripped the sheet of paper out of the notebook, wadded it up, and tossed it at the garbage can in the corner. It hit off the rim and landed in a pile of previously poorly aimed doodle rejects. Truth be told, at the moment, she was feeling a little like them. What could she have been thinking when she agreed to this ridiculous scheme?

A vision of Goldie's hopeful face filled Julia's mind, followed by the image of Rachel, carefree and lovely, dancing across the intersection and into the Hallmark store. Julia smiled. There had to be a way to help.

"Think like a jury consultant, Spielman. How would you research prospective jurors? You'd start by searching their social media footprint."

Julia opened a browser window and logged into her Facebook account. She did a search for Rachel. Sure enough, within seconds, her profile picture popped up. Julia clicked on Rachel's profile, and then perused the "About" section. Eureka!

As so many people did, Rachel gave plenty of information away. "Too much, actually." In this case, Rachel's openness gave Julia the perfect solution. She simply would send appropriate clients to Rachel's Facebook profile and leave the rest up to them. The solution was in keeping with maintaining Rachel's privacy, since she was in charge of what information she made publicly available.

Julia ripped off another failed drawing, wadded it up, and threw it at the can. This time it landed squarely inside the circle. Yes, indeed. She could do this.

Rachel paused at Mr. Crawford's front door. "I can do this." Her hand shook as she inserted the spare key he'd given her in case of emergencies into the lock. That was when she remembered that she'd left the door unlocked.

She imagined Freud standing directly inside the opening, waiting. "This is stupid." Sabrina was right—the dog had feelings too. Freud was probably scared and lonely.

Before she could lose her nerve, Rachel pushed the door open and stepped fully inside. Freud sat there, a sock dangling from his mouth. Hardly threatening. Unless you were the sock. Rachel burst out laughing.

Freud bounded forward, his tail wagging, and rubbed the length of his body against Rachel's legs. "W-what are you doing?" For a split second, she panicked, fear rising in her chest, nearly choking off her airway. She sucked in a breath.

As if sensing Rachel's impending implosion, the dog backed off and sat at her feet. More accurately, he sat *on* Rachel's left foot. He looked over his shoulder at her and blinked, the sock still protruding from either side of his mouth.

Rachel's heartbeat slowed ever so incrementally. Tentatively, she reached out and stroked a hand through Freud's thick coat. He tilted his head back, and Rachel could've sworn she heard him moan in delight. Maybe she could do this, after all. At the very least, she'd gotten in the door without getting eaten for dinner.

That reminded her… "Are you hungry?" Freud's ears perked up and he jumped to his feet. Rachel's heart raced again. She much preferred when the dog was sitting calmly. He jogged halfway down the hall, stopped, and looked back at her. When she didn't move, he let out a woof.

Rachel flinched. "Don't do that."

Freud took another two steps down the hallway, stopped again, and glanced backward. If Rachel didn't know any better, she would have thought he was beckoning her to follow him.

"He's a dog, not a person." *Dogs are people too.* "Please, God, don't let that mantra get stuck in my head." Reluctantly, Rachel moved forward. "Just in case you're a human in dog's clothing," she muttered.

With a swish of his tail, Freud trotted happily ahead until the hallway opened into the kitchen. He skidded to a halt in front of the pantry, sat, and dropped the sock on the floor.

Rachel scanned the kitchen. Dirty dishes sat on the counter next to the sink, as if Mr. Crawford was clearing his place when he fell ill. A single placemat devoid of any plates or silverware lent credence to her supposition.

Freud jumped up and pranced in place impatiently, reminding Rachel why they were in the kitchen. She noticed a pair of red ceramic bowls with white paw prints on them sitting on a rubber mat in the corner. One of the bowls was half full of water. The other was empty.

"Are you hungry?" she repeated.

Freud's entire body vibrated as he hopped up and down in front of the pantry door. Was it possible that he understood what she was saying?

Rachel picked up the empty bowl and walked over to the pantry. By this time Freud was practically apoplectic. She opened the door and peered inside. Freud pushed past Rachel and nosed at a large bin with a lid. The sign on the bin said, simply, Freud. Evidence was mounting that Freud spoke fluent human, at least insofar as food was concerned.

There were no instructions anywhere to be found, just a scoop inside the container. "I don't suppose you'd like to tell me how much of this no-doubt-yummy stuff you're supposed to get?" Rachel asked.

Freud blinked.

"Guess I'm on my own." Rachel set the bowl down on the counter and dumped scoops of the kibble into the bowl until it was full. The morsels looked so…dry. "Is this like cereal? Do you get milk in it?"

Freud blinked again.

"You're not much help, you know that?"

Freud whined.

"Okay. I get the point." Rachel picked up the bowl and scrunched up her nose. Dogs are people too. She would never eat a bowl of cereal without any milk in it. Why should Freud? She opened the refrigerator and hunted around until she found the container of milk on the door. The sell-by date indicated it was still good, so she poured the milk over the dog food until it reached the brim of the bowl.

"I need you to stay where you are until I get this bowl over there. I don't want to spill it."

Freud cocked his head to the side, even as his entire being continued to vibrate with excitement. Rachel took several careful steps with the bowl in the direction of the corner of the kitchen that obviously belonged to Freud. The dog jumped up and danced around her.

Rachel felt the fear rise again. She stopped halfway across the kitchen. Freud sat down in front of her. *He only wants the food. He only wants the food. He's not interested in you. It's about his dinner, and you're not on the menu.* "Stay put, please." Perhaps politeness would help.

Freud blinked and wiggled, his tongue lolling out of his mouth. Rachel hazarded another step forward. Freud looked as if he would spring to his feet, but his rear end remained affixed to the floor.

As quickly as she could manage with the food bowl overflowing, Rachel covered the rest of the distance to the corner. She'd barely bent to place the bowl on the mat before Freud muscled his way past her to stick his face in the bowl.

She stepped back, out of the dog's way. He was gobbling the contents of the bowl as if he hadn't eaten in a month. "Slow down." Hadn't Mr. Crawford taught this beast any manners? He was eating so quickly Rachel was certain he couldn't even taste the food. Milk slopped over the sides of the bowl and onto the mat.

Rachel found a roll of paper towels in the pantry. She tore off several sheets and used them to clean up the mess, careful not to turn her back to the dog. She needn't have worried, though, as Freud never even picked his head up from the bowl.

Freud finished lapping up the last of the milk and burped loudly.

"Charming." With a start, Rachel remembered Sabrina's admonishment that Freud would need to go out directly after eating. "Where's your leash? I don't suppose you want to point me in the right direction, do you?"

As if on cue, Freud trundled out of the kitchen and into the mud room. He stood at the back door with his nose practically on the knob. That was great, except that he hadn't shown Rachel where to find the leash. She opened the closet. No leash. She looked behind the door. No leash. By this time, Freud was dancing in place.

"I'm doing the best I can. Honest." Finally, she noticed the hooks on the wall. A leash was draped over the middle hook. She grabbed it. "I'm going to clip this on you. Please be nice to me while I figure it out."

Freud's nose never moved from the door knob. Haltingly, Rachel touched the collar that was barely visible through the fur.

Please don't bite me. Please don't bite me. She thought she might be safe, since Freud just finished devouring half a bin of dog food. She fumbled around some more, until her fingers found a metal ring on the collar. She clipped the leash to the ring, opened the door, and stumbled headlong through the opening as Freud took off.

Rachel barely managed to stay upright as they bounded down the stairs leading to the back lawn. "Whoa! Whoa, Freud," she screamed. The dog yanked harder against the leash, unbalancing Rachel and sending her sprawling onto the grass. "Darn it all. Stop!" The arm still holding the leash felt as if it would fall off any second.

Just as she was sure this beast would drag her to her death, he stopped. Rachel struggled to her knees. Freud's head was lurching and his body was convulsing.

Oh, my God. He's having a seizure. I killed the dog. Rachel scrambled to her feet. As she stood up, Freud opened his mouth and deposited the vast majority of his clearly undigested food on the ground.

Eww. Rachel felt the dry heaves coming on. She'd always had a weak stomach. The sight of anyone throwing up made her nauseous. Apparently, that extended to canines, as well. She swallowed bile just as Freud lifted his leg and peed on a bush. *Lovely.*

The dog strained against the leash again. This time, Rachel was more prepared. She tugged back. He pulled forward. She tugged back again, determined to win this battle of wills. Finally, he gave up. Or so she thought. With one last surge, Freud yanked the leash out of Rachel's hand.

"Stay. Don't move." If Freud ran away, it would break Mr. Crawford's heart.

The dog shook his head, then turned in a circle, squatted, and pooped a mountain of diarrhea. When he was done, he straightened up, shook himself, and jogged back into the house, the leash trailing behind him.

Rachel followed Freud into the house, closed the back door, locked it, and tried not to think about the messes in the yard. "Well, that was fun." When she turned around, Freud was lying with his head on his paws, groaning. Rachel wasn't sure what had happened there, but at least they'd both survived. It was a start.

Great Bones

CHAPTER FIVE

G oldie sat on the edge of the sofa, fully made up and dressed in her mint-green pantsuit. Today was the day Ida's granddaughter, Julia, would come and report in. True, the girl had seemed reluctant at first to help, but eventually she had warmed up to the task, hadn't she?

Rap, rap, rap.

"Come in, it's open."

Julia stuck her head in.

"Don't be shy. Come in, come in." Goldie pointed to her recliner. "Sit. I can't wait to hear."

Julia sat, folded her hands in her lap, and said...nothing.

"Well? Surely you have some news. Rachel told me she was going on a date when I saw her last Friday."

Julia shifted in the seat.

Goldie's heart sank. "What happened? What's wrong? Did anything happen to my Rachel?"

"No." Julia cleared her throat. "No, it's nothing like that."

"Then, what?"

"I'm not sure this is a good idea, Mrs. Horowitz."

"Goldie. And what 'this' are you talking about? The helping my beautiful granddaughter find true love? Or the telling me about it?"

Briefly, Julia gazed out the window that overlooked the courtyard.

"The suspense is killing me, here," Goldie said.

"Okay. Yes, Rachel went on a date with a woman I sent in her direction, based on the profile I created mostly from information you supplied."

"And?"

55

Julia crossed and uncrossed her legs. "Didn't you tell me that Rachel didn't have any pets?"

Of all the things she'd expected Julia to say... "She doesn't."

"Are you sure about that?"

Goldie stiffened. "I'm positive. You think I don't know my own granddaughter?"

"No. No. It's just that I sent her a woman who's allergic to dogs. It seems that she spent the entire date sneezing, coughing, and using her emergency asthma inhaler because Rachel was covered in dog hair."

"I don't know who that woman you're talking about met, but trust me, it wasn't my Rachel."

∾⸱⸱⸱∽

"I don't even own a dog and already he's ruining my love life."

On the other end of the phone, Sabrina laughed.

Rachel poured a generous amount of Hershey's chocolate syrup on top of her Ben & Jerry's Peanut Butter Cup ice cream. "It's not funny. I could've killed the poor girl."

"You didn't know she was allergic to dogs."

"She asked me if I had any pets, and I said 'no.'"

"So, you answered honestly."

Rachel scooped a spoonful of ice cream into her mouth, causing her next words to be slightly garbled. "Generally speaking, one doesn't ask a question like that without reason."

"What are you eating?"

"Ice cream. And don't judge. It's a food group."

"Whatever you need to tell yourself, Rach."

"Anyway, that's not why I called. While I was at the hospital with her—"

"Wait a minute. At the hospital? With who? The date?"

"I told you, she had an asthma attack."

"And it required hospitalization?"

"No. Just a trip to the emergency room. She didn't have the right inhaler with her or something."

"Is that all?" Sabrina teased.

Misery covered Rachel like a shroud. This was the second recent date that ended with medical intervention. *What am I, the Grim Reaper?*

"Not helping. As if I don't feel horrible enough already." Rachel stuffed another spoonful of ice cream in her mouth, chewed on a chunk of peanut butter cup, and swallowed. "Before we got sidetracked there, I started to tell you that after my date's mother showed up—"

"The girl called her mother? How old is this woman?"

Rachel sighed and prayed for patience. "Are you going to let me finish this story, or what?"

"Sorry. But a grown woman called her mother because she had an asthma attack?"

"She called her mother because she needed a ride home and she sure as heck wasn't going to take another ride in my car, since that's where she had the attack to begin with."

"Personally, I'd have called a cab, but that's just me." There was a pause in the conversation. "Did you actually put the dog in your car?"

"No! Of course not."

"Then how did the hair get there?"

"I stripped off my sweater and threw it in the backseat after I went over and fed him that afternoon because, no surprise, it was covered in the hair of the beast."

"Hello? Dogs are people too, Rach. He's not a beast. And please, God, tell me you didn't leave him staying in his house by himself."

"Of course I did. It's where he lives."

"Rachel Wallach! You don't leave a dog alone overnight."

"How am I supposed to know that?"

"Common sense. How many days has it been?"

"Forget that and let's talk about how long it's going to be." Rachel pushed on before Sabrina could interject again. "I've been trying to tell you. While I was at the hospital, I saw Mr. Crawford."

"I'm sure you've told me this, but who's Mr. Crawford?"

"The dog's owner. Apparently he had a second, worse stroke after they transported him. He's going to be in the hospital for a while, and then the nurse said they'll have to send him to rehab at a skilled nursing facility."

"That's terrible."

"I feel awful for him."

"What about the dog?"

"I don't know what to do. I can't very well board him for months on end. Mr. Crawford asked me to take care of him. It's the least I can do."

"Well, you can't leave him in the house by himself. You're going to have to take him over to your place."

"Are you kidding me?" Rachel's voice rose so high it squeaked.

"No. Dogs are pack animals. They're not meant to stay by themselves."

"But every time I feed him he throws up and has diarrhea. I don't want that in my house."

"He's having digestive issues? What are you feeding him?"

"His food." *I'm not a moron.*

"Dry or wet?"

"Dry."

"How much?"

"A bowlful."

"How much does a bowl hold?"

"What is this, twenty questions? I don't know. Probably four or five cups." Rachel knew her irritation was beginning to show.

"Four or fiv... Oh, my God. He probably shouldn't get more than one cup or a cup-and-a-half."

"It's not like I made him eat it dry. I added milk."

"You added milk?"

"You know. Like cereal."

"Oh, my God."

Now Rachel did feel like a moron. "You said that already."

"That's because I don't know what else to say. Rachel. The dog should be fed twice a day, probably one cup each time, with just a little bit of water to moisten the food. You're way over-feeding him. That's why he's having digestive issues."

"Okay. I didn't know."

"Didn't you look online?"

"Of course I did. I spent the better part of an hour looking. But everything I read was so vague: It depends on the food, the dog, the age of the dog. Blah, blah, blah." In fact, the more she read, the higher her anxiety level rose, until Rachel no longer could see the words on the screen.

"And you have to take him into your home. There's no way that puppy should be left alone overnight."

Rachel felt the heat rise to her cheeks. Sleep while the dog was in her house? What if...

"Rach? I can hear you hyperventilating." Sabrina's tone gentled. "Take it easy. This puppy doesn't sound like he's a danger to you or anyone else. If you want, Trudy and I will come over and assess the situation and feed him once with you so you can see how it should go. And we'll help you get your place puppy-proofed and pet-friendly. We'll even show you how to walk him properly and stay for one night so you can get comfortable with him in your home."

"You'd do that?"

"Yes. We'd do that."

Rachel was speechless.

"You can do this, Rach."

Rachel was less positive, but it wasn't as though she had any other viable options. Mr. Crawford was counting on her. His world already had been turned upside down by the stroke. The least she could do was take care of the one thing in the world that mattered more to him than any other.

"Rach? You still there?"

"I'm here. What are you guys doing later this afternoon?"

"You look nice, Gold-e-lah. Are you going to services with the family?" Ida joined Goldie on the bench in front of the main entrance to Shady Acres.

"Just to my daughter's for the break-fast. God help me."

"You don't want to go? What's wrong with your kid?" Ida asked. She wrapped her scarf more tightly around her neck.

Goldie didn't want to get into a discussion about Deborah's many shortcomings. "You look awfully swanky, yourself, Ida. Is Julia picking you up?"

If Ida noticed the evasion, she didn't let on. "She is. We're going to her father's—my son's. To tell you the truth, I think the poor girl just likes to take me along as her shield. It's inexcusable the way my son and daughter-in-law treat Julia. She's such a lovely girl, and those two don't have an ounce of warmth in their bones for her. I don't understand it a bit."

"That's a real shame. She seems like such a nice girl."

"Speak of the devil." Ida pointed toward the parking lot.

Goldie shaded her eyes from the sun. A shadowed figure resolved itself into Julia's outline. She was walking toward them. But something, or, more accurately, someone else, caught Goldie's eye.

"Oh, dear." She clutched her chest.

"What is it? Gold-e-lah, are you all right? You look ashen."

"We have a problem."

"We do?"

This time it was Goldie who pointed. "That's my Rachel getting out of the car next to where your granddaughter parked. What are we going to do? They're bound to run into each other." She and Ida hadn't planned for this contingency. What if…

"Goldie? Yoo-hoo? Earth to Goldie Horowitz, come in, please."

Goldie turned to Ida. "What are we going to do?" How could she not have seen this coming?

"What do you mean, what are we going to do? We're going to go with our respective granddaughters to Yom Kippur break-fast, that's what."

Julia was less than twenty feet away. Rachel trailed her by perhaps ten steps.

"What if Rachel figures it out?"

"Why on earth would she figure it out? Our granddaughters are coming to pick up their bubbes and take them out for the holiday meal. That's all."

"But Julia knows me."

60

"Of course my granddaughter knows you, Gold-e-lah. You're one of my best friends. Just act natural. For God's sake, you're as jumpy as a cat."

Goldie turned to the left, as if she was looking away. No. That wouldn't look casual. She swiveled to the right so that she was facing Ida, as if they were in deep conversation.

"Could you be any more obvious?" Ida asked under her breath. Julia arrived in front of them. "Hello to my favorite granddaughter. You look lovely." She stood and kissed Julia on the cheek.

"Hi, Grandma. Hi, Goldie. You both look like a million bucks."

At that moment, Rachel strode up alongside Goldie. "Hi, Grandma."

"H-hi, darling. You look very fetching." And Rachel did, Goldie thought, dressed up in a fancy pantsuit, high-heeled pumps, and a silk blouse that showed just a little bit of cleavage.

"Yes," Ida stepped in. "You look beautiful." Ida turned to Julia. "And you look stunning, young lady." With a sweep of her hand, she gestured at both Rachel and Julia. "Look at the two of these girls, Gold-e-lah. Aren't they something?"

"I don't believe we've met." Rachel blushed to her ears. She held out her right hand to Julia. "I'm—"

"You must be Goldie's granddaughter, Rachel. She's told me so much about you. I'm Julia Spielman, Ida's granddaughter."

"Nice to meet you." Rachel fixed Goldie with a look and narrowed her eyes. "Grandma? Have you been telling tales out of school again?"

Goldie knew she must look like a deer in the headlights. *Think of something. For Pete's sake, think of something.*

"I'm only kidding, Grandma. Are you okay?"

"Okay? Of course she's okay, aren't you, Gold-e-lah?" Ida poked her hard in the ribs.

"Me? I'm fine."

"Look at the time." Ida made a show of checking her watch. "We'd better get going. You know how your mother is about late arrivals," she said to Julia.

"Sounds like my mother," Rachel commiserated. "I was born two days after she went into labor, and she never lets me forget it." *Why in the heck did I say that?*

61

"Right, then," Julia said. "Shall we?"

As they started forward toward the parking lot, Ida let go of her walker and grabbed Goldie by the arm, nearly unbalancing both of them. They fell behind Rachel and Julia.

"What are you doing?" Ida hissed. "You'll ruin everything. Get a grip!"

"Ouch. Seems like you've already got that covered." Goldie looked pointedly at Ida fingers, wrapped around her arm.

"Are you two slowpokes coming?" Rachel asked, turning around to address the grandmothers.

"Right behind you," Ida called. "Act normal, Gold-e-lah. She doesn't suspect a thing, and she won't unless you keep acting like a crazy person."

❧❦

"You make me crazy, Mother," Deborah said to Goldie. "If you'd just put the damned hearing aids in, everybody wouldn't have to repeat themselves ad nauseam."

"Deborah, cut Goldie a break," Richard intoned sensibly from his end of the dinner table. "We don't get to host her very often anymore. Can't we just get along?"

Rachel smiled at her father in silent thanks. Her mother's foul mood had started an hour ago when she forgot the rolls in the oven and burned them to a crisp.

"You." Deborah pointed her fork at Rachel. "You're not helping here. Wipe that smile off your face and eat more pot roast. You're getting too thin."

"I am not getting too thin, Mother."

"Do you need money for groceries? If you had a real job that you could support yourself with, you could have food in your refrigerator."

Rachel started counting to ten, but only made it to five. Why was it that her mother could push her buttons like nobody else's business? *Don't engage. Don't engage. Don't engage. Aww, hell.* "For the last time, I have a real job, in a real profession at which I excel, and for which I am well compensated. I'm not having this discussion with you again." For good measure, Rachel pushed her plate away without finishing the mashed potatoes.

An awkward silence ensued until Goldie interjected. "How about them Yankees?" Her eyes twinkled with mischief.

Rachel and Richard busted out laughing, prompting Deborah to shove her chair back, get up from the table, and stalk into the kitchen.

The remainder of the evening was spent in frosty monosyllabic give-and-take until Rachel couldn't stand it anymore. Goldie yawned, and Rachel saw it as the perfect excuse to make a clean getaway.

She and Goldie took their leave and managed to get out the door without being saddled with Tupperware containers filled with leftovers.

Five minutes into the drive back to Shady Acres, Goldie said, "I'm sorry."

"For what, Grandma?"

"For raising a daughter who would speak to her daughter with such disrespect and disregard."

Rachel stole a glance sideways at her grandmother, sitting in the passenger seat, looking disgusted and sad. Her heart ached. "This isn't your fault, Grandma. You didn't 'make' Mother this way. She's an adult, fully responsible for her own stuff."

"I raised her to be better than this. I don't know where I went wrong."

"You didn't. Honestly, I think she's just jealous. I went to college and grad school and have a successful career. She got married and was a stay-at-home mom. She's never earned a penny of her own, never held a job outside the home—not that there's anything wrong with that. Raising three children is a full-time job. What I'm saying is, she probably feels as though she got cheated out of something."

"Nobody forced her to marry Richard. Not that we didn't love your father," Goldie hastened to add. "Your grandfather and I told her she was too young to marry. She should wait a little while. Live a little. Experience life. But not your mother. She was as stubborn as an ox. If we said the sky was blue, she would argue that it was red."

Rachel nodded knowingly. That was her mother to a "t."

"We were probably the only parents in the world not in a rush to have grandkids." Goldie touched Rachel on the arm, "Not that we weren't thrilled to pieces when each of you was born. But your parents were so young. They needed time together like Morris and I had, to establish themselves as a couple, to put together a home, to save some money, to enjoy each other's company. Instead, they had Paul almost nine months to the day after they married."

Goldie fell quiet, and they continued the drive in silence until Rachel pulled up in front of the assisted living facility. She turned off the car. "I love you, Grandma."

"I love you too, bubbeleh. And I am so proud of you. You were always such a sensitive child, so introverted and quiet—like a little mouse. I worried for you, being overpowered by your mother and your siblings. I worried that you would get lost in the shuffle."

"Oh, Grandma. You shouldn't have worried—"

"I wasn't finished." Goldie wagged her finger at Rachel. "But here you are, a strong, independent, brilliant, beautiful woman, filled with purpose and talent. So, so much talent. Don't you ever hide your light under a bushel, bubbeleh."

Rachel wiped away tears. "I won't, Grandma. I promise."

"Okay, then. I'll just toddle these old bones inside the castle here, and you'd best be on your way. It's late, you have a very long drive, and I worry about you."

"I'll be fine, Grandma."

"Even so, please call me when you get there and let me know you're all right."

"It will be late."

"I know. I don't care. You can let the phone ring twice and hang up. We don't have to talk."

"And letting the phone ring twice won't wake you?"

"Don't argue with your elders, darling. Just do as I say."

"Uh-huh."

"I mean it." Goldie fixed Rachel with her most stern look, which, in truth, wasn't very stern at all.

"I love you, Grandma."

"I love you too, my Rachel. Now get going."

CHAPTER SIX

Julia escorted Ida to her room at Shady Acres, said her goodbyes, and jumped back in the car for the ride home. Running headlong into Rachel hadn't been in her plans. In fact, it made her decidedly uncomfortable.

Still, maybe it was for the best. After all, it would only be natural for their paths to cross at Shady Acres, wouldn't it? Besides, interacting with Rachel gave Julia more insight into her personality. That, in turn, would help with the matchmaking.

Julia had no trouble conjuring up an image of the love in Rachel's eyes for her grandmother. She was an open book. "You need to make sure whoever you send her will treat her heart tenderly," Julia mumbled to herself. It wasn't that Rachel appeared fragile, exactly, it was more that she seemed…innocent. She had a purity about her. Julia imagined that her heart was easily bruised, that she was often misunderstood, and that the genuine Rachel…

"Jesus, Julia. You've met the woman once, observed her from a distance one other time, and read greeting card sentiments she created. And, what? You think you know her deepest self? Get a grip."

Julia punched the power button on the audio system and tuned in to National Public Radio's hit show, "Wait Wait…Don't Tell Me!" It was time to focus on something else. Besides, she'd already sent the next three women the link to Rachel's Facebook profile. It was out of her hands.

❧❧

"I don't understand why the sudden interest in me." Rachel sat on the sofa, inhaling a Dairy Queen Reese's Peanut Butter Cup Blizzard and talking to Freud, who had positioned himself in front of her on the floor, his tail thumping a staccato rhythm. Occasionally, he cocked his head to one side or the other as she spoke.

"It makes no sense. Two months ago, my phone never rang." She waved the spoon in Freud's direction. "Well, except for robo calls and scams. Nobody was knocking down my virtual door after looking at my profile picture, wanting to meet me, either."

Freud laid his head on his paws, his eyes on Rachel. He let out a groan. Or maybe he was passing gas. It was hard to tell.

"Now, I get local women sending me private Facebook messages, wanting to talk and get to know each other. What changed?" Rachel scraped the bottom of the Blizzard cup, ate the last spoonful, and set the empty container on the coaster on the end table. She swiveled around so that her feet were on the couch and laid down, propping her head on several decorative pillows.

Freud's eyes followed her every movement, although he never lifted his head off his paws.

"Don't look at me like that. I'm not complaining. I'm just asking questions. That's healthy. Right?"

Freud blinked.

"It's probably Facebook changing its algorithms again. Social engineering. Human behavior experimentation." Rachel readjusted a pillow. "Still, some of these women look promising."

She turned her head so that she was facing the dog. He blinked again. "What? You think it's something else?" She pushed herself to a sitting position again and hugged one of the pillows to her chest. "Maybe Malinda's right. The energy of putting myself out there and telling the world I'm available to date is drawing in similar energy. I don't know about that, but, whatever the reason, I'm not going to look a gift horse in the mouth."

Freud yawned.

"I know it was a cliché. I don't need you to tell me that. Everybody's a critic." Rachel waited for Freud's reaction. None came.

"Mr. Crawford would be proud of me, you know." Rachel smiled at the thought. "It's only been a week and I'm not even afraid of you anymore."

Freud stood up and shook his entire body, and Rachel flinched.

"Point taken. In my defense, I'm still learning canine body language. You have to give me credit. I'm so much better than I was."

Freud approached her and put a paw on the sofa.

"Don't push it, mutt." Rachel rose, collected the empty Blizzard cup, and threw it out on the way to her home office. She had three new anniversary sentiments due by the end of the week. Between Freud and her new-found popularity with the women, she'd fallen behind on her work, and that wouldn't do at all.

Over her shoulder she said, "Are you coming? I want you where I can keep an eye on you." *Did I just willingly invite the dog to follow me?* "Rachel Wallach, I don't even recognize you anymore." She thought about that for a minute. Maybe this was a good thing. She'd been in such a rut. A fresh start would do her good.

✧❧

"You're a fresh voice. This could be your big break, Rachel. Imagine it—you're going to be the face of the industry."

"I don't know. I like the anonymity of being a freelance writer who creates words from the heart. I don't like having attention called to myself."

"Then why did you retain me?"

"I hired you because my therapist said I needed to stop cocooning and raise my profile both personally and professionally. Since I'm no good at promoting myself, it seemed to make sense to find someone like you to do it for me.

"Right. So let me do my job. I'm telling you, if you want to take your career to the next level, you're going to have to get outside your comfort zone. If you do this magazine interview and photo shoot, you'll have more orders coming your way than you can possibly fulfill in a lifetime. They accepted my pitch to do a story on you, Rachel. That doesn't happen every day. Cut me a break here."

Rachel swung around in her office chair and stared out the sliding glass doors that led to the deck and backyard. Money never had been her primary consideration. Where her work was concerned, she simply wanted to do what she loved and to love what she did. She was following her passion. She had a good life. She wasn't struggling royalty check to royalty check.

Freud, who had been lying on the brand-new L.L. Bean dog bed Sabrina had sent him, chose that moment to stand up, stretch, trot over to the sliding glass doors, and scratch at the door to go out.

"Not now," Rachel whispered to him.

"If not now, when?" The public relations expert asked, his exasperation clear.

"I wasn't talking to you." Rachel appreciated Tony. He worked hard on her behalf and never bugged her unless it was something important. She returned her attention to Freud. "I'll take you out when I get off the phone."

"What did you say?"

"Nothing."

"Come on, Rachel. I busted my ass to get you this opportunity. The least you can do is say you'll do it."

Freud pawed the door again.

"Stop it."

"Stop what? Getting you invaluable publicity?"

"No. I wasn't…talking to you." Rachel grunted as she grabbed for the dog's collar, missed, and nearly fell off the chair.

Freud howled.

Oh, my God. "Cut it out."

"Rachel? What's going on over there? Are you being attacked by a pack of wild coyotes or something?"

Freud howled again.

Rachel fumbled with the receiver and slammed the button to take the call off speakerphone.

"Rachel?"

"I'm here. Sorry. I was talking to Freud."

"You were… If I've been pushing you too hard—"

"What?" Recognition dawned. "He's a dog. Freud is a dog."

"Oh." The line fell silent.

"It's a long story. I'll spare you the details."

Freud howled again.

"If this is a bad time…"

"No." Rachel watched as Freud danced from foot to foot on the rug. If she didn't get him out in the next minute... "I'll do it. I'll do the interview. Email me the details."

"You won't regret this, Rachel."

As Freud lifted his leg, Rachel already was regretting it.

৯৯

"Gold-e-lah? Is this kosher?"

Goldie risked another peek around the corner. Not a staff member in sight. "We're not prisoners here, Ida. We can leave anytime we want."

"If that's true, then why are you acting like the Birdman of Alcatraz about to escape?"

"I said we were free to come and go as we please. I didn't say I was allowed to take the car," Goldie said.

"So we're breaking the rules? Oh, this is fun!"

"Less talking, more walking. Come on." Goldie led the way out the side door and to the parking lot. It took her several minutes to locate where Rachel had left her prized car, a cascade-blue 1972 Buick Electra Deuce-and-a-Quarter, and then another little while to pack Ida's walker in the trunk and adjust the driver's seat so that she could reach the pedals.

She started the car, put it in gear, and stomped her foot on the gas. The car lurched forward, and she clomped on the brakes.

"Gold-e-lah? You have a license to drive this whale, yes?"

Goldie didn't answer. Instead, she maneuvered the car out of the parking space, negotiated the turn from the parking lot onto the main street, and headed toward Melvin's Diner. "You'll thank me when we get where we're going. Best chocolate malted in town."

"I haven't had a good malted in years, since they closed the old ice cream shop on the Lower East Side. You remember it?"

"Who doesn't? It's where I met my Morris, God rest his soul."

"He was a good man."

"He was the best."

"Cancer?"

"What else?"

"Speaking of matches made in Heaven," Ida said, "what's going on with your Rachel? Anything yet?"

"I'll tell you when we get inside. Right now, I need to concentrate." Goldie drove around the block three times, until she finally found a parking space that didn't require parallel parking.

They got a table near a window and ordered two chocolate malteds.

Goldie said, "Rachel has been so busy lately, I don't think she's had much time to go out on dates."

"What could be more important than finding a match?"

Goldie sat up a little straighter. "I couldn't wait to kvell about it. I'm so proud I could burst a button."

"What is it already?" Ida asked, as the server brought them their drinks.

"My Rachel is going to be a big magazine star."

"You don't say?"

"Yep. She's going to be featured in the holiday issue of *People* talking about her work."

"Good for her." Ida took a noisy slurp of her malted. "Oh, my God. This is a slice of Heaven, that's what this is."

"I told you." Goldie took her first sip and savored the rich, sweet flavor on her tongue. "Just the way I remember it."

"It's a good thing that you're so supportive of the girl's accomplishments, Gold-e-lah. Grandmothers are supposed to cheerlead. It's just…"

"It's just, what? You want I shouldn't be happy for Rachel?"

"Of course not."

"This is important, Ida. It's a big deal for her career."

"I'm sure it is. But girls these days, they put so much emphasis on their work lives. It's no wonder she hasn't found the right one yet."

"I beg your pardon?" Goldie pushed the malted away.

"No offense meant, Gold-e-lah. Your Rachel is a very beautiful young woman. I'm not saying that she can't find the perfect match. I'm just pointing out that if she's working so hard, maybe finding a match isn't a high enough priority for her."

"You don't know what you're talking about. These days, young women have happy home lives and careers at the same time. They want it all, and they can have it all."

"Listen to yourself. You sound like a television commercial." Ida waved a hand dismissively.

70

"And you sound like an old fuddy-duddy."

Goldie grabbed her malted and sucked the last third of it down. She didn't care that the resultant brain-freeze made her head hurt like nobody's business. Ida had no right to rain on her parade like that.

Goldie had been planning to tell Ida about Rachel taking in the neighbor's dog as a good deed too, but now... Now she wanted to get back to Shady Acres and leave Ida to her own negative thoughts. Since when had she become such a cynic?

After several uncomfortable minutes of silence, Goldie pointed to Ida's malted. "Finish that. We need to get back before that Evan figures out that we've flown the coop. He watches me like a hawk."

"I like Evan. He's a good boy."

"Figures," Goldie mumbled under her breath.

"What did you say?"

"Nothing. Drink up and let's get going."

৶৲৵

"Mother, I have to get going or I'll be late." Rachel pulled yet another silk blouse off a hanger to try on.

"Were you expecting snow? Is it slushy? How are the roads? Do you have a pair of dress boots? Do they supply the clothes for the photo shoot? What are you going to wear?"

"No. Yes. I don't know, much to my chagrin I'm not on them yet. No. I don't know. And I have no idea." Rachel drew the blouse over her head, careful not to pull the Bluetooth out of her ear, straightened the sleeves, and looked in the mirror. *Bleh.* She stripped the shirt off and selected another one.

"Don't get smart with me, young lady."

"I'm not, Mother. I'm just trying to figure out an outfit." Of all the times to be having a "What are you wearing?" conversation, this wasn't it, and her mother wasn't the person who should be on the other end of the phone line. "I have to go. I'll call you later."

Rachel reached for the phone and the "end" button. She never trusted that simply turning the Bluetooth off severed the connection.

"By later, you do mean right after you're done with the interview, right?"

Oh, good Lord. Please stop talking. "'Bye, Mother."

Rachel once again sorted through her outfit options. Snow in late October was not unheard of in Albany, but this freak storm rolled in overnight without any warning. It was cold and raw outside—more a day for boots and wool pants than a skirt suit and heels.

Although they seemed terribly passé these days, Rachel dug out a pair of smoke gray pantyhose to match her charcoal gray suit. Those ought to keep her legs warm, at least.

Red silk blouse with a bit of cleavage? Or teal cashmere turtleneck sweater for warmth? Rachel stood in front of the full-length mirror and held the sweater and the suit jacket up against her torso. Too staid and school-marmish. She tossed aside the sweater and replaced it with the red blouse. Red was a power color. She always got compliments whenever she wore red. It was her signature color. Red it would be.

Rachel eyed the clock. She needed to be dressed and out the door in less than forty-five minutes, and she hadn't even applied her makeup yet.

Thirty minutes later, she congratulated herself on her efficiency and eyed the results in the mirror. Not too bad. *I am successful. I am accomplished. I am enough. I am successful. I am accomplished. I am enough.*

Rachel picked up her black purse and strode with purpose toward the door to the garage. She snatched up the car keys from the kitchen table and her black London Fog dressy raincoat from the closet in the mudroom. Still ten minutes to spare. On a miserable weather day like today, being early would be a plus, especially given how hard it was to find parking in downtown Albany, where the magazine had rented an office suite for the interview and photo shoot.

Just as she opened the door to the garage, she heard it. Freud let out a howl loud enough to make her teeth clench. She turned around and there he was, looking forlorn and prancing from foot-to-foot. "Please, Freud. Not now. You can't possibly have to go out now."

The dog howled again. He definitely needed to potty. Rachel looked down at her outfit. If he got close to her now it would take her twenty minutes with a lint brush to get the fur off her coat.

"Unbelievable." If she simply took off the coat, Freud would ruin her suit. Coat or suit. Suit or coat. Rachel knew she was running out of time. "I'm a problem solver." She whipped off the coat, turned it inside out, and reached for the leash. Oh, no. If Freud left fur on the inside of the coat, when she reversed it the fur would be stuck to her suit. *Think, Rach. Think.* Got it! She took off the coat, threw on her rain slicker, dumped the high heels, removed the skirt, jumped into her rain pants and winter boots, snapped a leash on Freud, and yanked him out the back door.

By the time Freud finished his business, Rachel was freezing and running late. *I am successful. I am accomplished. I am enough. I am successful. I am accomplished. I am enough.*

She repeated the mantra five times—the amount of time it took her to re-dress, fix her hair and makeup, and get into the car. So much for perfect planning and running early.

CHAPTER SEVEN

Julia bounded into Ida's apartment, bursting to tell her about the breakthrough she'd achieved by utilizing Rachel's Facebook profile as the conduit to send her potential matches. "Hi, Grandma Ida!"

But she skidded to a halt inside the door. Something was terribly wrong. The blinds were drawn and the room was pitch dark, save for cracks of light seeping through the slats. It took a moment for her eyes to adjust.

A shadow in the corner resolved into Ida sitting in her chair, wrapped in a blanket.

"Grandma! What's wrong?" Julia snapped on the nearby lamp and Ida shielded her eyes. Her hair was uncombed and her eyes appeared watery.

"Turn it off, for God's sake. Are you trying to blind me?"

Julia started to comply, then thought better of it. "Why are you sitting in the dark? Do you feel okay?"

"Can't an old woman sit in the dark without someone playing twenty questions?"

Julia crossed the room and sat on the end of the sofa nearest the chair. She took Ida's hand and spoke gently. "It's the middle of the afternoon, you're still in your nightgown, you haven't combed your hair or put on your makeup, all of which are completely out of character for you. So no, you can't sit in the dark without me asking what's wrong."

"Give it a rest, Julia. I'm fine." Ida withdrew her hand and shifted so that her face was turned toward the wall. "I just want some peace and quiet."

"Can I get you a nurse? Do you need a doctor?" Ida's appearance, her behavior... It was so unlike the buoyant, boisterous, center-of-attention woman Julia had known and loved as long as she could remember. "Look at me, Grandma." She waited for Ida to face her. "I'm not going anywhere until you talk to me and give me some answers."

Ida sighed heavily. "Can't an old woman mourn the death of a friendship in peace? Julia, darling, I love you, but you need to get out and leave me to myself for a little while."

Julia frowned. Had she heard correctly? Was Ida losing her mind?

"Why are your feet not moving? Don't just sit there like a lump on a log. Get out!"

"I love you, Grandma. I'm not going anywhere until you explain to me what in the world you're talking about."

Ida scowled at Julia. "If I tell you, will you leave already?"

"I'm not making any promises." Julia crossed her arms. "Start talking and we'll see."

"We'll see," Ida mocked. "Now you sound like your mother. Do you remember when you were a little girl and you used to come to me whining that every time your mother said 'We'll see' what she meant was 'no'?"

In this case, Ida was right, but Julia had no intention of letting her know that. "Good thing I'm not my mother," she replied.

"Well, I have to agree with you there." Ida squirmed in the chair, her physical actions clearly mirroring her emotional discomfort. "Goldie's not talking to me anymore. I rang her doorbell, no answer, although I know she was in there. I tried to sit with her at breakfast, she wouldn't give me the time of day. I even slipped a note under her door. She pushed it back into the hallway."

"What?" Of all the things Julia expected to hear, that Ida and Goldie were fighting would've been last on the list of possibilities.

"You heard me. It's true. Every word of it."

"What happened?"

"I don't want to talk about it." Ida crossed her arms over her chest, reminding Julia of a recalcitrant child.

"Grandma, Goldie is your best friend. It doesn't make any sense. There must've been some precipitating event. What was it?"

Ida made a motion as though locking her lips and throwing away the key.

"Seriously?"

"Serious as a heart attack."

Julia shook her head. "I guess I'll just have to go and ask Goldie about it." She thought the threat would be enough to make her grandmother talk. Instead, Ida sat in stony silence.

"Okay, then." Julia rose, kissed Ida on the forehead, and walked to the door.

"Where are you going?"

Julia looked back. "I told you, to talk to Goldie."

⋘⋙

"Who is it?"

"It's Julia."

"Are you alone?"

"I am."

Goldie cracked the door open. When she was certain that Ida wasn't along, she opened the door fully and motioned Julia to come inside.

"Do you want some coffee?" Goldie asked, as Julia settled herself in a chair. Regardless of the circumstances, Goldie's upbringing would never allow her to forget her hostess duties.

"Love some, thanks. Just black is fine."

Goldie puttered around the tiny kitchenette, taking far longer than necessary to brew a pot of fresh coffee. She could just imagine why Julia was here. No doubt Ida sent her. Well, Goldie had no intention of forgiving Ida anytime soon.

"Is that a new picture?" Julia asked. She picked up the framed photograph from the end table and held it up so that Goldie could see it through the pass-through from the living room to the kitchenette.

"No, I've had that one a while." If Julia was trying to make conversation to cover up the awkward silence, Goldie wasn't about to help her.

Finally, when she couldn't stall any longer, Goldie carried a mug of hot coffee and a napkin into the living room and handed them to Julia.

"Thank you."

"You're welcome." Goldie remained standing. Maybe Julia would think she had someplace she needed to be and so wouldn't stay long.

Julia ran her finger around the rim of the mug. Goldie continued to say nothing.

"So," Julia finally began, "you've probably figured out that I've come because of whatever is going on between you and my grandmother."

"Oh?"

"I don't want to pry, Goldie, and I'm sure it's none of my business."

"You're a very nice girl, Julia. I like you a lot. But what's between your grandmother and me is between your grandmother and me. It doesn't concern you."

"You're right, it doesn't." Julia sipped her coffee. "What does concern me is that two women I care about, who've been dear friends for almost eighty years, are both miserable and aren't talking to each other." She put her mug down. "Do you realize that my grandmother is over there crying because she thinks she's lost her best friend? And you don't look any too upbeat either, I might note."

Goldie wanted to take satisfaction in Ida's pain, but she couldn't. The whole thing made her sick to her stomach. She sighed. It didn't look as though Julia was going to take the hint and shove off, and Goldie's bunions were killing her. She sat on the edge of the sofa.

"You don't owe me an explanation," Julia said softly, "but I'd appreciate if you'd help me understand."

Goldie chewed her lip. What difference did it make if Julia knew how rude Ida had been and the awful things she had said?

"All right." Goldie folded her arms. "Your grandmother said my Rachel wasn't good enough to make a match."

Julia, who had been taking a sip of coffee, spit it out in a spray that left her choking and gasping for air. "What?"

"I'm sorry. But that's what she said. How could she say such a thing?" Much to her mortification, a tear leaked out of Goldie's right eye. She wiped it away.

"That's ridiculous. My grandmother would never say that. Rachel is beautiful, and desirable, and... Are you certain you heard her correctly?" Julia blotted her lips and blouse with her napkin.

The hair rose on the back of Goldie's neck. "Are you accusing me of lying?"

"Of course not." Color rose to Julia's cheeks. "It's just that I can't imagine what would possess my grandmother to think that."

"My Rachel is perfectly capable of having a love life and a successful career."

"Absolutely," Julia agreed. "You know, I just remembered I left something in the car I meant to give you. I'll be right back, I promise." She shot up out of the chair and jogged out the door before Goldie could say another word.

Goldie cleared away the coffee cups and washed them in the sink.

Julia returned minutes later, just as Goldie finished plumping the chair cushion. It wasn't until Julia was inside that Goldie recognized the telltale tennis balls on the wheels of a walker trailing her through the door.

Ugh. She turned her back and faced the window.

"I thought you said Goldie asked for me to come." Ida sounded puzzled.

"Goldie, Ida," Julia said, "we're going to sit down and talk through this, because I can't believe what I'm hearing."

Goldie spun around. "You're treating us like children."

"You're acting like children," Julia countered.

"I'm going. It's clear that Goldie has no desire to see me. You tricked me."

Julia barred the door. "Nobody moves until I get the straight skinny from both of you and we resolve this situation, which I'm sure is a misunderstanding." Julia motioned for the two friends to sit.

Reluctantly, Goldie sat in the recliner. Ida continued to lean on her walker. Neither said a word.

Julia looked from one to the other. "Okay. I'll start." She pointed to Ida. "Grandma? Goldie says you disparaged Rachel and her ability to find a match. Is that true?"

"I did no such thing."

79

"You did too!" Goldie blurted out.

"Did not." Ida said, defiantly.

"Grandma? Exactly what did you say?" Julia asked.

"I simply told the truth. Goldie was telling me that Rachel was going to be featured in some big-deal magazine—"

"She is?" Julia wheeled around to face Goldie.

"She is." Goldie sat a little taller. "She's being interviewed today, as a matter of fact, for *People* magazine. There are even going to be pictures."

"That's amazing!"

"—And I was explaining, quite reasonably, that it's wonderful that the girl's doing so well, but it's likely that her focus on work makes it harder for her to find a match."

"Grandma! That's not true."

Ida bristled. "So, you're siding with her?" She jutted her chin in Goldie's direction.

"See? I told you," Goldie said.

"I'm not 'siding' with anyone." Julia pointed to Ida. "You need to apologize. What you said was not only inaccurate, it was insensitive."

"I will not—"

"Grandma Ida…"

Ida huffed out a breath. She still wasn't looking at Goldie. "If you disagreed with what I said, I'm sorry."

"Not good enough," Julia said. "I've made plenty of great matches for women who are very successful at their jobs."

"Gold-e-lah? I'll allow that it's possible that I could be wrong about this. If so, I'm sorry."

"That's an apology?" Goldie waved a hand to dismiss it.

"Goldie," Julia said. "Ida is conceding that she made a mistake."

"I did not—"

Julia held up a hand to forestall whatever it was Ida was going to say.

Ida fell silent.

"I accept, I guess."

"Excellent. It's a start," Julia proclaimed. "Now I want you two to hug it out."

"Do what?" Both elderly women exclaimed at once.

"Make up with each other."

"Absolutely not," Ida said.

"I'd rather eat chicken livers without ketchup," Goldie said.

"I've tasted your chicken livers," Ida shot back. "I wouldn't eat them without ketchup, either."

"Your Bernard never complained. He cleaned his plate every time. In fact, he used to ask for seconds."

"You leave my Bernie out of this." Ida took a threatening step forward with her walker.

Julia slid into her path. "For heaven's sake! Listen to you two. Stop it. Right now."

Goldie's cheeks burned red with anger, so much so that it felt like a hot flash, and she hadn't had one of those in almost forty years. She stared hard at the woman who used to be her friend. Ida was staring back at her, her ample bosom heaving.

"Julia?" Goldie tried to modulate the shaking in her voice. "I appreciate what you're trying to do. I'm sorry to disappoint you. Truly, I am. I like you a lot. But I have no intention of letting bygones be bygones with a woman who clearly has so little regard for me and for my granddaughter."

Ida thrust out her chin. "This was a mistake. I should've known better than to think you actually wanted to come to your senses. You were pig-headed as a girl, and you still are. Come on, Julia. We know when we're not wanted."

After several false starts in which she was thwarted alternately by the wall, the kitchen pass-through, and a bench, Ida freed her walker and made her dramatic exit.

Julia lingered in the entryway.

"You'd better go with her. Regardless of the circumstances, I don't want to come between a granddaughter and her bubbe. Thank you for working to make a match for my Rachel. I'm sure she'll find the right girl when the time is right. Give me your mailing address and I'll write you a check for your services."

"I don't want your mon—"

"Oh, no." Goldie interrupted. "I'm going to pay you. I don't want your grandmother saying I'm a welcher. Here's a piece of paper and a pen."

"Goldie—" But it was no use. Julia wrote out her address.

"Go on, now." Goldie shooed Julia out of the apartment and closed the door behind her. *Good riddance, Ida. My Rachel will show you a thing or two. She's going to be a big star.*

⋘⋙

Rachel resisted the urge to scratch her nose. The pancake foundation the makeup artist had plastered on her face made her feel like a mannequin at Madame Tussaud's Wax Museum. The false eyelashes were so heavy she was having a hard time keeping her eyes open. And the platform heels the dresser had given her to wear instead of her patent-leather pumps were so high she was sure if she fell off them it would be a three-story drop.

"Turn a little to the left, love."

Rachel complied.

"That's it. Now, swivel just your head this way and smile like you just spotted your boyfriend coming toward you in a crowded airport after an extended military deployment."

Who thinks of these things? Rachel wondered what in the world made this unwashed, unkempt, scrawny pipsqueak of a man think that imagery would result in a dazzling smile. Still, she understood what he was after, so she conjured up a vision of Gal Gadot, dressed as Wonder Woman, striding toward her with purpose.

"Beautiful! That's it. Tilt your head a smidge to the right. Yes! Oh, yes! That's the look. That's it."

The photographer's shutter whirred away, and Rachel tried to forget how exposed and embarrassed she felt. It was just her and Gal, alone on Paradise Island.

"Right. That's a wrap! Thank you, love."

Rachel blinked and worked to adjust to the darkness as the photographer's assistant snapped off the klieg lights, and the room once again transformed into the rented downtown Albany office space *People* had secured for the photo shoot and interview. She removed the uncomfortable platform heels, traded them for her own shoes, grabbed her coat, and followed the assistant's directions to the corner office down the hall where the interview would take place.

⋘⋙

Julia sat in the darkness of her living room. The only sound was the howling of the wind outside the trio of picture windows overlooking the front of the house. Her logical self told her that she hadn't truly been fired. It was just Goldie's hurt pride talking. She would come around soon and everything would get back to normal. Not only that, but Ida would realize she'd been a Class-A horse's ass and make a more heartfelt apology. Goldie would accept it, and Julia would be back on the case of finding Rachel the perfect match she deserved.

Julia picked up her iPad from the coffee table and opened Facebook to Rachel's page. So far, the feedback she'd gotten from potential matches she'd sent there was that Rachel looked "interesting," "cute," "intriguing," "friendly," and "not-like-a-serial-killer."

One of the matches reported back that she and Rachel had corresponded a few times via the Messenger app and met to have coffee. That sounded promising, until the client became concerned that Rachel might be mentally unbalanced, because she kept referencing conversations she'd been having with Freud. Just to be sure she had her facts right, the client came home and Googled the father of modern psychoanalysis to determine that yes, indeed, he was deceased. The client cancelled plans for a second coffee date.

Julia chalked that experience up to miscommunication. Perhaps the coffee shop had been loud and the client had misheard Rachel. After all, Julia had met her and didn't find any reason to suspect that Rachel was anything but a lovely person.

She obviously was successful at what she did. Hadn't Goldie boasted that Rachel was going to be featured in *People* magazine? That was huge! Julia popped open a note app and wrote a reminder to check into which week Rachel's story would appear. Raising her professional profile most certainly would help Rachel find a match. Women would be clamoring to date the queen of hearts— the ultimate romantic.

It would make Julia's job a piece of cake... Except that, thanks to Goldie and Ida's petty squabble, Julia no longer had that job. She'd lost clients before; no big deal, right? But this one made her unaccountably sad.

CHAPTER EIGHT

Rachel took a deep breath and relaxed into the cushy black leather seat. Although she'd been nervous at first, the interview had gone smoothly. She'd even managed to ignore the smell of the reporter's leftover Chinese takeout food that permeated the room, although it left her craving chicken with broccoli.

Rachel guessed the reporter to be roughly her age, or perhaps a little younger. She had thick, curly blond hair and an athlete's body. More importantly to Rachel, she'd clearly had done her homework, including a statistical analysis of romantic greeting card sales over the past decade, a profile of card buyers, and demographics on areas with the heaviest concentration of greeting card purchases.

"I want to read you a few quotes from consumers who recently bought your cards."

Rachel tried to hide her surprise. "You talked to card buyers?"

The interviewer laughed. "Don't look so shocked. Did you think we randomly selected you to talk to? When your publicist pitched the story to us, we did some checking. You were everything he promised us you were and more. In fact, in a single store, eight out of the ten consumers we surveyed had a sentiment you'd crafted in their hands at checkout."

"Eight out of ten?"

"Eight out of ten," the interviewer agreed. "We were as surprised as you look right now. We expected to find a cross-section of brands and authors at various types of stores and geographic locations. Not the case."

Rachel knew both Tony and Claudette were pushing hard to get her to increase production, but she simply assumed that was tied to the usual seasonal uptick in romance greeting card production in advance of Valentine's Day.

"Can I ask which stores you staked out?"

"I don't see any harm in telling you. Two Hallmark stores, three Walmarts, and four Target stores, from the Northeast to the Southwest. Plus one in Guam."

Rachel soaked in the information. It was overwhelming. It was one thing to find a random shopper reading one of her cards. But a cross-section of stores in a variety of geographic areas carrying her cards? And buyers in at least one location overwhelmingly choosing her sentiments? This was the mother lode.

"As I was saying," the interviewer returned to her notes, "I'm going to read you a few quotes. I'd love to hear your reaction."

"Okay."

"This card says what I would've said myself, if I were smarter and more romantic." The interviewer looked up from her notes. "That was from a sixty-two-year-old man who was about to propose to his twenty-one-year-old girlfriend."

Rachel tried to scrub that image from her mind. She was glad she didn't know which sentiment he'd bought—it probably would've ruined the words for her forever.

"How does that make you feel?"

Like I want to go home and take a shower. "I hope he got the desired outcome."

"Fair enough. Here's another one. This guy said, 'Now, I don't have to figure out what to say. I can just hand my girlfriend this card and, boom, I'm a hero.'" The interviewer once again glanced up expectantly.

"Let me guess. He's in his early twenties and from Long Island or one of the five boroughs."

"Close enough. He was twenty-six and we caught him buying one of your cards in the Walmart Supercenter in Secaucus, New Jersey."

"I hope he remembered to buy flowers to pair with that sentiment."

"Touché. I doubt it. He seemed more likely to buy her tickets to a heavy metal concert."

Rachel smiled. "Nothing says love like an ear-splitting electric guitar solo."

"You're funny, you know that? Very quick-witted."

Rachel wanted to argue with the interviewer. She wasn't anything of the sort, which was why she spent so much of her time alone in a room, creating beautiful sentiments for others to share with their loved ones.

"Were all of the buyers men?"

"No." The interviewer turned a page in her notebook. "You might find this one interesting. It's a quote from a forty-two-year-old woman, who purchased the card for her wife."

Rachel blinked and studied her inquisitor for any sign of judgment.

"Does that surprise you?"

"That a woman would buy a romantic card for another woman? Not at all. Love is love."

"Fair enough. She said, 'This card speaks from my heart. It says everything I feel so succinctly, and it does so in a way that's applicable to our lives. I appreciate that.'"

"Lovely."

"Did you intend that sentiment to be for same-sex couples?"

"No, but I'm happy to know that the words are universal enough to speak to every heart." Of course lesbians felt what everyone else in love felt and deserved to have greeting cards appropriate to express their emotions.

Still, Rachel had no intention of getting sucked into a conversation about same-sex couples and romance. It hit too close to home. Although she wasn't exactly in the closet, she didn't feel the need to talk about her sexuality with the hundreds of thousands of readers of *People* magazine.

"Okay. Last question."

Rachel's attention snapped back to the moment. This time the interviewer stared directly at her without consulting her pad.

"So, Ms. Wallach, you're the Queen of Hearts, the woman whose words touch lovers around the world..."

Rachel's gut tightened as she anticipated where this was going. *Don't ask it. Don't ask it.*

"I'm assuming there's someone special in your life. Do you write your own romantic sentiments for him? And how in the world does he romance you? Do you critique the greeting cards he gives you for occasions?"

You had to go there. Rachel's mind raced. The clock on the wall sounded loud in the silence. She put on her best poker face. "I never mix business with pleasure. My private life is my own, and I'd like to keep it that way."

"Oh." The interviewer, clearly taken aback, fiddled with her notebook. "I'm sorry. I didn't mean to intrude."

"No worries." Relief coursed through Rachel's veins as she realized that the interviewer wouldn't push the point. "I just like to keep things separate, you know what I mean?" She smiled kindly at the interviewer.

"Yeah. I get it. I wouldn't want someone prying into my personal life, either, if I had one." The interviewer stood up. "I've got plenty to work with here. Thank you for coming."

"Thanks for asking me." Rachel shook the interviewer's hand, gathered up her coat, and headed for the reception area and out the glass doors leading into the second-floor hallway.

⊰⊱

Rachel stood frozen in the corridor. She spied an exit sign some twenty feet away and to the right. Another exit sign glowed red directly over a door opposite the office where she'd just completed the interview.

She wished she'd paid closer attention when she arrived. Instead, she'd been consumed with Freud, the nasty weather, and the lack of parking spaces making her late.

She'd taken an elevator to the second floor, hadn't she? But there was no elevator in sight. Well, no matter. The stairs would do just fine. She certainly could use the exercise. Besides, she needed to get home to let Freud out, and indecision was getting her nowhere.

Once again, Rachel eyed both exit signs. Surely, all roads led to Rome and all exit signs led to the first floor and the main building entrance. "To heck with it." She turned the knob of the closest exit door and shouldered her way through. She found herself standing in a space without any stairs. In front of her was another door with an exit sign above. She pushed it open and walked through.

It wasn't until that door clicked shut behind her that she felt the cold air sting her legs. What in the world...? Rachel looked around. The fire escape? How could she possibly have ended up out on the fire escape?

She grabbed the handle of the door she'd come through and yanked. Nothing happened. She tugged again, with the same result. Her heart hammered in her chest so loud she could hear it in her ears. She knocked on the door. No one came.

"Deep breaths. Take deep breaths," Rachel admonished herself, even as she struggled to take in air. "Hyperventilating won't get you anywhere." She fished in her pocket. She'd just call for help. Her heart sank at the realization that her cell phone was sitting in the console of her car, in her purse, right where she'd left it so that she truthfully could answer her mother that she hadn't heard the no-doubt twenty-seven calls asking her how the interview went.

Big, fluffy snowflakes dotted her coat and landed in her hair, and a gust of wind sent a chill through her. The smell of rotting garbage permeated the air. Rachel surveyed her surroundings. There were no windows overlooking either side of the fire escape. The good news was, no one from *People* magazine would see her out there making a fool out of herself. The bad news was, no one would see her to help her.

Across an alleyway was a building Rachel recognized as the Albany Public Library. The entire first two floors on the alley side of that structure were solid brick. From her position on the landing, Rachel shielded her eyes and focused on the third-floor windows. Could there be someone up there who could see her dire predicament? The glare prevented her from seeing inside. What could anyone at the library do even if they saw her? Run next door, take the elevator to the second floor, find the exit leading to the fire escape, and let her in? That clearly wasn't going to happen.

They could call the fire department. *And tell them what? That there's a crazy lady standing outside on the fire escape next door in a nice coat and heels?* Rachel estimated the likelihood of someone from the library coming to her aid at less than two percent.

"Well, you can't keep standing out here." Rachel turned around and pounded on the door one more time, with the same result as the last. She peeked over the edge. The drop ladder from the fire escape stopped about eight feet off the ground. It appeared sturdy enough.

Tentatively, Rachel took a step forward. Her high heel caught in the landing's iron grating. She reached down and freed it, minus a sizable chunk of the leather. Could this situation get any worse?

Gingerly, slowly, she picked up her left foot and took another step, this time making sure only to balance on the ball of her foot, thus saving her one good heel. The drop ladder was within reach. Experimentally, she gave it a shake. It didn't budge. She examined it more closely. Surely there was a way to get it to release and reach the ground.

"You, the one lesbian in the universe who doesn't even own a roll of duct tape, think you're going to figure out how this sucker works?" Rachel examined the ladder one last time. Still, the answer eluded her.

The snow was falling harder now, coating her hair and dripping down the back of her neck and the front of her coat. If she stayed here any longer, her footing would be too treacherous even to attempt it. She grabbed the ladder with her right hand, swung herself around so that her body was pressed against the cold iron, and wrapped her left hand around the other side. Why had she left the house without gloves?

She shivered and her teeth chattered. *I will get down safely. I will get down safely. I can do this.* Carefully, she placed her left foot on the first rung. Not too bad. She reached with her right foot for the next rung. It was farther down than she anticipated, and it took her several seconds of feeling around with her by-now-nearly-numb foot to find it.

Rachel tried to ignore the niggling voice in her head repeatedly insisting that she should've worn more practical footwear. After all, who plans on getting locked out on a fire escape and having to shimmy her way down?

Step by step, slowly, painstakingly, Rachel made her way down, until she reached the bottom rung. So far, so good. There was only one problem—she still was nowhere near touching the ground. "WWWWD," she mumbled out loud. "What would Wonder Woman do?"

"That's easy, she'd wrap her lasso around the bottom rung and effortlessly swing to the ground."

The absurdity of the situation made Rachel giddy.

"Wallach? There's no place to go but down. Stop stalling." Rachel realized that talking to herself was a sign of mental instability, but since no one was here to see it, it hardly counted, right? "The way I see it, you've got two choices. Jump from this height, or use your arms and lower yourself down."

An eight-foot drop in high heels seemed foolish, so Rachel settled on option number two. After three false starts trying to twist herself into a pretzel, she finally managed to get a good grip on the bottom rung, slide her right foot past her hand, swing her left leg out and away from the ladder, and use those muscles her personal trainer insisted she needed more work on, to lower herself to the ground.

Any second, her arms surely would dislocate from their sockets. How many times had she cheated on those pull-ups at the gym? "Lower yourself slowly. Feel the burn." Her trainer's voice mocked her as her arms shook. She extended them fully. She should look down. She needed to know how far she was from the ground, didn't she? Before she could finish the thought, her ice-cold hands slipped from the iron cross bar.

Rachel screamed as she plummeted to a certain death... Roughly six inches later, her feet hit the snow-covered pavement. How was that possible? She shook the snow from her hair.

"Oh, my God! It's a flipping arithmetic problem!" Rachel slapped herself in the forehead with the palm of her hand. Word problems—arithmetic problems involving stories—were the bane of her existence. "If the drop is eight feet, and my arms are two feet long, and my body is five feet six inches tall...subtract ten inches for the distance from the top of my head to my shoulders... With my arms fully extended, how far would my feet be from the ground?"

It didn't add up. She should've fallen farther—sixteen inches, to be exact. "Solve for 'X'. What's wrong with this picture, apart from the fact that you failed to account for the height of the heels?"

Rachel chuckled, although it sounded more like a cackle to her ears. "What's wrong with this picture is that you're standing out in the freezing cold, having locked yourself out on a fire escape and successfully negotiated a way down, and you're doing a math problem instead of rejoicing at your ingenuity and real-life problem-solving skills."

She checked her watch. If she hurried, she could get home before Freud lost his bladder on her favorite rug. Rachel turned in a circle, trying to orient herself. Which way was her car?

Word problems, engineering feats, and directional challenges—in less than half an hour, the universe had hit the trifecta of her weaknesses.

Well, she'd gotten through the tough spots, hadn't she? She should be proud of herself. Now, the only thing left was for her to exit the alley with her dignity intact. With as much confidence as she could muster, Rachel strode toward the sounds of traffic. That must be the front of the building.

When she got close enough to see the street, Rachel's knees went weak. Standing between her and salvation was a ten-foot-high chain-link fence, topped with barbed wire. "Don't freak out. There's a gate. You just need to open it." Her voice caught in her throat as she spied the massive chain and padlock. She turned her back to the street and slumped against the cold steel. What more could go wrong?

Where there was a front, there must be a back. Of course. Rachel pushed off the fence and headed back in the direction from which she'd come. The warming temperature was turning the snow into slush, the unevenness of her heels made her walk like Quasimodo, and wetness seeped into her shoes so that her feet made a squishing sound with every step. Big fat snowflakes stuck to the false eyelashes, making Rachel wish she had windshield wipers for her face.

No! It couldn't be. "A brick wall? Seriously?" The wall spanned the distance between the building from which Rachel had exited and the library. She was effectively boxed in. In frustration, she reached down, picked up one of the copious empty Styrofoam cups that littered the alley, and threw it as hard as she could.

If she thought tears wouldn't have frozen her eyes shut, Rachel would've cried. Instead, she yelled at the Heavens. "Okay, that's it. I've had it. Enough, already!"

Back she trudged to the front of the alley, where she confronted the fearsome fence. Maybe she could fit through the space between the gate and the fence. It was a tiny opening, but if she turned sideways… Rachel wedged herself as far into the space as she could manage, and shoved against the steel. It didn't budge.

Okay. Time to reconsider. The only way out was over. "You're going to climb a ten-foot fence and two feet of barbed wire? You've lost your mind." Rachel imagined her hands and legs cut to shreds. She couldn't do it. There was no way. Except that she had to do it. There were no other options.

She wrapped her fingers through the chain links and hoisted herself up. The metal dug into her palms and fingertips. The openings barely accommodated her toes and up to the balls of her feet. The soft leather soles offered no protection whatsoever. The skirt and raincoat impeded her progress even further.

After what seemed an eternity, Rachel chanced a glance downward. She closed her eyes as despair welled up within her. How was it possible she'd progressed so little? She hung in the stillness, suspended on a barbed wire fence, the wind buffeting her, stinging her cheeks, the grayness of the day making her wish she'd never gotten out of bed that morning.

"Onward, Wallach. Stop feeling sorry for yourself." She counted the number of rows she could bypass in one stretch. Four rows up with her left arm and she wrapped her fingers through the next opening. Then up the same number of rows with her right foot, followed by the right hand, and the left foot. And on, and on, and on for what seemed like an hour.

Finally, finally, she reached the last two rows before the barbed wire. Exhaustion and cold took up residence in her bones. More than anything, she wished she were curled up in a blanket on the couch at home, a fire in the fireplace, and a good book in her hands. She wouldn't even complain when Freud passed gas.

Reality, in the form of a fresh blast of cold wind, forced her back to the present. Rachel peeked up through the false eyelashes to gauge the distance to the top of the barbed wire. Even if she could manage to get enough momentum, there was no way she could propel her arms and legs over the barbs without any part of her body touching them. Now what? Hadn't she already met her problem-solving quota for the day? *More like for the year.*

What body part was she willing to sacrifice? She needed her hands to work, so they were out. Where were the major arteries in her legs, again? Bleeding out would be an ignominious end. What would they put on her epitaph? "Here lies Rachel Wallach. She lost her life in a bold bid for freedom from imprisonment in an alleyway?"

Too wordy.

Oh, how she wished she'd paid more attention in anatomy class. Professor Rusk was right, after all. Anatomy would come in handy in the real world. Who knew?

The hairspray the makeup artist liberally applied gave up the ghost, leaving Rachel's hair plastered to her head, the stickiness dripping down her neck and inside the back of her blouse.

"WWWWD, Wallach?" *She'd use ingenuity, that's what. She'd improvise.* And that was the moment. That was when Rachel figured out that she could take off her raincoat, tie it over the barbs, and use it as a buffer. It was the only option that made sense.

In practice, she ripped her pantyhose in three places, and scratched her hands and legs several times through the material of the coat, but, lo and behold, she found herself in one piece on the other side of the fence. "It worked! It worked!" Belatedly, Rachel realized she was using her outside voice.

She untied the coat and let it flutter to the ground. As fast as she was able, she lowered herself down the fence, repeating the process she'd used on the other side. It sure was easier going down than it was climbing up. When she was three feet from the ground, she kicked off her shoes and jumped, landing with a splash in the slush. She didn't care. She'd made it. She'd done something she didn't think she could do. She held her hands up like a gymnast sticking a landing and awaiting her score. Then, with as much dignity as she could manage, she gathered up her shredded coat and her shoes and headed for her car.

Thank God no one had been there to see that.

CHAPTER NINE

Julia's computer chimed, alerting her to an incoming email. Absentmindedly, she clicked on it, as she continued to stare at pages thirty-two and thirty-three of her copy of *People* magazine. Rachel looked positively stunning in the full-color spread of photographs that accompanied the article. Her eyes were bright and vibrant, but in them Julia noticed a sense of vulnerability that matched the shyness of her smile. The effect was adorable and alluring.

She certainly won't need my help, or anyone else's, to get a date after this.

Julia popped two more Tums into her mouth. Lately, she'd been suffering from a serious case of heartburn. She'd cut out anything spicy from her diet and eliminated as many other obvious causes as she could. If this persisted, she'd have to make an appointment for a check-up.

As she put the bottle back on her desk, the open email caught her attention. It was from an old friend she hadn't heard from since she'd moved upstate. The subject line read, "Have you seen this? Isn't this in your neck of the woods?"

Julia read the body of the email.

> Hola, chica. Long time no talk to. I thought I remembered that you'd hung your shingle in the Albany area. Am I remembering that right? This gem made me LOL. Then I looked at the description, and it was shot in downtown Albany. That made me think of you. Do you recognize the

building? Anyway, just thought I'd share. Hope
you are well. XO.

Curious, Julia clicked on the YouTube link embedded in the
email. The description of the video said, "Captured on film outside
a downtown Albany, New York building. MacGyver's got nothing
on this woman."

Julia hit play, and the musical soundtrack from the old
Keystone Kops silent movie chases circa 1906 blared from her
computer speaker. The clip unfolded in black and white, made to
look like a comedy from that era, complete with the action
accelerated to enhance the comical effect.

A well-dressed woman stood on a snowy fire escape balcony,
pounding on the door to get back inside. When no one answered,
she shook the ladder to no avail, and then climbed down, stopping
where the steps left her stranded to... Julia squinted at the
screen... What in the world was she doing? Having a conversation
with herself?

"Oh, my God. That's too funny." Julia laughed even harder as
the woman played her own personal version of the game Twister
in order to bridge the distance between the last step and the
ground, and guffawed as the woman spotted the barbed wire fence
and turned around in the narrow alley looking for another way...

The laughter died on Julia's lips. "Oh, my God." She paused
the video and pushed her chair in so that she was practically on top
of the screen. "It can't be." She fumbled for the mouse, moved the
arrow back over the play button, and un-paused the movie.
Quickly, she hit pause again. The woman was a little closer now,
and facing the camera.

Julia's heart stuttered. She jumped up, ran into the bathroom,
and rummaged through her drawers until she found her
magnifying glass. She hustled back to her office, shoved the chair
out of the way, leaned forward on the desk until again she was
virtually on top of the monitor, and held the magnifying glass up
to the screen.

Rachel's unmistakable, beautiful face filled the glass. Julia felt
for the chair, pulled it toward her, and sank down heavily into the
seat. For long seconds, she sat there paralyzed, torn between the
need to watch the rest, or turn away.

The arrow hovered over the play button. Watching felt like a betrayal. Not watching meant not knowing what other embarrassing footage was floating around the internet. What if Rachel wasn't aware of the video's existence? What if she was? What if there was something even more offensive? If Julia saw it, could she report it and have the movie taken down?

Reluctantly, she clicked on play. By the time Rachel landed on the other side of the fence with her hands raised triumphantly in the air, Julia didn't know whether to cry or cheer.

Poor Rachel. Apart from the horror of finding herself in the middle of a hair-raising predicament, was the indignity of having been videotaped and streamed around the world as the butt of a joke.

Julia checked underneath the video thumbnail. Over 65,000 views in just under three hours. Maybe, if the fates were kind, neither Rachel nor anyone else who knew her would see it.

Rachel sat on a bench in the park, watching Freud play with a dead leaf. The Darth Vader theme from the original "Stars Wars" movie pierced the silence, and Rachel snapped up her cell phone. Paul was calling? Her brother never called. He'd probably heard from their mother about the upcoming piece in *People* and was calling to congratulate her, however grudgingly.

"Hello, Paul."

"Hi, squirt. Did you get my email?"

"What email?"

"That answers that question. You'd better check your email. You're a star!"

"You talked to Mom about the *People* magazine article?"

"What *People* magazine article?"

"The one I'm featured in. It's coming out next week."

"Hell, no. Your video is trending on YouTube. It's viral. Holy shit, I haven't laughed that hard in, like, forever."

"What video?"

"What, do you live in a cave? Never mind. I know you live in a cave. Just check your email, will you? I'm related to an honest-to-God internet celebrity. Who knew?"

Paul's laughter rang hollow in Rachel's ear. What in the world was he talking about?

Freud was happily chasing his tail, so she opened her email app and found Paul's note, which consisted of nothing but a YouTube link and his automated signature.

Rachel clicked. Five minutes and forty-four seconds later, she still sat rooted to the spot, her hands shaking uncontrollably, and her phone forgotten in her lap.

"Your dog is so cute."

"He's not my dog," Rachel responded, somewhat peevishly.

"Oh. I'm sorry. I didn't mean to offend you."

Rachel glanced at the woman who'd sat down next to her on the bench. "No, I'm sorry. You didn't offend me. It's just that it's a long story, and this is royally bad timing."

"I get it. Lord knows I have moments when I want to be alone too. I'll just leave you to it, then." The woman got up and walked away without uttering another word.

This isn't a "moment" I want to be alone. I want to disappear for the rest of this life and the next. Rachel rose and tugged on Freud's leash. "Come on. Let's go home before anybody else sees me and starts pointing."

When they reached the house, Rachel took Freud inside, unsnapped the leash, and grabbed a pint of Ben & Jerry's Chocolate Chip Cookie Dough ice cream from the freezer, along with a spoon. If ever there was a full-pint emergency, this was it.

She threw herself on the couch. The dog, no doubt aware of the sense of doom permeating the air, laid down a short distance away, his head on his paws, his eyes on her.

"Just when I thought things were finally starting to go my way, this happens." Rachel pried the top off the container, tossed it on the end table, and spooned out the first therapeutic dose of creamy goodness. She closed her eyes briefly and let the ice cream melt on her tongue.

"Of course," she mumbled around the next mouthful, "it would have to be my dolt of a brother who saw the flipping thing. It couldn't be someone who would understand how devastating this could be to me and would break the news gently and sympathetically."

Rachel stabbed the spoon into a chunk of cookie dough and extricated it. "No. It had to be the one person who will gleefully share the news with the rest of the family and every single one of his jerky friends."

Rachel's phone rang again. This time the ringtone was "I Feel Pretty," from the musical "West Side Story." Rachel groaned. Did she have the strength to talk to her sister? *If you don't answer, she'll keep calling.*

Rachel hit the speaker button. "Hi, Erin."

"Oh, my God, Rach. I'm so glad you answered. Are you okay?"

Rachel blinked her eyes and swallowed to keep the tears at bay. "No, I'm not okay. Would you be?" She shoveled another spoonful of ice cream into her mouth. "Wait," she slurred around a chunk of cookie dough, "that's a stupid question. You'd never have gotten yourself into that situation in the first place."

"You don't know that."

"Come on, Erin. You're too perfect and far too put together for that. God, I wish I could be more like you."

"You *what*?" Erin asked.

"You heard me. Please don't make me repeat it."

"Rachel Wallach, you listen to me. I don't know why you've never seemed to understand this, but I'm going to put it in plain English for you. You want to be like me? You've got it backwards. I'm the one who always wanted to be like *you*."

"Bullpucky."

"Truth. I swear to God, Rach."

"Erin, you're gorgeous, outgoing, successful... You've got the world by the tail. Why would you ever want to be like me? What? You want to have anxiety attacks every time you have to deal with people? You want to be so socially awkward that millions of strangers laugh at you on YouTube?"

"Stop it, Rach." Erin's voice was soft, but commanding. "Right now. Nobody talks about my sister that way, including you. Do you know that growing up, I idolized you?"

"Pfft."

"I did," Erin said. "You were the brightest person I knew. You were sensitive, and compassionate. Who else rescued every salamander from being dissected by the boys? Who was the one who saved that bird with the broken wing, bottle fed him, and released him back into the wild? Who got straight-As and was the valedictorian of the class? Who got in early action to Princeton?"

"Maybe those things are true, but I'm the great disappointment in the family. I'm the misfit, the outlier, the one with the job nobody thinks is a real job. Mom's disgusted with me. Not only am I a lesbian, but I can't go on a date without making a fool of myself, or worse. I have zero people skills. I'm not like you. Everything comes easily for you."

"Rach, that's not true. I struggle too."

"You've always been the 'good' daughter—the golden girl, Erin."

"That's so bogus. You were Mom's favorite, Rach. You were everything Mom wished she was but never could be. You had so much potential. That's why she pushed you so hard."

"And look at me now. One great big disappointment."

"Not true. She's been bragging to anyone who'll listen about *People* doing a feature on you."

"Uh-huh."

"Let me let you in on a secret. You think I'm successful? If I am, it's because of you."

"Me?"

"Yep. Watching you, I never felt like I measured up. So I tried three times as hard to be successful so Mom would think half as much of me as she did of you. You were my hero."

Rachel shook her head. "You're just trying to make me feel better."

"Trust me, I wouldn't admit that to make you feel better. By the way, I tried to track down the scumbag who posted that video."

"You did?"

"You bet I did. Unfortunately, YouTube wasn't helpful about it. They wouldn't tell me who it was and they wouldn't take it down. I'm sorry."

"I-I can't believe you did that." Erin did that…for her?

"Of course. I told you, no one messes with my sister. I love you, Rach."

"I love you too, Erin."

"Don't let the idiots in the world drag you down. And for Heaven's sake, don't go into hiding. Hold your head up. You're a rock star. I've got to go. Hang in there."

"Thanks. 'Bye."

"See you around."

Rachel put the phone down. "What do you think about that, Freud? My sister stood up for me. Imagine that."

Freud thumped his tail on the hardwood floor.

Rachel scooped up another spoonful of ice cream. "I don't believe for a second that Erin idolized me," she told Freud. "But it sure was nice of her to say so, and to come to my defense." Don't go into hiding, she'd said. She knew Rachel too well.

"What am I going to do?"

Freud blinked twice.

"I can't simply pretend it never happened. That's not a viable solution." Rachel shoveled another spoonful of ice cream into her mouth. "I'll just never go out again, and if I have to go out, I'll wear a paper bag over my head."

Freud groaned and rolled onto his side.

"Okay. That's not practical. How do you expect me to think clearly at a time like this?" She sat up and nabbed her laptop off the other end of the couch and booted up.

Freud covered his eyes with his paws.

"I recognize that watching it again is cruel and unusual punishment, but I have to know what it looks like on a regular-sized screen, don't I?" Rachel toggled to her email, opened Paul's note again, and clicked on the link.

The play button loomed large in the center of the screen. Rachel's gaze alighted on the information below. Views: 1,247,862. Comments: 322. "Oh, my goodness." The ice cream settled like lead in the pit of her stomach. It was like a train wreck. Rachel couldn't stop herself from reading the comments.

> "This is the funniest thing I've seen in ages. Thanks for the laugh. Anyone know who this woman is?"

> "My wife and I watched this just now and nearly peed our pants. What idiot gets locked out on a fire escape? Worse still, why the hell didn't she use her cell phone to call somebody?"

"Maybe because she didn't have her cell phone with her," Rachel muttered.

"OMG! Please tell me this was staged. Nobody could be that inept for real."

Rachel's eyes filled with tears. How could people be so mean? Hadn't they ever done anything embarrassing before?

Freud whimpered.

"I know, stop reading. No good can come of it." Rachel grabbed a tissue and blotted her eyes, took a deep breath, and hit play. As her plight played out on the screen in triple-time, the tears overflowed. She'd thought that she was alone out there. Judging from the angle of the video, someone had been standing in one of those third-floor windows at the library. Why hadn't they tried to help her instead of using her predicament to make fun of her?

As the video finished, Rachel dropped her head into her hands and sobbed. She felt so violated. Something cold nudged her and she jumped. Freud was sitting so close they were practically nose-to-nose. He licked her face.

"Eww."

He licked her face again and pulled back. The expression in his eyes was so kind, so understanding.

"This totally blows, Freud."

Again, he licked her face, and this time it was obvious to Rachel that what he was doing was licking away her tears. The gesture was so human—well, not the licking part, but the compassionate part—why couldn't more humans be like Freud?

She nuzzled her cheek against his, and Freud nuzzled her back. She wrapped her arms around his neck and hugged him, hard. He seemed to relish the closeness. How could she ever have been afraid of this intuitive soul?

Rachel smiled through her tears and scratched behind Freud's ears. She pulled away to snatch a tissue from the nearby box.

Freud's howl morphed into a belch she could smell from several feet away.

"Good job ruining the moment, pal."

⋙⋘

Goldie checked her watch for the umpteenth time. Rachel should've been here nearly an hour ago, and she was never late. What could be wrong? Was she in a ditch somewhere? Maybe she'd gotten mugged! Had the train derailed? Should she call the police?

Goldie stepped out the door and headed toward the front entrance. From there, she should be able to see Rachel coming. She rounded the corner and stopped short. Ida, the turncoat, was headed straight for her. Goldie ducked quickly behind the post. She'd count to ten and then risk a peek. Maybe she should make it twenty; Ida was so darned slow with that walker.

At the count of fifteen, Goldie couldn't stand it anymore. She poked her head around the corner. Ida was almost to the front door. She looked gaunt and haggard. Goldie wondered if she was feeling all right. No, she couldn't care. Whatever was going on with Ida was none of her beeswax.

The automatic doors slid open and in walked Julia. She looked only slightly better than her grandmother. Goldie watched them embrace. It was so tender. It reminded her of the way she and Rachel were together.

Rachel. Where in the world was Rachel? She jumped when she felt a tap on her shoulder from behind. Her hand flew to her chest, where her heart was beating a staccato rhythm. A shadowy figure stood too close, a large pair of sunglasses masking his eyes and the black hood of a sweatshirt covering his head and obscuring most of his face.

"I have mace. Back off, or I'll spritz you and scream bloody murder."

"Shh. It's me, Grandma. It's Rachel."

Goldie lifted the sunglasses.

"What are you doing?" Rachel asked. She pulled the shades back down.

"I just wanted to be sure. Why are you wearing that ridiculous get-up?"

Rachel ignored the question. "Why are you skulking around hallways?"

If Rachel wasn't going to answer her, then she didn't need to answer Rachel, either.

Goldie shot one more glance in Ida's direction before retreating down the hall toward her apartment, Rachel in tow. When they were seated, Goldie asked, "Are you planning to let me see that beautiful face any time soon?"

Rachel got up, closed the shades, and removed the disguise. Her eyes were puffy and red.

"Bubbeleh. Have you been crying? What's wrong? And why are you so late? I've been worried sick."

"I'm okay, Grandma." Rachel looked away.

"Now see here, young lady. I know that routine. Something's bothering you. Something's wrong, and I'm going to get to the bottom of it before you leave here."

"Nothing's wrong."

"You know you haven't been able to lie successfully to me since I first taught you how to play gin rummy as a little girl. 'Fess up."

"I brought you something."

It was clear that Rachel had no intention of addressing the elephant in the living room. Well, Goldie would wait her out and find an opening.

Rachel fished in the briefcase next to the chair and pulled out one of several copies of *People* magazine. "This is the article about me. It came out a few days ago."

Goldie snatched up the magazine. "Thank you. But changing the subject isn't going to work this time. Isn't the story any good?"

"It was great."

Patience wasn't Goldie's strong suit. To heck with waiting. "Okay. So whatever's bothering you isn't about that. What is it, already? Maybe I can help you."

"You can't help with this, Grandma."

Aha! That was progress. "So, good. Now you admit something did happen. Does whatever it is explain why you gave me three extra gray hairs by being so late today?"

"Please, Grandma. I'm not playing twenty questions with you," Rachel pleaded. "Just let it be."

"I see."

Should Goldie do nothing when her favorite granddaughter was this miserable? "Letting it be when something's wrong? That's not in the grandmother/granddaughter contract, darling," she said softly.

"It's just horrible, that's all." Rachel wrung her hands.

"What is, bubbeleh? What has you so upset? You know you can tell me anything."

"I made a little mistake that turned out to be huge, and now everybody in the world can see it. They're making fun of me in countries I've never even heard of." Rachel said the words in a rush as her tears flowed.

Goldie couldn't stand it anymore. She leaned over and gathered her granddaughter into her arms. "There, there, sweetheart. I don't know what you're talking about, but I can tell you that if someone is making fun of my Rachel, they're going to have to answer to me."

Rachel sniffed and blew her nose noisily into a Kleenex she extracted from her pocket. "Thanks, Grandma. You always have my back. But you can't fix this one."

"Not even with my extra special chocolate chip cookies?"

Rachel shook her head. "Did you forget that you don't have an oven in here?"

"Minor detail."

"Nothing can fix this one, Grandma. Not this time."

"I can't believe that. What do you mean everyone can see it? And what mistake is it you think you made?"

Rachel chewed her lip, as if trying to reach a decision. "What did you do with that present I brought you a while back?"

Goldie's brows drew together. "What present?"

"The one with the pink bow."

"Oh, that." Goldie pointed to the bookcase by the window, where the polka-dot-wrapped gift sat unopened on a shelf.

Rachel retrieved the package and unwrapped it. "I bought you an iPad."

"I have plenty of pads laying around here."

"This isn't a pad of paper, Grandma. It's electronic." Rachel opened the gizmo and images appeared on the screen. "I'm going to show you something. You have to promise not to laugh."

"Cross my heart and hope to die." Goldie made an "x" across her chest.

Rachel's fingers moved so fast Goldie gave up on trying to follow what she was doing. She heard her mumble about why and fi-something, going on a safari, and chrome, although why she would be thinking about Africa and car bumpers was a mystery.

Finally, Rachel came and sat next to her. "Remember, you promised not to laugh."

"Have I ever broken a promise to you?"

"Never."

"So show me, already." Goldie could feel Rachel trembling next to her. She reached out and wrapped her arm around her. "Whatever it is, it will be okay. You'll see."

Suddenly, music blared from the device. Goldie recognized the tune from the movies of her childhood. She loved the Keystone Kops! Just as she was about to say so, she realized what was happening in the movie. The poor woman on the screen was in danger. Why didn't someone help her?

A few seconds later, the woman's face came fully into focus. Oh, no. Goldie's heart sank. So this was the embarrassing thing. Oh, dear. The drama continued to unfold on the screen, but Goldie had seen enough. Poor, sensitive, shy Rachel, her trauma laid bare for the world to see.

The movie ended, and Goldie took her granddaughter's hands in her own. "You know what I see in that movie?"

"An inept, foolish girl."

"Absolutely not. I see a brave, resourceful young woman who got stuck with lemons and made lemonade."

"You have to say that. You're my grandmother."

"I don't have to say any such thing. I'm simply calling it the way I see it."

"Read the comments, Grandma. Everyone is saying vicious, hurtful things."

"Then stop reading, bubbeleh. They don't know you from Adam." Goldie could feel the misery pouring out of Rachel. "How do you make one of these comments? I've got something to say."

"What? No, Grandma." Rachel pulled the iPad away and closed it.

"Why not? If other people can have their say, I can too."

106

"I appreciate the gesture, but, no." Rachel returned the device to the bookshelf. She paused, and partially opened one window blind. "Grandma? Why is there an ambulance outside?"

"There's an ambulance?"

"Yes." Rachel covered her mouth with her hand. "Oh, no. That's your friend Ida on the gurney."

CHAPTER TEN

Julia could never remember being this frightened. Ida looked so small and frail on the gurney. When she'd called and started the conversation by telling Julia not to worry, Julia knew it must be serious. Then when she'd arrived and gotten a good look at her grandmother, she knew there was no time to waste. Her color was wrong and her breathing was shallow.

"I'm telling you, it's nothing. Stop worrying. That crease in your forehead will become permanent."

"I'll be right behind you in my car, Grandma. I'll meet you in the emergency room."

"Ma'am?" The paramedic addressed Julia. "We'll need you to step out of the way now." He hung an IV on a portable pole. "Mrs. Pinsky? Please stop gesturing with your hands. We need you to lie still."

"You're such a handsome young man. Are you married? My granddaughter there is single."

"Grandma!"

"What? Well, you are."

"I'll meet you at the hospital," Julia called, as the paramedics loaded Ida into the ambulance.

As she turned to run to her car, Julia collided with a body. "Sorry, I…"

"Um. Hi," Rachel said. Nervously, she tucked an errant strand of hair behind her left ear. "I don't know if you remember me. We only met briefly. My grandmother is Goldie Horowitz, your grandmother's friend. I saw what was happening from her window. She sent me out to find out what's going on and if there's anything we can do to help."

"They think it's her heart. I'm on my way to meet her at the hospital."

"We're going too." Goldie appeared under the portico. She was carrying her purse. "Aren't we, Rachel?"

Rachel's eyebrows rose up into her hairline, but she didn't miss a beat. "That's right. Come on, I'll drive."

"No. That's okay. I have no idea how long we'll be."

"Nonsense. Rachel and I have nothing but time. Rachel? Get the car."

"But, you're not even talking to each other," Julia said to Goldie.

"There's no such thing during a crisis. We stick together. That's how it's always been, and that's how it always will be until we're cold and in the grave. When this is over, Ida will come to her senses and apologize."

"In a pig's eye," Julia muttered. It would take more than a heart attack—more like a complete frontal lobotomy—for stubborn Grandma Ida ever to admit that she'd made a mistake.

Goldie was being just as pig-headed about this trip to the hospital. Julia realized she'd have more luck dealing with Rachel. "You don't..." Where was Rachel? She'd been standing there just a minute ago. Julia spotted her thirty yards away in the parking lot, just getting into her car.

"See? Rachel's already on her way. There's no point arguing. We're taking you to the hospital and that's that."

Goldie crossed her arms, her pocketbook dangling from one forearm. At another time, it would've been comical. Now... Now it was a truly kind gesture.

What would Ida say? She'd tell Julia to remember her manners and mind her elders. "Thank you."

Rachel pulled up to the entrance in the Deuce and a Quarter, jumped out, and opened both the passenger and back passenger doors. Goldie started to get in the back seat.

"No. You ride in the front," Julia said.

"I won't hear of it. Besides, you'll need to tell Rachel how to get there. She has her father's sense of direction."

Goldie folded herself into the back seat and buckled her seatbelt, Julia followed suit in the front seat, and Rachel stepped on the gas.

"Watch out for the…" The words died on Julia's lips as the car flew over the speed bump, bouncing them into the air.

"Sorry," Rachel said, fighting to be heard over the radio, which mysteriously had turned itself on with the impact. Glenn Miller's "Chattanooga Choo Choo," blared from the front speakers.

"That's weird." Rachel snapped the radio off.

"You like music from the 1940s?" Julia asked.

"What? No. I mean, yes, but that's not what I was listening to last time I was in the car. I have no idea how it could've changed itself to another station."

Julia heard a choking sound from the backseat. "Are you okay, Goldie?" Julia turned to see the oddest look on Goldie's face.

"I'm fine, dear. So tell me about Ida. What happened?"

Julia thought Goldie still appeared red in the face, but she no longer was coughing. "If you're sure you're all right."

"Yes, yes. I'm sure." Goldie waved away Julia's concern. "Nu? Tell us about Ida."

"Ever since your spat, she's been out of sorts." Julia noted the consternation in Goldie's expression and immediately regretted her choice of words. This health scare with Ida had her so she wasn't thinking straight. Well, she couldn't take the words back now. "Her blood pressure's been high, she's been retaining fluids, and she hasn't been sleeping or eating normally."

"You and Ida had words? That's why you shut me down every time I ask you how she's doing?" Rachel was watching Goldie in the rearview mirror. "Why didn't you tell me?"

"You didn't need to know. It doesn't matter." Goldie's tone brooked no discussion, but Julia bet that Rachel wouldn't let the issue go so easily.

"Of course it matters. That explains why you've been moping around. You two were thick as thieves, Grandma. Nothing should've come between you. Ida is in bad shape, and you're not doing so hot, yourself. This has to stop."

The entire time Rachel was talking, Julia kept an eye on Goldie. Would she tell her granddaughter that the argument had been about her and her dating appeal? Julia shifted uncomfortably in her seat. Would Rachel find out that Goldie had employed her to find Rachel a romantic partner?

"Hush. What's between Ida and me is between Ida and me. Butt out."

"Grandma!"

"I mean it." Goldie pointed her finger at Rachel. "No more talk about this. Right now, we need to focus on Ida's health, and poor Julia, here, who must be frightened out of her mind and anxious about her bubbe." Goldie turned to Julia. "You'd better start giving her directions or we're liable to end up in Chicago."

঵঵

Rachel hazarded another sideways peek at Julia. Ida had been taken into surgery more than an hour ago for an angioplasty. The doctors had determined that one of the arteries in her heart was ninety-five percent blocked.

Julia was handling this with such calm and grace. If the roles were reversed, Rachel would be a wreck. "I'm sure they'll tell us something soon," she said to Julia.

"I'm certain you're right."

"Would you like something to eat? I could go get you something from the cafeteria."

"No, thank you. I'm fine."

Rachel turned to Goldie, who hadn't said more than five words since they'd gotten the news of Ida's condition. "Are you okay, Grandma?"

Goldie patted her on the hand. "I will be, darling. We have to go sometime. If this is Ida's time, so be it. But I hope not."

"Me too." Rachel debated whether to bring up the feud again. Goldie nearly bit her head off when she raised the issue in the car. She knew in her heart that, although Goldie and Ida might be mad at each other, they loved each other practically like sisters. This pettiness needed to end.

"Grandma?"

"Yes, bubbeleh?"

"If...no...when Ida gets through this health crisis, you two need to make up."

Goldie's eyes flashed ever so briefly with anger and then softened. She said nothing, and Rachel could see that the fight had gone out of her.

A nurse wearing scrubs walked by. Rachel had seen her earlier when Ida was being prepped for surgery.

"Excuse me?"

The nurse paused. "Yes?"

"Can you give us an update on Ida Pinsky?"

The nurse sighed wearily. "When the doctor is done, he'll... Wait a minute... You're her. Oh, my God. You're her, the girl from the internet! Holy shit! Right here in my hospital."

Rachel felt her face flush bright red. How could she make this stop? She jumped to her feet and bolted out of the surgical waiting room, down the hall, and kept going until she'd reached the automatic doors leading to the visitors' parking lot, all the while praying for the ground beneath her feet to open up and swallow her.

"Hey."

Rachel spun away from the gentle touch on her shoulder.

"Rachel?"

Rachel closed her eyes. She couldn't face Julia now. She couldn't face anyone now.

"Rachel? Please. It's okay." Julia moved around in front of her.

Rachel's bottom lip quivered. It wasn't okay. It never would be okay again. A sob escaped her lips. Her hands shook.

"Rachel? Please. Don't let idiots like that get to you." Julia wrapped her arms around her.

Rachel tried to turn away. Julia held her fast. The touch was comforting and comfortable and confusing at the same time. Finally, when she realized Julia wasn't about to let go, Rachel gave in.

The tears flowed freely now, as Rachel's pent-up shame, anger, mortification, and helplessness poured forth.

"Shh." Julia rubbed circles on her back. "That's right. Let it out. Get it out of your system."

Eventually, the fog lifted and Rachel became aware of several things. First, she was freezing. Second, she'd managed to soak Julia's sweater with her tears. And third, she was in desperate need of a Kleenex. She pulled away and fumbled in her pocket for a tissue.

"Oh, wow. I can't believe I lost it like that. I'm so, so sorry." Rachel blew her nose noisily. "I hope I didn't ruin your sweater."

"It's fine. Truly."

Rachel shifted from foot to foot. If she felt self-conscious before, she felt even worse now. "I'm such a dolt. Here you are, dealing with your grandmother undergoing life-and-death surgery, and you're having to comfort me."

Julia took a step closer. Rachel took another step backward. "You're going through a traumatic time too. Nobody expects to have a private moment made fun of and splashed all over the internet."

Rachel gasped. "You saw it. You know." Could the situation get any worse? Where else could she run to? Maybe if she moved to Siberia... Then again, somebody probably had seen it there too. How did people join the witness protection program? Could she get her face changed? And assume a new identity?

"Whatever it is you're thinking right now? Please don't do it," Julia said.

"What?" Rachel refocused on the conversation.

"The look on your face," Julia said, as if that explained everything.

"What look on my face?"

"The one that screams, 'I wish I could just disappear without a trace.'"

Rachel's eyes widened. Had she been that transparent? It was time to shift the focus. "You saw the video."

Julia shrugged. "I did."

Even though she'd known the answer, Rachel felt it like a punch in the gut.

"Please don't run again," Julia pleaded. "I saw it after a friend forwarded the link to me because the footage was shot near my office and she wanted to know if I was familiar with the location. I didn't know it was you."

"You must have. You just said so."

"I meant that I didn't know it was you when I clicked on the link. When I saw your face, of course I recognized you. Yes."

Rachel hung her head. Everyone knew.

"Please, Rachel. Don't make assumptions. I saw the video, and I saw that it was you. I'd just finished reading the *People* magazine article online, which was fabulous, by the way. I realized that whoever posted the video was mean-spirited, and I hated that for you. But I never once thought that you were anything less than enterprising and resourceful. You were in a horrible situation, and instead of panicking and giving up, you fought through it and solved the problem. I was in awe of your spirit."

"You don't have to say that." Rachel continued to stare at the ground, misery filling every cell in her body.

Julia ducked down so that she forced eye contact. "You're right. I don't have to say that. But I'm telling you that because it's the truth. It's the truth of how I felt at the time, and it's even more true now. What you did was courageous, Rachel. Not many women would've gotten out of that jam the way you did. I'm proud of you."

"Yeah, well. Most women wouldn't have gotten themselves into that mess in the first place."

"You don't know that."

"I—"

"Ms. Spielman? I've been looking everywhere for you." A different nurse approached from the hospital entrance. "Your grandmother is out of the recovery room and would like to see you now."

"How is she?" Julia and Rachel asked simultaneously.

"The doctor is with her now. If you hurry, you can still catch him. She's on the trauma floor. Room 6, third floor."

⋖⋗

Ida looked tiny and helpless in the bed. Goldie approached slowly and on tiptoes, in case Ida was sleeping.

"Why are you sneaking around my hospital room?" Ida's voice was raspy and sounded tired.

"I thought maybe you were asleep."

"You thought maybe I was dead. It's okay. I did too, for a while there."

"You're too stubborn to die."

"Takes one to know one."

"Fair enough," Goldie conceded.

A lengthy, awkward silence ensued. What could she talk about that wouldn't lead to another argument? They could discuss the weather. *Trite.* How about the best recipe for matzo ball soup? *No.*

Discussions about who was the best cook would lead to another disagreement. Politics? *No.* The state of the world? *Depressing.*

"Gold-e-lah? You look like a fish out of water, standing there wondering what the heck to say to me. Life is short, my friend. Why don't we just let bygones be bygones and move on? You and I, we've buried so many of our friends and family. There aren't many of us left."

"And most of those who are left aren't really here, if you know what I mean."

"Exactly. We go back a long way, you and me, Gold-e-lah."

"We do."

"We've gotten through, and over, much worse."

"We have." Goldie nodded. Ida was right. "Nothing is so terrible that it can't be resolved over a cream soda." It was something her father used to say.

"Wiser words were never spoken." Ida coughed, and Goldie gripped her hand.

"Are you all right?"

"Meh. I've been better, that's for sure. But as you said, I'm too stubborn to die. So, nu? Tell me what's been going on with you. How did you get here, by the way? Did you drive again?"

"No. Rachel brought us."

"Us? Who's us?"

"Me and Julia, of course."

"I figured she'd driven herself. You brought my granddaughter to the hospital?"

"Yes. Rachel saw you being loaded into the ambulance and we couldn't let poor Julia be by herself at a time like this."

"Gold-e-lah? You did this for me and mine?" Tears dotted Ida's eyelashes.

"Naturally. You'd do the same for me, I know you would."

"Count on it. But Gold-e-lah? We weren't even on speaking terms."

Goldie shrugged. "It's like you said, we go back a long way. You're my best living friend. I needed to be here."

"You're a mensch, you know that?"

"Oh, speaking of driving, I forgot to tell you. I almost got caught."

"I thought you said you didn't do the driving."

116

"I didn't. But somehow, the car radio turned itself on. It was on our favorite station—you know, the one that plays Benny Goodman, Perry Como, and Tommy Dorsey."

"Oy!" Ida exclaimed. "What did the kids say?"

"Julia—"

"Grandma! You're awake!" Julia came running into the room, followed closely by Rachel. "Did we miss the doctor? What did he say?"

"Shh. Not so loud. Yes, I made it. Go figure. The doctor says I'll live to be one hundred."

Goldie stepped back to let Julia get closer to her bubbe. Under her breath, she asked Rachel, "Are you okay, darling? You ran out of that waiting room like your hair was on fire."

Mutely, Rachel nodded. Goldie thought she looked a little pale. "Don't you let anyone rain on your parade. You hold your head up high. They're just jealous, that's all."

"Jealous of me making a fool of myself? I don't think so."

Goldie nudged Rachel with her shoulder. "None of them got a fancy set of pictures in a big deal magazine."

"None of them is the laughingstock of the internet, either," Rachel said glumly.

"Mother Ida? Are you okay? Where's the doctor?"

A middle-aged woman in tight pants and a long fur coat swept into the room, shoving Goldie and Rachel aside as she strode over to the bed. A man who strongly resembled Ida's deceased husband followed two steps behind.

Goldie noted that neither of the newcomers even acknowledged Julia's presence. Already, she didn't like them.

"Hi, Mom." The man kissed Ida on the cheek.

"Hello, Stanley. Hello, Lois. Why are you here?" Ida failed to hide her lack of enthusiasm for these interlopers.

"Why are we here? We're your family, that's why," Lois answered indignantly.

"Your daughter has been by my side the entire time. I've been well cared for."

Lois wheeled on Julia. "Why didn't you call us? You should've called us right away."

Before Julia could answer, Ida broke in. "I told her not to."

"You...what?" Lois and Stanley stammered simultaneously.

"That's right. I told her not to. There was no reason for you two to come. Julia had everything well under control."

"You." Lois poked her finger in Julia's chest and Goldie wanted to bop her upside the head. "You had an obligation to call us."

"How did you find out I was here?" Ida drew the attention away from Julia and back to herself.

"The hospital called. You do remember that Stan is your health care proxy? We came as soon as we could."

Lois looked around the room, as if noticing Goldie and Rachel for the first time. She immediately took an aggressive stride toward Rachel, and Goldie stepped in between them.

"Who's that?" she spat at Julia. "Your new 'friend?' How could you bring her here at a time like this?"

Goldie watched as Julia's eyes opened wide in horror. Rachel's expression wasn't much different. Ida's gaze swiveled from Lois, to Julia, to Rachel, and back to Lois again.

"What in the world are you talking about?" Ida asked, genuinely perplexed.

"What? You haven't told her? You just bring your concubine around without explanation? Shame on you. Go ahead, Julia. Tell your grandmother your dirty little secret. Tell her about your perversion."

"Moth—"

"Now see here." Goldie shifted again so that now she was directly in between Lois and Julia. "First. I don't care who you think you are. You have no business being here. My friend, Ida, said you weren't welcome. You should listen to her wishes. She's the one in the bed."

"Who, exactly, are you?" Lois asked derisively.

"I," Goldie puffed out her chest, "am your mother-in-law's best and oldest friend." She beckoned for Rachel to join her and looped her arm through Rachel's arm. "This beautiful young woman is my granddaughter. She's a lesbian, I love her, and she's a lot less perverted than you are, you—"

"Grandma!" Rachel squeezed Goldie's arm.

"Right, then. I don't know anything about whether your Julia likes boys or girls—"

"Oh, she likes girls. She's made that perfectly, disgustingly clear," Lois said.

In response, Goldie looped her free arm through Julia's. "In that case, good for her. She should love whomever she pleases. She and my Rachel are not an 'item' as you are intimating, but if they were, I would be the proudest grandma that ever walked the earth. Two wonderful young women. We should all do so well in our love matches."

"Hear, hear," Ida croaked weakly from the bed. "You tell them, Gold-e-lah." Ida broke into a coughing fit, and Julia filled a water glass, placed a straw in it, and gently placed the glass in her grandmother's shaking hands.

When she'd stopped hacking, Ida lay still with her eyes closed.

"Grandma?" Julia asked softly.

"I'm still here, dumpling." Ida opened her eyes. "Lois? You get out. Now. And take that no-good, sanctimonious son of mine with you. I raised you better than this, Stanley. Shame on you. Turning your back on your own daughter. She's the best part of you two."

"Mother Ida, you don't know—"

"I know perfectly well. I've got heart trouble, but at least I have one. Now get out! I don't want you here."

"This is your fault." Lois pointed at Julia. "You've brainwashed her."

"You heard Ida." Goldie stood up as straight as she was able. "She doesn't want you here. Skedaddle."

Lois and Stanley swept out of the room, sucking the air out with them.

"Come on." Goldie tugged on Rachel's arms. "Let's give those two a little time alone."

CHAPTER ELEVEN

Julia couldn't decide which would be worse—following Goldie and Rachel out of the room, or staying to face the music with Grandma Ida.

For a time, the only sounds were the beeping and whirring of the apparatus attached to Ida and the patient's uneven breathing. Julia watched her with trepidation. Her eyes were closed, her skin sallow. The events of this day had taken so much out of Ida, Julia feared she might not recover.

That her mother would start a confrontation in her grandmother's hospital room was outrageous. As Julia sorted through her emotions, she realized she was angrier about her mother's callous disregard for Ida's precarious health situation than she was about being outed so publicly.

"I can feel you fuming, you know." Ida's voice was little more than a whisper.

"You can?"

"Of course I can. I'm your grandmother. If it's any consolation, I'd be hopping mad too, if I had the energy for it."

"Grandma, I—"

"Stop right there." Ida opened her eyes and pointed her finger at Julia. The IV tube taped to the back of her hand swayed with the motion.

"But—"

"But, nothing. I don't have a lot of energy, so please let me speak what's on my mind. Then, if you still have something you're just dying to say to me, you can have your say."

Julia nodded and averted her gaze. A knot of dread filled the pit of her stomach. Sure, Ida had defended her in front of her parents.

That didn't mean that she accepted or approved of Julia's sexual orientation.

"Julia? Look at me."

Reluctantly, Julia complied.

"I'm an old woman. I view the world through an old woman's eyes. That doesn't mean I can't open my mind. To me, you are the same beautiful child I held in my arms the day you were born.

"I'll be honest with you," Ida continued after several shallow, rasping breaths, "when Goldie first told me her Rachel preferred girls, I was a little taken aback. But I watched how Goldie loved and accepted Rachel, and I watched how Rachel loved her bubbe. Honestly? I admired Goldie for her fierceness in defending her granddaughter. I wondered if I would have it in me to do the same." Ida paused to take a sip of water. "I guess I did." Her laugh morphed into a cough.

"Grandma—"

"I'm not done yet. Did I say I was done? I just need to catch my breath." Ida struggled to push herself up in the bed.

"Let me help." Julia grabbed the bedside controls and pushed the button to raise the head of the bed. "Is that better?"

"Much. Thank you." Ida took another sip of water. "As I was saying, I'm not crazy about the idea of you being one of those girls…"

Julia stiffened. Here it was. This was the moment when her grandmother would turn her back.

"…but not for the reason that your parents object. Eh. I've seen it all in my line of work. Love is love. Finding the right match is hard. If you find the right one, that's what matters. The problem is," Ida reached out for Julia's hand, "I'm afraid the rest of the world is more like your parents than like Goldie. You're in for a rough time of it, and that worries me for you."

Julia wanted to weep with relief. "Grandma…" Julia paused. "Is it my turn to say something yet?"

"Why not? I'm tired of talking."

"Your support means the world to me. I only ever wanted to make you proud. I was afraid to tell you. I was afraid you'd react the same way my parents did. When I was in college and Mother found out, she told me I could never tell you."

"You'll pardon me for saying so, but your mother is a horse's ass. Always was."

Julia nearly choked at Ida's candor.

For the first time since the ordeal had begun, Ida had that old glint of mischief in her eyes. It warmed Julia's heart beyond measure.

"What? I'm just telling the truth."

"You are so right, Grandma."

"I love you, my granddaughter-the-lesbian, or whatever you are."

"I love you, Grandma." Julia kissed Ida's cheek.

"Now, if you don't mind, I need to get some shuteye."

∽⋙⋘⋧

"You should've seen her in action," Rachel told Freud. She was lying on the couch in her sweats and slippers. It was past two in the morning, but she was too amped up from the day's events to sleep. "I've never seen Grandma Goldie be confrontational before. She was a real badass. You would've been impressed."

Freud, who had been gnawing on a new Nylabone, stopped mid-chew and cocked his head to the side inquisitively.

"I know. I wish you could've seen it too. Also, I'm sorry you got stuck at the pet sitter's for so long. I didn't expect to be running so late."

Freud blinked and resumed his chewing. Lazily, Rachel reached behind her on the end table and felt around for her phone. She'd put it on mute and intentionally avoided looking at it all day. The last thing she wanted was to see more fallout from her debacle. If she didn't see it, then she couldn't be upset by it.

Her fingers latched onto the phone and she pulled it toward her. "Twelve phone messages? Holy cow!" Rachel opened the phone app and pressed the speaker button to listen to the first voicemail.

"Rachel? This is your mother speaking. Where are you? It's almost sundown. Hurry up." Rachel deleted the message and clicked on the next one.

"Rachel? Are you intentionally ignoring me? Because if you are…" Her mother didn't finish the threat. "If you're stuck in

traffic, let us know. We're holding dinner a few minutes for you."
Again, Rachel deleted the message.

"Rachel? This is your mother…again. This isn't funny. It's
very disrespectful for you not to answer my calls, young lady."
Rachel sighed and pressed the delete button again.

"Squirt? It's Paul. If this is about that video thing, I've already
shown it to Mom and Dad. They promise not to bring it up at
dinner, and I promise to try not to bust a gut laughing when I see
you. You'd better show up soon. Mom is spitting nails." *Delete.*

"Rachel? This is your dad. Listen, kiddo. I just want you to
know that I'm proud of you. You scaled that fence like one of
those contestants from that reality television show. You know, the
one I can never remember the name of. Um, anyway, your mother
is worried about what might've happened to you. I told her not to
worry, that you were probably just fine, but you know how she is.
Anyway, pretty soon she's going to make me call out the National
Guard. So come home, okay? 'Bye." *Delete.*

"Rachel Wallach. You answer this phone right this minute. I'm
not holding dinner for you anymore. If I don't hear from you in the
next twenty minutes, I'm going to send your father over to the
assisted living place to your grandmother's." This time, her
mother didn't even say goodbye. *Delete.*

"I just called your grandmother. She's not answering the
phone. Not that that's news. She can't hear half the time when she
does answer anyway. But if you're there, you'd better answer that
phone, in case there's something wrong with your cell phone."

Rachel rolled her eyes. "Mother, if there was something wrong
with my cell phone, telling me what to do in a voicemail left on
that phone wouldn't do much good, now would it?" She hit the
delete key again and moved on to the next message.

"She still doesn't answer. I don't know why she doesn't
answer. Am I dialing the right number? She didn't change her
number and not tell us, did she?" Rachel's mother either didn't
realize she hadn't disconnected the call, or didn't care.

Rachel scrolled through two more similar messages.

"Rachel? You call us the minute you get this message. We
don't care what time of night it is. Do you hear me?"

This time, Rachel heard genuine panic in her mother's voice.
She glanced at the time on the phone—2:27 a.m. She knew her

mother. Chances were she was still awake and waiting, assuming the worst. Worse yet, she might've called the police and they might be out searching for her in ditches throughout Westchester County. Rachel knew she would have to call her mother.

There was one remaining message on her voicemail. It was from an unfamiliar number in her own area code. Curious, she pushed play.

"Rachel? This is Julia Spielman, Ida's granddaughter. I hope you don't mind. Goldie gave me your number." Five seconds of silence ensued, and Rachel wondered if Julia had hung up. "I don't know what to say here. I guess, first, I want to apologize for that ugly, ugly scene with my parents at the hospital. I can only imagine how awkward that must've been for you, and I'm sorry you had to witness that."

Rachel could hear the strain in Julia's voice and her heart went out to her.

"I also want to thank you. I don't know what I would've done without you and your grandmother. You both were a godsend to me and to Grandma Ida, and I'm so grateful. I know the ride home was one big awkward silence, and I'm sorry it took me until now to say what I should've said in the car. I suppose I was still processing and looking for the right words. I'm still processing, even now. But I felt like I needed to let you know how much I appreciated your support—both of you."

More silence ensued.

"Anyway. I guess I'll see you around sometime. 'Bye."

Rachel held the phone against her chin. "Goodbye, Julia. I'm glad we were there for you too." She paused over the delete button, then pulled her hand away. Instead, she added Julia to her list of contacts and saved the message.

When she was done, Rachel returned to her recent calls and selected one of her mother's calls. Her mother picked it up on the first ring. It was going to be a long conversation.

❧❧

"So? You're feeling better?" Goldie sat on Ida's velveteen sofa eating lunch off a snack tray. Ida, still in her nightgown, was propped up in the lift chair, her meal—chicken soup and half a grilled cheese sandwich—balanced on a portable breakfast tray.

"Eh. You know how it is. I'm glad to be back, I'll tell you. The food is much better." She slurped from a flexible straw. "Now this? This is what I imagine Heaven is like." She wiped her mouth with a paper napkin. "How in the world did you manage to get a chocolate malted delivered here?"

Goldie laughed. "Delivered? Who said anything about delivered?"

"Goldie Horowitz. Have you been naughty again?"

Goldie adopted her most innocent expression. "I have no idea what you're talking about."

"So, you didn't sneak away in your car and go to the malt shop?"

"Oh, no. I definitely did that."

"I'm proud of you, Gold-e-lah. You're turning into a rebel in your old age. Mazel tov!"

"You taught me everything I know, my friend." Goldie raised her ice cream soda in salute. It felt so wonderful to joke and visit with Ida. She'd made the right decision to put their disagreement in the rearview mirror.

They ate in companionable silence. When Ida was finished, Goldie picked up her tray and took it to the kitchen.

When she returned, Ida said, "So, Gold-e-lah. About what transpired with my daughter-in-law-the-horse's-ass…"

Goldie waved a hand in a dismissive gesture. "Not my affair."

"You were there, so that makes it your affair, at least indirectly. I'm sorry you had to bear witness to such ugliness. Usually, she's too concerned about appearances to let her slip show in public, if you know what I mean."

"I do." Goldie nodded. She had no idea what to say. It wasn't like her family was perfect. After all, the whole reason she was at Shady Acres was to get away from her own daughter.

To share such a thing would be too embarrassing, though. Or would it? Who was worse, her Deborah or Ida's Lois? Maybe they were equally bad. Then again, Ida had inherited Lois by marriage. Deborah? Deborah was the product of Goldie's own loins.

"Nu? Gold-e-lah? What's with the expression on your punim like you just ate the bitter herb at Passover, or some bad lox?"

126

"Let he who casts the first stone... I was thinking about my daughter, who can also be...challenging."

"Challenging is one thing. An outright dark stain on humanity is another issue entirely."

"Is Lois really that horrible?"

Ida pretended to spit off the side of the chair. "Worse. What mother turns her back on her own child simply for being different? You didn't turn away your Rachel. You embraced her even more."

Goldie's heart swelled with pride. "She's a special one. Always the brightest kid in the class—and the most sensitive. She got bullied a lot in school."

"Because she liked girls?"

Goldie shook her head. "No. I don't think she understood that she preferred girls back then. I'm talking about elementary school and high school. I think her problem was that she was too smart for her own good. She was every teacher's pet because she always knew the answers."

"Ah. The goody-two-shoes everyone loved to hate."

"Exactly."

"Good thing you and I never needed to worry about that." Ida laughed heartily, and it morphed into a coughing jag.

Goldie jumped to her feet. "Can I get you something? Water?"

Ida, who was red in the face from coughing, waved her away. When finally she was able, she took a deep breath and settled back into the chair.

"Are you sure you're all right? Maybe you left the hospital too early. Or maybe you should've gone to the rehab place where they wanted to send you."

"I'm fine. Getting old isn't for sissies, Gold-e-lah."

"No kidding."

"If I went into one of those long-term places, I might never get back out."

Goldie nodded mutely. What could she say? Ida was right.

"Anyway," Ida said, "I wanted to thank you for stepping in and defending me and Julia, and for putting my daughter-in-law in her place. She got what she deserved."

"You're welcome." Goldie didn't want to pry, truly, but she was worried, so... "Have you seen Julia since—well, since then?"

"I had her pick me up from the hospital and she and I had a good talk on the way home. I told her I changed my health care directives. I want her to be in charge from now on."

"Good for you."

"I also told her I called Stanley—"

"Who?"

"My son—Julia's father. He was the one dragging behind the horse's ass."

"Oh, right."

"I told him I want a family meeting, here, day after tomorrow. I have some things to say."

"Are you sure you're up to it? You just had heart surgery."

Ida leaned forward conspiratorially. "That's why I want to do it now. I want to get to them while I still have the sympathy vote. If they become belligerent or disagreeable, I'll just do this." Ida clutched at her heart, leaned back, and shut her eyes.

"Ida?" Goldie rose again in alarm. "Ida? Are you okay?"

Ida opened her eyes and grinned. "See? It works every time."

"You stinker! You scared me."

"Sometimes, Gold-e-lah, I scare myself."

Mr. Crawford's eyes were closed when Rachel walked into the room at the long-term skilled nursing facility. Even though the nurse had warned her that her neighbor was not doing well, she hadn't been prepared for the shrunken, disheveled man in the bed.

No wonder he'd refused to see or talk to her before now. If this was an improvement, she couldn't imagine what kind of shape he'd been in before.

Rachel approached the bed and touched Mr. Crawford on the hand. He stirred slightly but did not open his eyes. "Mr. Crawford? Mr. Crawford, it's Rachel. From next door."

Slowly, as if it took great effort, he opened his eyes, though his gaze remained unfocused for seconds longer. "Rachel?" Her name came out so garbled she almost missed it.

"Yes, Mr. Crawford. How are you?" In the ensuing silence, it occurred to Rachel that the question might have been too complex. The nurse had told her to keep it short, simple, and easy for him to process. The stroke had badly affected his speech, his memory, and his ability to hold onto thoughts and to sustain conversations.

"What was that?"

Mr. Crawford mumbled something Rachel couldn't make out.

"Howmbee?"

Rachel's brows knitted together. "One more time?"

"Howmbee?" Mr. Crawford asked, more loudly.

"How is..." Rachel saw the desperation in his eyes to be heard and understood.

"Dig," Mr. Crawford said.

"How is dig?" What on earth could he mean? "Are you asking about the farm?"

"No." Mr. Crawford shook his head. He pursed his lips and tried to form a word.

Rachel leaned closer.

"Oof."

"Oof?" What the...?

"Woof!" Mr. Crawford blurted out.

"Oh! You want to know how Freud is doing. The dog, right?"

Mr. Crawford smiled and nodded.

"He's doing great, except he misses you. I'm a poor substitute, I'm afraid. Here, I've got a picture of him for you on my phone." Rachel fumbled in her purse. When she looked back up, Mr. Crawford had tears streaming down his face.

"Oh, no. No, no, no. Please, don't cry. Don't cry." Rachel located a box of tissues on the bedside tray and grabbed them. She gave a tissue to Mr. Crawford, but he could only clutch it in his hand. She took it from him and blotted his face gently.

"Miss hem."

"He misses you too." Rachel thought Mr. Crawford might not be the only one to cry. She cleared her throat and busied herself searching the photos on her phone.

"Here's a good one." She held out the phone for Mr. Crawford to see. It was a shot she took a few days ago of Freud lying on his bed, a Nylabone hanging from his mouth. He looked as though he was smoking a good cigar and grinning.

Mr. Crawford swallowed hard, as tears once again formed on his lashes. "Good bee."

This time, Rachel needed no translation. "Yes, he is a good boy. I promise you," she paused as her voice shook. "I promise you, I'll take excellent care of him and love him as best I can until you get back home."

Rivulets of tears rolled down Mr. Crawford's cheeks. He pointed at Rachel with a shaky finger.

"Me? Me what?"

The certified nurse's assistant bustled into the room with a blood pressure cuff and some pills in a plastic cup. She glanced at the picture Rachel was showing Mr. Crawford. "Cute dog."

"It's Mr. Crawford's. His name is Freud. I'm just taking care of him until Mr. Crawford comes home."

The woman gave Rachel an odd look, but said nothing. She opened Mr. Crawford's hand to give him the pills and held a cup with a straw for him so that he could swallow water with the medications. As she was getting ready to leave, she motioned Rachel to join her in the hallway.

"Hasn't anyone told you?"

"Told me what?" Rachel asked.

"Your Mr. Crawford is never going to be able to live independently again. And he most certainly isn't ever going to recover sufficiently to be able to take care of a pet. I'm so sorry to be the one to tell you that."

Rachel stumbled a step backward and braced herself against the wall for support. "Are you sure? I thought he was getting rehab."

"Positive. The doctors and therapists have told him as much. I'm afraid this is going to be his home from now on."

Rachel's heart ached for her neighbor. "Surely the dog can live with him here, with some assistance to take him out and feed him."

"Nope, sorry. No pets allowed in this facility. I'm afraid you're going to have to make other arrangements."

"Other arrange..." Rachel's voice trailed off and her resolve kicked in. Send Freud to live with some stranger where Mr. Crawford wouldn't know where the dog was? That wasn't going to happen. She pushed off from the wall. "As long as he lives, that dog will always have a home with me. I promised Mr. Crawford that I would take care of him, and that's exactly what I'm going to do."

"That's a lot to take on. You're a good friend. He sure could use one of those," the nurse's assistant said. Her eyes were soft, brown, and filled with compassion.

"It's the right thing to do," Rachel answered. She returned to Mr. Crawford's bedside. Once again, his eyes were closed.

"Mr. Crawford?" Rachel shook his arm gently and he focused on her again. "I know you're not allowed to have pets in this place. I need you to know," she paused as her voice choked with emotion. "I need you to know that I keep my promises. You asked me to take care of Freud for you, and I swear to you right here, right now, that I will keep Freud and treat him as my own until you're ready to have him back." She didn't have the heart to tell him that was never going to happen.

"Nobody, except for you, of course, will love him more than I do. Do you understand what I'm telling you?"

Mr. Crawford nodded and held out his hands, beckoning Rachel to come closer. He gripped her shoulders and looked deeply into her eyes.

"You're welcome." It was the clearest thing he'd said.

Rachel thought it ironic that the most understandable words Mr. Crawford had spoken were the opposite of what he was trying to convey, which was his thanks.

CHAPTER TWELVE

With great effort, Julia put one foot in front of the other. She imagined this was what her ancestors must've felt like as they were being led away from the safety of their homes and to Gestapo headquarters for interrogation. Their whole lives hung in the balance and depended on the answers they gave, and the mood of the interrogator.

Julia's memories of the last family meeting were painfully fresh, even now, more than a decade later. Shortly after her mother discovered her with her paramour, Julia received a summons to the stuffy law offices of her parents' attorney. She still could see her mother's face, pinched and closed, void of all emotion save contempt.

"Julia? Do you know why you're here?" the lawyer intoned in his nasal voice.

"I have no idea. I'm supposed to be in my dorm room, studying for finals."

"Young lady, this is very serious. You'd do well to lose the smug expression and impertinent attitude." He glared at her over his half-glasses.

"I was being serious," Julia answered.

"Let's get this over with," Julia's father interrupted the contest of wills.

Julia noted the dark circles under his eyes and the slump of his shoulders. She almost felt badly for him. Almost. Her mother, on the other hand, appeared calm, cool, and as collected as if she wanted to check this box off on her list of daily tasks and move on to the next item on her to-do list.

"Your parents came to me last week. Do you know why?" the attorney asked.

"No. But I'm sure you're going to tell me." Julia thought she had a pretty good idea what this was about, but she had no intention of making it easy for her parents.

"Right, then. I'll get to it. Your parents have asked me to handle this matter as a neutral third party and the attorney of record for their estate." He cleared his throat and sifted through a pile of papers on his desk.

Julia was certain the pause in the action was more for dramatic effect than for any other reason. She supposed this moron enjoyed the misery of others. Perhaps he was a frustrated school principal.

"You may be unaware of it, but your parents have a sizable estate, worth approximately six million dollars at this time."

Was Julia supposed to be impressed? It was no secret that her mother had received a large inheritance from her father, Julia's grandfather. He'd made his fortune in banking. He hired Julia's father after her parents married and groomed him to take his place upon his retirement. When her grandfather dropped dead of a heart attack three days before retirement, the bank board unanimously selected her dad to take over the helm.

"The original estate plan," the lawyer was saying, "left you as your parents' sole heir. Perhaps you will have some grasp of the magnitude of their generosity?"

Julia was an only child, who else were they going to leave the money to?

"Your folks tell me that certain…facts…have come to light that necessitate that they now reconsider their plans. Your judgment has been called into question. While they have not shared the particulars with me, your parents assure me that your behavior is sufficiently egregious that, rather than name you as sole beneficiary, they are setting up a charitable foundation to direct their money to certain worthy causes."

Bile rose in Julia's throat, not because she stood to lose millions of dollars—she would much rather make her own way in the world than to accept blood money. What sickened her was that she well knew the kinds of conservative, homophobic, mean-spirited causes her parents supported.

"Your parents want to be sure you understand what is at stake. Now, before you lose hope and freak out, as you kids would say..."

The lawyer smiled slyly at her, his upper lip curling over his teeth, and the sight made Julia want to throw up.

"There's still a way for you to turn this situation around. If you apologize—"

"Apologize? To whom? And for what?" Julia interrupted. She couldn't stand it anymore.

"...and guarantee in writing that you will forego these unnatural urges and behaviors..." the attorney droned on as if she hadn't said anything.

"Unnatural urges? What the hell are you talking about?"

"Julia. Sit down and let the man finish," her father admonished.

Julia hadn't even realized she'd shot to her feet. Reluctantly, she sat back down. She gripped the chair arms so tightly her knuckles turned white.

"As I was saying," the attorney continued. He looked as though he'd swallowed a whole lemon. "Here are your parents' terms. If you admit that you were brainwashed into committing certain perverted acts and testify against the other party at an expulsion hearing before the college deans—"

"You want me to lie and rat out my girlfriend," Julia blurted as she jumped up again. "What is wrong with you?" She wheeled around to face her mother. "Why would you want to destroy someone who's done nothing but love me?"

"Sit down," her mother hissed. "And shut your mouth. You'd do well to listen closely and choose carefully."

The lawyer waited until Julia reclaimed her seat. He pushed a small stack of documents toward her, uncapped a pen, and held it out to her. "If you do those things, and guarantee in writing here and now that you will henceforth conduct yourself in a manner befitting your family name and station, as defined in a document I drafted at your parents' instruction, then your claim to the estate will be reinstated with prejudice. If, at any time between now and the disposition of the estate, you violate or otherwise circumvent these terms, your right to the inheritance will be forfeited."

"And if I refuse to sign my name to such a piece of garbage?"

"Then we're done here." The attorney pushed the half glasses farther down his nose and leaned closer across the desk so that they were practically nose-to-nose. *"You're* done here." He pointed his finger in Julia's chest.

This time, Julia stood deliberately, strode directly over to her mother, taking satisfaction in seeing fear in the woman's eyes, and leaned over her, a hand placed on either arm of her mother's chair. "Let me say this as slowly, and as clearly as I can, so that even you can understand. I am not now, nor have I ever been, an abomination or a sickness to be cut out of the family tree. I will never, ever live a lie, especially not in order to inherit your filthy money, earned on the backs of hard-working people just trying to live their dreams."

Julia watched as her mother's lips curled in anger, her nostrils flaring. She'd seen that look before. It was taking everything her mother had not to lose her composure in front of the lawyer. That, after all, would be unseemly.

"You do realize, dear daughter, that that 'filthy' money is putting you through college?"

Julia's eyes widened. Her parents would never withdraw support for her education. It would be too much of an embarrassment if she were forced to drop out. How would they explain it to their friends?

"Ah, so that hit home, did it?" Her mother primly crossed her legs. "What? Speechless now?"

"I will never sign that piece of paper. Never!" Julia shook her head.

"Don't be an idiot, Julia!"

"What would be idiotic would be to submit to your pitiful blackmail attempt. You can take your threats and the inheritance and stuff them—"

"Enough!" Julia's father grabbed her by the arms and led her out of the room.

"Look, Julia. It was all I could do to get your mother to agree to even the possibility of a way out for you. Don't blow this."

Julia searched her father's face for any hint of the man who used to lift her in the air as a child and spin her around, the man who bought her cotton candy and spirited her out of school to go to the Museum of Natural History so that she could see the dinosaurs. She found no trace of him.

"Take your hands off of me. You're both pathetic. You think I can flip a switch and magically like boys instead of girls? You think our love doesn't count, because Jill is a girl? You think I'd turn my back on her to save my own skin? You don't know anything about me."

"You're sealing your own grave."

"You think money's that important? Without your millions I won't be able to make it on my own? Maybe so. But at least I'll be able to sleep at night."

Even now, Julia still could see the look of disappointment on her father's face as she'd pulled free of his grasp, turned her back, and walked away.

Shortly after the incident, Julia went to court to legally change her surname to Spielman, Grandma Ida's birth name.

She'd paid her own way through her remaining two years of school, working two jobs, and moving into off-campus housing that she shared with five other girls.

True to their word, her parents had revoked any right Julia had to her inheritance. Jill eventually left her, and, after several years during which she and her parents rarely spoke, they had achieved an uneasy détente when Ida suffered her first heart attack.

Julia hesitated as the automatic doors slid open. This was Shady Acres, not a lawyer's office, and it was Ida who had demanded the meeting, not her parents.

Now is not then. You're not that scared young girl, and they don't have any power over you anymore. There's nothing they can threaten that can hurt you now.

Goldie made a right-hand turn into the street leading to the Shady Acres parking lot. She tightened her fingers around the steering wheel and used the leverage to hoist herself higher in the driver's seat. The car swerved to the left, and she compensated quickly by yanking the wheel to the right. Her teeth knocked together as the right front tire climbed up the curb, and she adjusted the wheel again to get off the curb.

"This is what happens when you rush," she muttered. The way she saw it, she had no choice. She needed to hurry, or that nosy-but-nice Evan would be the least of her problems. Rachel would be arriving within the hour.

Goldie had forgotten how long "Gone with the Wind" ran. But the opportunity to see Clark Gable on the big screen one more time was worth it.

"Oh, no." Goldie's stomach flipped as she turned down the row. Rachel was standing in the middle of the parking lot, in the assigned space for Goldie's unit, right where the Deuce should have been. She was turning in circles.

"Deep breath. Time to face the music. Act natural." Goldie honked the horn, plastered a smile on her face, and waved.

Rachel jumped and put her hand to her heart, as she whirled around and locked eyes with Goldie. The startled look on Rachel's face morphed into consternation.

"Uh, oh." Goldie finished pulling into the space, put the car in park, and rolled down the window. "Hi, there, sweetheart. You're early."

"Goldie Horowitz, what on earth are you doing driving that car? You don't even have a current license." Rachel wagged a finger at her, and Goldie felt like a schoolgirl in for a scolding.

"Who says I don't have a driver's license?" Goldie winked.

"You do?"

"Of course I do. It was your meddling mother who thought I shouldn't be driving anymore." Goldie rolled up the window, grabbed her purse, got out of the car, and locked the doors.

"You kept a set of keys?"

"I did."

"Does Mother know?"

"Absolutely not, and I intend to keep it that way."

"You're wicked, Grandma."

You have no idea. Goldie bit her lip. Should she come clean about the rest of it? Should she 'fess up about the state of her hearing? Now that Rachel knew one secret... Eh, one secret was enough for today, although it would be nice not to have her granddaughter screaming in her ear anymore.

"So, where were you?"

Goldie winced as she looped her arm through Rachel's and they made their way toward the building. "Frankly, my dear, I don't give a damn." Goldie said, in a horrible Southern accent.

"You went to the movies to see 'Gone with the Wind?'"

"I couldn't help myself. It was at the revival house. Clark Gable makes me swoon. Those eyes, those shoulders!"

"Grandma! You brazen hussy, you."

"Well, I'm not dead yet, my dear."

"Oh, good Lord. I'm never going to get that image out of my head. Stop. Please, stop."

They were almost to the door, when Rachel pulled them up short.

"What are you...?" Goldie's voice trailed off as she saw where Rachel was pointing. Julia was pacing up and down the sidewalk, seemingly lost in thought.

"She looks upset," Rachel whispered. "Maybe we should go to her."

"No," Goldie answered quickly. "Leave her be for now."

"But, Grandma. What if it's Ida?"

"Don't argue with me, Rachel. Come. We can go in the back door. I'll explain on the way."

Rachel looked as though she would protest again, but she went along with Goldie. "Is Ida okay?"

"I suspect Ida is just fine. She called a family meeting for this afternoon. What time is it?"

"Four o'clock."

Goldie nodded. "The fun is just about to begin."

"Fun? Julia didn't look like she was having fun. More like she was getting ready to go to her own funeral."

"It will be all right. You'll see." Goldie patted Rachel on the arm. "And if it isn't, we'll take Julia out to my favorite diner for a milkshake. There's nothing in the world a good milkshake can't fix."

Julia heard the yelling before she even turned the door knob. It was her mother's shrill voice.

"We'll have you committed and declared incompetent!"

"You'll do no such thing," Ida answered.

"You forget, I have your power of attorney." Julia heard the controlled rage in her father's threat. It was the same tactic he'd used on her many times.

"And you forget that I am your mother. I gave birth to you. I cleaned your tush when you were learning to use the potty, I taught you how to walk and to eat. I fed you, I clothed you, I taught you to drive, and your father and I supported you throughout your college years as you squandered your education. How dare you come in here and threaten me, especially just days after I left the hospital."

"You don't know what you're doing. You're not in your right mind. Anyone with half a brain can see that," Julia's mother sneered.

"That description leaves you out, you no-good—"

Julia threw open the door and strode through the kitchenette and the living room and into Ida's bedroom, where she was lying in bed, propped up on some pillows. "Is this a private shouting match, or can anyone join?"

"This doesn't concern you," Julia's father said. "Step out of the way."

"On the contrary," Ida waved a bony hand. "This has everything to do with Julia." She smiled up at her granddaughter. "Hello, darling. What took you so long?"

"I—"

"No matter, you're here now. Just in time for the fireworks." Ida winked at her.

"Julia? Get out." Stan crossed his arms.

"Grandma asked me to be here. It's her apartment."

"Have you no shame? Whatever you've done to brainwash her, it isn't going to work." Lois started toward her, and Julia steeled herself for whatever would come next.

"Enough. Please, Mrs. Pinsky, back away." The stranger who appeared in the bedroom doorway looked as though he'd just stepped out of an ad for Brooks Brothers. His suit pants were sharply creased, the handkerchief in his breast pocket perfectly matched his neatly tied tie, and his shoes were polished to a high sheen.

When Julia's mother didn't budge, he moved toward her.

"Who are you?" Stan asked.

"He is Jacob Levine, my attorney," Ida said from the bed.

Stan looked positively stunned. "He's not your attorney. You've been using our lawyer ever since Daddy died."

"Yeah, well, I decided it was a conflict of interest, so I hired myself a new lawyer."

Mr. Levine stepped fully into the room, reached into his inside jacket pocket, and pulled out a stack of business cards. He handed cards to Stan and Lois, and then gave one to Julia, as well. She turned it around to read it. He was with a large, well-known New York City law firm. She was impressed.

"When did you do that, hire a new lawyer?" Lois asked, as if it were any of her affair.

"Right around the time you became such a horse's ass."

Julia wondered when that might've been, as her mother had been a horse's rear end as long as she could remember.

"If you don't mind, I'd like to get to the business at hand," Mr. Levine said. He pulled two folders from his briefcase, passed one of the folders to Stan, and the other to Julia.

Lois grabbed the folder out of her husband's hands and rifled through it. Julia decided to hold off on reading the materials, as her mother's face told her everything she needed to know.

"You can't do this."

"Actually, Mrs. Pinsky, your mother-in-law has every right to do whatever she pleases with her assets and to assert her own wishes. As you can see, there are several signed affidavits in your packet from Ida's doctors attesting to her fitness to make her own decisions and determinations."

Lois zipped through the documents as if she was being tested for an Evelyn Wood speed-reading course. With each devoured page, the color in her cheeks darkened and her eyes got wider. "You won't get away with this. And even if you do, you'll live to regret it."

"Eh," Ida said, "living is overrated. But in the time I have left, I'm certainly going to enjoy myself."

"As you can see," Mr. Levine broke in, "the elder Mrs. Pinsky has named her granddaughter, Julia, as her sole heir in a new will signed and witnessed this morning. She also has appointed Julia to be her health care proxy, to hold her medical and general powers of attorney, and to manage her finances, all of which have been removed from the bank at which you serve as CEO, Mr. Pinsky."

"Where did you move the money?" Stan turned on his mother. "When did you move the money?"

"My money and managing my accounts, Stanley, are no longer any of your business."

"You've completely lost your mind," Stan said.

"More like I've opened my eyes," Ida countered.

"To prevent you from interfering with her wishes after she is deceased, Ida already has transferred to Julia the deed to the family home in Port Chester, along with the material items within the home, as well as some property upstate in Saratoga County."

Stan's face went white. "My father built our family home with his own sweat."

"Yes, he did. It was his wedding gift to me," Ida said.

"I grew up in that house."

"It appears to me, son, that you might've grown older, but sadly, you never grew up." Ida broke into a coughing jag, and Julia slipped behind her and lifted her higher on the bed to help her breathe.

"I thought you only made me your health care proxy. The house? The land? You shouldn't have done that, Grandma. You didn't need to sign those things over to me."

"Oh, my dear. I've set aside plenty of money to see me through for whatever time I have left. Truthfully, I'm only sorry it took me until now to take care of you. I should've done this a long, long time ago, right when those hard-hearted parents of yours cut you off when you needed them most."

Julia stiffened. "You knew about that?"

"It didn't take a genius to see that something had changed in your life, sweetheart. Out of the blue, in addition to your schooling, you were working your tail off. Every time I called you, I got one of your roommates who told me you were at one job or the other. And you changed your name to match my birth name. Do you think your bubbe is so unobservant that she couldn't put two and two together and come up with four?"

Julia didn't know what to say. Her parents were standing there, mouths set in thin lines of disapproval and desperation. Grandma Ida squeezed her hand.

"What I was never able to figure out, until the other day in the hospital room, was why your parents turned their backs on my beautiful, talented granddaughter. Now the whole picture is clear, and I'm ashamed that I didn't step in sooner to help you. I can't imagine how hard it must be to be you. And to go through it alone, without the support of your family? Unfathomable."

Ida wagged a finger at Stan and Lois. "You two ought to be drawn, quartered, and hung out to dry. This is the perfect moment to quote from the McCarthy Hearings. 'At long last, have you no decency?' You, Stanley, are of my loins. I carried you inside me and spent twenty-eight agonizing hours in labor with you. I expected better from you. I raised you to be better than this. I raised you to be kind and accepting. You can't even see your way clear to do that with your own daughter. Your own flesh and blood! Shame on you.

"And you?" Ida shifted her gaze to Lois. "You grew up with every advantage, went to the best schools, got the best education, and took lessons in etiquette. Your parents came to Bernie and me and begged to make a match with our son. Begged, I tell you. My Bernie, your father," Ida glared at Stan, "is rolling over in his grave right now from this. If we had known what kind of a miserly, miserable mother you would be, we would never have agreed to the match."

"Mother? That's enough." Stan stepped in between Ida and Lois.

Ida sighed heavily. "For once, you're right. It's enough. I'm an old woman, and while I'm still mentally sharp as I ever was, I grow weary and tired of so much hatred and narrow-mindedness. Stanley, I can't believe it's come to this, but you've left me no choice. Get out, and take that horse's ass with you."

"Mother—"

"Don't 'Mother' me. Get out, and don't come back unless it's to apologize to your daughter in front of God and me."

"Mother Ida, you're going to be sorry..."

Stan grabbed Lois's arm. "Don't make threats." He glanced at Levine, who stood calmly, watching and listening.

Ida said, "Lois, I'm sorry already that you're still here. Get out and stay away from me and my granddaughter. If she wants to see you, that's up to her, but I'm going to advise her against it."

"Julia—" Lois turned to her.

"Mother, for once in your life, stop talking and listen. I'm done. I'm done tiptoeing around, trying to pretend everything is all right and that your emotional abandonment was in any way acceptable behavior toward me. I'm done appeasing you and your 'sensibilities.' I'm just...done. Period."

"You both deserve each other," Lois pointed at Ida and Julia. "And you'll both rot in hell together."

"Lois? Jews don't believe in hell. You should've paid more attention in temple," Ida said.

Julia followed as Mr. Levine escorted Stan and Lois out of the bedroom and the apartment and closed the door behind them. They returned to the bedroom.

"Is there anything else you need from me right now, Mrs. Pinsky?"

"No, Mr. Levine. That was just perfect. Now, if you both don't mind, I'm tired, and I need some rest."

"Of course. Julia? You have my card. I'll be in touch in a few days to finalize the details of the property transfers, to go over the financial documents, and to answer any questions you may have."

"Thank you." Julia didn't know what else to say. Her head was spinning.

"Your grandmother is one special, special lady."

"She's the best," Julia said. She glanced over at Grandma Ida, who already was asleep.

"I'll just see myself out," Mr. Levine said.

When they were alone, Julia brushed the hair from her grandmother's forehead. She curled up on the bed with her and watched her chest rise and fall. "I love you, Grandma."

"I love you too, bubbeleh," Ida mumbled. "Always remember that."

CHAPTER THIRTEEN

Rachel stared out her office window and sighed for what seemed like the hundredth time in the last hour. Claudette was waiting for the next sentiment in the "Love, Always," series she'd been working on, but the only thing Rachel could think about was the troubled look she'd glimpsed on Julia's face the last time she saw her. There was something haunted about it, like a pall that hung over her. Such sadness.

Rachel reflected on the scene in Ida's hospital room. If she had parents like Julia's, she'd be sad too. "So says the girl who's been avoiding her family like the plague since the YouTube debacle."

Rachel grimaced. Sooner or later, she was going to have to face her parents and Paul again. Erin said her mother railed for the entire Sabbath meal last week about her absence.

Rachel was only putting off the inevitable. Perhaps if enough time passed, her family would forget about it. Then again, the volume of YouTube comments that continued to appear daily from people who had seen the video made it pretty clear that no one was about to let her forget those few moments of infamy any time soon.

Inexorably, Rachel's eyes alighted on the twenty-three messages awaiting her in the Facebook Messenger app. She bit her lip. Why would she want to look? Undoubtedly, these notes were more of the same—cracks about her problem-solving skills, her appearance, her wardrobe choices. She couldn't take much more of this.

She glanced over at Freud, who was in his usual position, lying on the rug, his head on his paws, his eyes watching her every move. "What would you have me do? Read every one of them?"

He cocked an eyebrow.

"I'm telling you, it's a bad idea."

Freud belched. Or maybe he was blowing her a raspberry. It was hard to tell.

"Yes, I know there might be one in there that could be a serious request for a date." When was the last time she'd been on an honest-to-goodness date? Rachel opened her calendar app. Weeks ago. What would Malinda say about that? *She'd tell you to get your butt back out there.*

She eyed the messages again. Surely there must be one woman on the planet who hadn't seen the video. What about those women who'd sent her messages before what she'd come to think of as, "That Day?" Maybe one of those was waiting among the rabble. Would it be worth it to risk a peek and potentially to suffer through more shaming and embarrassment?

Freud whined.

"Of course you'd think so. It's not your ego that's taking a beating."

Her finger hovered over the Messenger app, where the little red circle with the number twenty-three in the upper right-hand corner glowed brightly. What was the worst that could happen? Rachel closed her eyes and tapped on the app.

She cracked open one eye and peeked at the name and first line in the first message. Both eyes popped open wide and she deleted that message without opening it. The second message was a repeat of the first, only with a little nicer language.

Rachel worked her way down the list, deleting as she went, until she got to a message from a woman whom she'd met at the gym last month. The first line of the message read, "I enjoyed chatting with you over ab crunches. Do you think you'd like to catch a movie some time?"

Would this woman still feel the same way post-"That Day?" Rachel drummed her fingers on the desk. What did she have to lose?

"I'd like that," Rachel typed. "What are you doing this Saturday?" She hesitated momentarily before hitting the "send" button.

Seconds later, the response came. "Going to the movies with you." This was followed by a smiley emoticon, and a back-and-forth discussion of which movie to see and at what time. Maybe things were looking up, after all. They discussed whether to do something else after the movie, like have a late dinner, but Rachel was only interested in taking baby steps at the moment. A movie date was plenty enough interaction for her.

⊰⊱

Rachel searched the lobby. They'd agreed to meet by the larger-than-life-sized three-dimensional cutout advertising the next upcoming blockbuster Marvel movie. Now, there was a movie Rachel would love to see.

As she and her date, Holly, both thought seeing a romance would be a bad idea on a first date, they'd settled on a thriller. How could you go wrong with a psychological thriller? Still, left to her own devices, it wasn't a movie Rachel would've chosen.

"You're that girl—the one from YouTube! I recognize you." A barely pubescent boy pointed at her and nudged his friends. "That's her. I'm sure of it."

Rachel turned her back.

"I'm telling you, that's her." The boy's voice was loud enough to carry through the din in the lobby.

Rachel's palms began to sweat. She started looking for an escape route.

"There you are." Holly, seemingly oblivious to the hubbub, came up alongside Rachel. She was carrying an extra-large bucket of popcorn and two large soda cups. "I didn't know what kind of soda you wanted, but you fill your own at those machines over there, so I figured we could just do that." Holly nodded in the direction of the soda dispensers. She looked good in her faded jeans and Henley shirt. Unlike at the gym, where she'd sported a ponytail, her hair cascaded down her back. Rachel liked the effect.

"Great. Thank you." Rachel guided Holly as far away from the teens as she could manage without being obvious, sighing with relief as the boys exited the lobby. "Nice to see you again, by the way!"

"Nice to see you again too." So far, so good.

"I thought we were going Dutch treat?" Rachel asked.

"We were. But the lines were long, and I was early, so... I figured you wouldn't mind too much if I took care of the concessions. Besides, you paid for the tickets online and got us the assigned seats."

"Right." Rachel hadn't planned on getting any popcorn. Every time she ate the stuff... What if she simply said she didn't want any? *Holly bought that huge bucketful; do you think she wasn't planning to share it?*

"Let's grab the sodas and get in there. The previews are going to start any second."

They reached their seats just as the lights dimmed. The theater was nearly sold out, save for the front row and the single seat on the other side of Holly. Rachel put her bag on the floor beneath her and spread her coat over the back of the seat. Holly set the popcorn bucket between them and handed Rachel some napkins.

"Do you like salt?"

There was no turning back now, Rachel realized. She would have to eat the popcorn and pray for the best. "Sure."

Holly liberally sprinkled the packets of salt over the popcorn and shook the bucket as the previews ended and the movie got going.

"You're in our seats." A woman forced herself directly in front of Rachel, blocking her view. A small boy and a man hovered uncomfortably nearby.

"I'm sorry, I'm positive these are our seats. Give me a second and I'll check for you," Rachel whispered. She reached in her pocket for their tickets.

"You're in our seats." The woman repeated. She made no effort to modulate her voice. "Get out of our fucking seats!"

Rachel couldn't believe her ears. She looked at the small boy and the man next to him, both of whom showed no visible reaction. "Ma'am, I'm looking for our tickets. I assure you—"

"You're in our fucking seats, bitch. Now get out before I drag you out." The woman reached down and grabbed Rachel by the arm, yanking her to her feet. She shoved Rachel hard, unbalancing the popcorn from its perch on the armrest and spilling half the contents of the bucket on the floor.

Before Rachel could react, Holly was standing at her full height, glaring at the rude woman. "If you touch her again, I'll break your face. You talk like that in front of your kid?"

"Holly, I'll just get the manager," Rachel said. "Let's go."

"No. I'm not going to miss the movie because this rude idiot comes in late and thinks she can kick people out of the seats they paid for."

"You want trouble? I'll give you trouble." The woman swung for Holly, but Rachel was in the way, and the punch landed on Rachel's shoulder.

"That does it," Holly said. She raised her fists like a boxer.

"No," Rachel said. Surely, this couldn't be happening. People around them were reacting, one guy saying, "Hey, hey, calm down." Someone else got out her phone to capture on video whatever was going to happen. Rachel wanted to bolt. "Let's just get the manager and he can settle this. Come on." She grabbed what was left of the popcorn, along with her soda, and her bag and jacket. "Please, Holly. Just let it go."

Reluctantly, Holly followed her out to the lobby, where Rachel flagged down the manager, explained the situation, and showed him their tickets.

"I see the problem. We accidentally assigned you handicapped seats. That's why the usher seated you in the closest available seats, which must have belonged to someone else."

"Why didn't your usher tell us that was what he'd done?" Rachel asked.

"I can't answer that. Listen, I'm sorry that happened to you. I can give you a refund—"

"We don't want a refund," Holly broke in. "We paid for the movie, and we're going to see the movie. Not only that, but we want a refill of the popcorn, since that rude woman spilled it on the floor."

"I'll take care of your popcorn. The only seats we have together are in the front row. If you want those…"

Whatever desire Rachel had had to see the movie was long gone. What she wanted was to get away—away from the children taunting her about "That Day," away from the deranged woman who'd taken their seats, away from the popcorn she feared would give her gas, and away from her date, who had turned into Cujo the rabid dog, before her very eyes, thus calling more embarrassing attention to her.

"We'll take them, along with free passes for a future movie, since we've missed half of this one," Holly said.

Did Holly really think that after this debacle, Rachel would go on a second date with her? Dear God, could this night get any worse?

◈◈

"I'm telling you, Grandma, this was the worst date yet."

"Worse than the bicycle date?" Goldie asked.

"Worse even than that," Rachel acknowledged. "You know how much I hate confrontation."

Goldie drew Rachel close and kissed her on the temple. "You'll find the right one, bubbeleh. I promise you will." She glanced at the clock on the wall. "Let's go for a walk."

"Where to?" Rachel asked.

"Just around the halls. I'm going stir-crazy."

"I could take you out for an ice cream soda."

"No!" Goldie realized she said it too quickly. *Be calm. You need to act nonchalant. You're going to give it away.* "I mean, you'll spoil your appetite before dinner at your parents and your mother will blame it on me."

"She doesn't have to know we went out for a treat."

"No, darling. I just need to stretch my legs a little, that's all." Goldie rose and linked her arm through Rachel's. "Onward."

They stepped out into the hallway and nearly plowed into Saul Rabinowitz. "Oh, excuse me," Rachel said.

He looked nervously at Goldie, who jerked her head in Rachel's direction. "Right. Uh, no, actually, I was coming to your grandmother's place to see if you might be here."

"Me?" Rachel asked.

"You're Goldie's granddaughter-the-famous-writer, yes?" Saul asked.

"The famous...?"

Goldie practically kicked him in the shin, and Saul produced a copy of the *People* magazine he'd been carrying folded up in the waistband of his pants. "Would you autograph my magazine, please?"

"Autograph your…?"

"I have a pen here, somewhere." Saul patted his pockets.

"It's in your pocket protector," Goldie helpfully supplied.

"Right." Saul smiled sheepishly, extracted the pen from the plastic sheath tucked inside his breast pocket, and handed it to Rachel.

"Are you sure you want me to sign this?" she pointed to the magazine.

"Yes."

"Okay. Anyplace in particular?"

"Huh?" Saul cupped his hand to his ear.

"Do you want me to sign anywhere specific?" Rachel shouted.

"Oh. No. Anywhere will do."

Rachel opened the magazine to the story about her and scrawled her name on one of the pictures.

"Thank you," Saul said when she handed him back the magazine. "You're a real looker, you know. Chip off the old block. Your grandmother…" Saul whistled. "In her day she could stop a train just by crossing the tracks."

"Saul!" Goldie swatted him on the sleeve.

"What? It's the truth and you know it, Goldie. If you ever decide to come out of retirement—"

"Okay. That's enough." Goldie wrapped her arm through Rachel's again and tugged her forward.

"He sure is sweet on you, Grandma," Rachel said when they were alone again.

"Don't you start," Goldie warned.

"There's nothing wrong with that. I think it's kind of nice."

"Well, you would. Saul Rabinowitz isn't trying to get into your skirt. Then again, if he thought he stood a chance…"

"Grandma!"

They reached the end of the hall and turned the corner. "You're Goldie's granddaughter the-famous-author, right?" An elderly woman with a kindly face and purple hair stopped them in their tracks.

"I—"

"Yep, that's her," Goldie agreed. "That's my Rachel."

"I'm so excited to meet you," the woman exclaimed. "Would you do an old lady a favor and autograph my magazine?" The woman fumbled around in the seat of her walker. "I know I put it in here."

"Gertie? It's in your hand," Goldie said, "along with the pen."

"Right. Of course." With shaking fingers, she held out the pen and the magazine for Rachel to sign.

Rachel dutifully signed the magazine and handed it, and the pen, back.

"Thank you, dear. Such a pleasure to meet you. Any granddaughter of Goldie's is a granddaughter of Goldie's."

"Okay. Thank you, Gertie." Goldie nudged Rachel forward.

"Grandma?"

"Hmm?"

"You didn't—"

"Oh, dear. There you are. You must be Goldie's-granddaughter-the-famous-person." A woman in a motorized wheelchair practically ran over their feet.

"Hello, Selma," Goldie said.

"Hello, Goldie. Such a surprise running into you and your granddaughter like this." Selma gave an exaggerated wink.

"Yes, what a surprise," Goldie said.

"I wonder, young lady. Would you put your Jane Hancock on this copy of my magazine?" Selma reached into the side pocket of her electric wheelchair and pulled out a copy of *People* and a pen.

"Sure," Rachel drew the word out and glared at Goldie. "I'd love to."

Goldie shrugged innocently.

Rachel signed the magazine and handed it back. She wrapped her arm around Goldie's shoulder and pulled her out of the hallway traffic. "Grandma?"

"Yes, bubbeleh?"

"You engineered this."

"I don't know what you're talking about."

"Is that so? It's quite a coincidence, these lovely friends of yours just happening to have copies of the magazine in which I'm featured. I'm guessing a good percentage of them can't even read print that small."

"They can see pictures, can't they?"

"Grandma. You did this."

"Excuse me. Is this a bad time?" A finely dressed gentleman in a tweed coat and hat stepped up to them. "Allow me to introduce myself. I'm... I'm... I'm..."

"Isadore," Goldie offered.

"Right. I'm Isadore. You must be that girl." He tapped his temple in thought. "Let me see." He thought some more. "You must be that girl who did something, or won something, or..."

"Oh, for Heaven's sake! Give her the magazine to sign."

"The what?" Isadore scanned the hallway.

"The magazine." Goldie grabbed the magazine that was hanging out of his jacket pocket and waved it in front of his face.

"Right." He looked to Goldie again. "What am I supposed to do with this?"

Goldie closed her eyes and willed herself to be patient. "Ask my granddaughter to sign it."

"Yes, yes. Would you please sign this piece of paper?"

"You mean this magazine? Absolutely." Rachel signed her name, all the while narrowing her eyes at Goldie.

"Well, that was monumentally bad timing," Goldie said. She knew her goose was cooked.

"I love you, Grandma, but you didn't need to stage this."

"I just wanted you to feel better, Rachel. You've been so down in the dumps lately, what with that me tube thing."

"YouTube."

"Me tube, you tube, everyone a tube, tube. Whatever that thing is, it pulled your focus away from where it should be. Not everyone gets a full-color feature in a major magazine, you know."

"Yeah. And not everyone is the laughing stock of the digital age, either."

"See? You're looking at this all wrong. You're always going to experience disappointments, darling. The secret is to focus on the beautiful moments and let everything else take care of itself." Goldie tapped Rachel affectionately on the nose. "You're a talented, successful, attractive girl, bubbeleh. Lots of girls are wishing they could be you right now."

"I don't think so, Grandma."

"Trust me, I know these things. Chin up and own your success. You deserve it."

"I wish I could see the world the way you do, Grandma."

"You can. You just need older eyes. Minus the cataracts, of course." Goldie kissed Rachel's cheek. "Now, you'd better get going or you'll be late for dinner. You know how your mother gets."

Rachel hugged her, and Goldie smiled. She might've gotten caught, but she was pretty sure she'd achieved her objective just the same.

"I love you, bubbeleh."

"I love you, Grandma. See you next week."

"God willing, I'll be here."

CHAPTER FOURTEEN

How had she gotten here? Julia wondered. Not here, as in where she was standing, which was in the center of her grandmother's cozy, cluttered living room. How had she gotten *here*, as in out of the closet, a non-person to her parents, and now her grandmother's heir and the proud owner of a million-dollar house and two acres of prime land with a beautiful view of the Adirondack mountains?

Of the myriad scenarios she imagined in which she might tell her grandmother that she was a lesbian, having her mother break the news was never on the list. The irony of it, and the resultant fallout, made Julia positively euphoric.

It wasn't that she was gloating, because, in a way, she felt horrible and as though she'd made her grandmother choose between her own son and her granddaughter.

What had Ida said? "Let go of the Jewish guilt, darling. You didn't make me do anything. I was already preparing to change my will before this latest health scare. Honestly, your mother has given me heartburn for as long as I've known her. Did you know your grandfather and I sat your father down and begged him not to marry Lois?"

"You did?"

"We did. Didn't like her and her highfaluting ways from the outset. She always thought she was better than everyone else, including your father's parents. Stan couldn't see past his own nose, she had him so wrapped around her little finger, dangling a big job at her daddy's bank in front of him. And of course we should have known he would defy us, trying to assert himself. But he wanted the match, so we reluctantly agreed."

155

Ida sighed, then patted Julia on the hand. "The only good thing to come of Stan ignoring our pleas was you. You, my darling Julia, are one of God's greatest gifts to me. I thank Him every day for you."

Julia sat down on the couch as her eyes misted over, remembering the conversation and the tender way Ida had smiled at her and touched her cheek.

The shrill ring of her cell phone sounded loud in the empty house. She glanced down at the display and her pulse quickened.

"Hello? This is Julia."

"Oh. I expected to get your voicemail. This is Rachel Wallach, your grandmother's friend Goldie's granddaughter, if you followed that."

Julia smiled into the phone. "I know who you are."

"Right. Um..."

Julia imagined Rachel tucking an errant strand of her pretty chestnut hair behind one ear, as she'd seen her do on several occasions, especially when she was nervous.

"Anyway, I was just returning your phone call. You left a message the other night, and I hate it when people don't call me back so..."

"I'm glad you called. Thank you, again, for what you did when Ida was in the hospital. I don't think I could've gotten through that without you and Goldie."

"Oh, you'd have managed just fine, I'm sure. But I'm happy that we were there for you."

Rachel's voice was warm and soothing. Julia idly thought that if her GPS sounded like Rachel, she wouldn't get so stressed out every time she missed a turn. It took Julia a second to realize they were in the middle of an awkward silence, and it was her turn to say something.

"I never got to finish what I was saying about—"

"I don't want to talk about it," Rachel jumped in.

"I wasn't—"

"It's too late to do anything about the video anyway."

"Please, Rachel? Can I at least finish a sentence here?"

After several seconds of silence, Rachel said, "I'm sorry. That was rude."

156

"It's okay. What I was going to say was, I'd like to know more about what you do for a living. I loved the magazine interview. I was fascinated by your description of what defines a great greeting card sentiment."

"You were?"

"Absolutely. What you do is so specialized. It's like an art form."

"You're not just saying that to be kind?"

Julia laughed. "I'm not *that* kind."

"I think you are."

Yes. With a voice like that, Rachel could give her directions any time. "Maybe next time our paths cross at Shady Acres we could grab a cup of coffee afterward?"

"Sure. We could try my grandmother's favorite diner. Apparently, she's been sneaking out to catch old-movie matinees and drink ice cream sodas there."

"Goldie?"

"Yep."

"Who knew she was such a rule-breaker? Well, that explains the musical choice on the radio that night."

"Ha! I hadn't thought of that, but I bet you're right. She must've been sweating bullets thinking we'd figure it out."

"She's not supposed to be driving?"

"Heck no. That car is there that I can commute to my parents for the Sabbath on Fridays after I arrive via train. I found out recently that Grandma kept a set of keys on the sly. I know I should take them away. But it's hard, you know?"

"Gotcha. Well, I like a good ice cream soda too."

"Okay. I'm there every Friday afternoon around four o'clock."

"I'll try to get there next Friday, then," Julia said.

"But this week, I'm going to make an extra stop there on Wednesday afternoon to pick up her new dental bridge and bring it to her."

"I could make it on Wednesday at around four."

"That would be great."

"See you then?"

"See you then, Julia."

"'Bye, Rachel." Julia tapped the phone against her chin after she disconnected the call. Unaccountably, she felt much better than she had a little while ago. Much, much better, indeed.

❧❧

"Too dressy?" Rachel asked Freud, as she twirled in front of the mirror.

Freud raised an eyebrow.

"Too dressy." Rachel hung up that outfit and thumbed through the business casual section of her closet.

"Too big. Too small. Too frilly. Ugh. Shoulder pads? Who thought that was a good idea?" She pulled out and discarded half a dozen blazers. "Too...purple." She turned the jacket toward the light. "Definitely too purple."

Freud covered his eyes with his paws.

"I know, Freud," Rachel said, as she continued to fling clothes. "It's just a chat with an acquaintance, what's the big deal? Why am I so worried about what I look like?"

Her eyes alighted on her small collection of black leather blazers and jackets. Nothing said "classy-dressy-enough-but-not-too-dressy" like the perfect leather blazer. You could pair it with jeans or with dress khakis and feel properly attired for just about any occasion.

Twenty minutes later, Rachel finished fidgeting with her clothes, hair, and makeup, which was a good thing. If she had tried on and rejected one more outfit, she likely would have missed her train.

❧❧

Julia kissed Ida on the cheek.

"I wasn't expecting you today," Ida remarked.

"How are you feeling?" Julia was relieved to note that Ida was fully dressed and sitting in her favorite chair. She had more color in her cheeks today and that old sparkle was back in her eyes.

"If I was any better, they'd name a monument after me."

"They might do that anyway. But you didn't answer the question."

"Neither did you."

"You didn't actually ask me a question."

Ida crossed her arms and sat back in the recliner. "Don't get fresh with me, young lady. And I have to say, you look too nicely dressed just to be coming to see your old grandmother."

"I came from work. I always dress this way for work." The explanation sounded rushed and false, even to her own ears. Why was she feeling so defensive?

"Of course you do," Ida said.

"I do."

"Right. I just agreed with you."

"Okay, then."

In the ensuing silence, the oversized pendulum clock loudly ticked off the seconds.

Thirty-three, thirty-four, thirty-five...

"Well? Are you going to answer me, or what?" Ida asked.

"I thought we established that you hadn't asked a question."

Ida wagged a finger at Julia. "I already told you, don't get smart with me, missy."

"I would never do such a thing."

"You're doing it right now. So, bubbeleh... Wednesday is not normally a day I get to see your smiling face. Why are you here, today, specifically?"

"Can't a girl come see her favorite grandmother for no reason?"

"First, I'm your only living grandmother, so that's not such a compliment. Second, you could come see me for no reason, but you do everything with purpose, and I imagine this is no different. So... What's the occasion?"

"As it happens, I did want to see you. I'm worried about you and I wanted to eyeball you in person."

"Well, as you can see, I'm fine. What else?"

"Why does there have to be...?" Julia stopped herself. It occurred to her that the longer she drew this out, the bigger deal Ida was going to make of it. And, after all, it was only a friendly chat over coffee or a milkshake with someone she admired. Why not just tell the truth?

"I'm going to grab a cup of coffee with Rachel."

"Goldie's granddaughter Rachel?"

"Yes."

"Now we're getting somewhere!" Ida gleefully clapped her hands.

Julia shifted uncomfortably on the couch. "It's nothing, Grandma."

"No? Rachel usually only comes on Fridays. If you know she's coming on a Wednesday, that means the two of you had a conversation about it."

"If you must know, I called to thank Rachel for staying with me while you were in the emergency room."

"Uh-huh."

"That was the polite thing to do."

"Yes, it was. Good for you."

More silence ensued.

Ida gestured at Julia's outfit, a formfitting pantsuit and a button-front silk blouse. "You look very nice, by the way. Is that the way you dress for work every day?"

"Pretty much," Julia agreed.

"Very professional."

"Thank you."

"I'm sure Rachel will think you look very nice."

"I didn't dress this way to impress Rachel. I just happened to be wearing this for work. As I said, meeting up with Rachel is just a casual thing. Two intelligent women getting together for some conversation over coffee." Julia wondered if Ida had turned up the thermostat. The air felt overly warm in the apartment.

"If it's not a big deal, why do you keep watching the clock?"

"I'm not watching the clock."

Roughly a minute later, Ida said, "Oh, for goodness sake. Staring at the clock isn't going to make it move any faster. Go, already."

"I wasn't staring—"

"No. No. Of course you weren't. Listen, darling. It's just about suppertime in this joint. You know that this walker thingy takes time to maneuver. I hate to kick you out, but I'd better get started over to the dining room." Ida rose slowly and pulled her walker to her. "Goldie is probably on her way to dinner too, by the way. Not that that matters to you, since you're so busy not watching the clock for your no-big-deal meet up with Rachel."

160

"I love you, Grandma."

"I love you too, darling."

⋘⋙

"Goldie? Goldie, what are you doing?"

Goldie's heart pounded. "Don't sneak up on me like that!"

"Like what? You're busy hiding behind a plant. I can't imagine why anyone would think you were lurking."

"Shh."

"Well? What do you see? I'm assuming you're spying on Rachel and Julia?"

Goldie spun around so fast she felt dizzy. She grabbed onto Ida's walker for support. "You heard?"

"That our girls are going out for a no-big-deal cuppa together? Yes, I heard. Julia came to see me. Getting information out of her was like trying to pry a Kennedy half dollar out of my Bernie's closed fist back in the day. May he rest in peace."

"I had the same experience with Rachel just now."

"Which? Getting the half dollar, or information?"

"Very funny."

"Which car are they taking?" Ida asked.

"Not mine."

Ida poked Goldie. "Are you thinking what I'm thinking?"

"What are you thinking?"

"I think maybe we should go out for a ride. You?"

Goldie's eyebrows shot up. "You want to follow them? Like in a detective movie?"

"Why not?"

Goldie tapped her fingers on the walker.

"If you wait any longer to make up your mind, they're going to get away," Ida said.

"Okay. Okay, already. You know we're going to miss dinner."

"Dried out pot roast? Who cares! Let's go. Get your keys."

"They're right here." Goldie winked and produced the car keys from her purse.

"That's my Gold-e-lah. Always a step ahead. Come on."

⋘⋙

The hostess led them to a corner booth by the window. "Is this okay?"

Rachel looked to Julia. Did she prefer booths to tables? She seemed like a booth kind of girl. "Fine, thanks. Is it okay with you, Julia?"

"Perfect."

When they were settled in their seats and the hostess retreated, Rachel said, "I hope you don't mind coming to this place. I love diners, and the coffee is so much better than at Starbucks."

"Are you kidding me? This place has character. I adore out-of-the-way, locally owned spots. This is fabulous."

"What can I get you ladies?" the server asked. She had short pink hair and a sparkly nose stud. Her nametag said ZELDA.

"Just coffee for me, please," Rachel said.

"Make that two," Julia folded the menu.

"Wait," Rachel said to the server.

The server, who had begun to walk away, hesitated.

"Go ahead and have something to eat," Rachel told her companion. "I hear their cheesecake is delicious."

"No," Julia said. "Coffee is good."

Again, the server walked away. "Wait," Julia said. "Unless you'd agree to share a piece with me?"

"I hope you two don't have this much trouble picking out furniture and paint colors for your bedroom," Zelda said.

Rachel's eyebrows shot up into her hairline. "We're not..." She and Julia said in stereo.

"Oh, my bad. So, shall I bring the cheesecake and two forks along with those coffees?"

Rachel looked to Julia. She appeared as flustered as Rachel felt. "Sure."

This time the server did walk away.

"I can't imagine..." Rachel and Julia once again began talking at the same time.

"You go first," Julia said.

"No, you go."

"I was just going to say, I can't imagine why anyone would think that we..." Julia made a gesture with her hand that encompassed the two of them.

"I know. That's completely insane. Pffft." Rachel rolled her eyes and they both laughed.

"Anyway, tell me how you got started writing greeting cards for a living. What a fascinating line of work."

Rachel searched Julia's face for any sign that she was being facetious. "You're serious?"

"Of course I am. What you do is create art and express emotions in ways that speak to peoples' hearts, usually in fewer characters than a typical tweet. That's amazing."

"Huh." It was, perhaps, not the most articulate response, Rachel knew.

"Why do you seem so surprised that I would feel that way?"

"Probably because everyone in my family thinks I don't have a real job." It took a second for Rachel to realize that she'd said the words out loud. She stared down at the paper placemat, solved the "word search" and "unscramble these words" puzzles in her head, and prayed for the blush in her cheeks to subside.

"Rachel?" Julia's voice was quiet, and somehow soothing.

"Yes?" She still didn't dare look up.

"Please look at me."

Slowly, Rachel raised her head until she made eye contact with Julia. What she saw there was kindness and compassion.

"If you'll excuse me for saying so—"

"Here you go. Two coffees, cream and sweetener, and one piece of cheesecake, with two forks." Zelda slapped the plate down on the table, and then the cups and saucers. Hot liquid sloshed over the side of one cup. "Can I get you anything else?"

"Extra napkins, please," Rachel said, dryly.

"Your family can go scratch." Julia picked up where she'd left off. "I meant it when I said that what you do is admirable. It takes real talent. You teach people about love. You show them how to share their emotions, or maybe it's that you identify emotions for them they didn't even know they felt."

"I do? I mean, I do." Rachel said it with more authority.

"Extra napkins." The server threw a handful of paper napkins in the center of the table and hustled away.

"So, how did you get started?"

"It was an accident." Rachel poured five creamers in her coffee and added four packets of Splenda. When she glanced up again, Julia was staring at her, wide-eyed. "What?"

"Nothing," Julia said. She sipped her black coffee. "Go on. You said it was an accident."

"Right." Rachel picked up one of the forks and motioned for Julia to do the same. "Are you a front/back splitter or a split down the middle splitter?"

"Any way you slice it, it's a New York cheesecake."

"I saw what you did just then. Very punny."

"Thank you. I thought of it all by myself." Julia stuck her fork in and scooped up a mouthful of cheesecake from the side closest to her. "Oh, my God. That's fabulous."

Rachel, entranced by the expression of pure ecstasy on Julia's face, let her own fork go slack in her hand. It clattered to the table. She scrambled to catch it before it fell on the floor.

"Got it. I've got it." She sat up straight again, tucked the hair behind her ear that had fallen in her face when she leaned over, and placed the fork on the table as casually as she could.

"You've got to try this," Julia said, taking another bite.

"Right." Rachel picked up the fork, dug it into the pristine side of the cheesecake, and savored her first bite. "Heavenly." She closed her eyes and enjoyed the sensation as the creamy delicacy slid down her throat.

"You said you became a greeting card writer by accident?" Julia prompted.

"Yep. I needed a topic for my masters' thesis and I was running out of time. A friend of mine saw an ad in the paper for a small startup company looking for someone who could write sentiments that would set their cards apart. I did some research on the greeting card industry, both the financial and artistic sides of it, and went to my thesis advisor. I pitched the idea of exploring the greeting card sentiment as a form of artistic expression, and whether or not the worth of that was quantifiable as represented by the number of cards with my unique sentiments that were manufactured and purchased. When he approved the concept, I spent something like seventy-two straight hours writing romantic greeting card sentiments and got myself hired by the startup."

Rachel glanced up and waved her empty fork with a flourish. "The rest, as they say, is history."

"Speaking of which…" Julia stole the last bite of cheesecake.

"You rat! I was going to flip you for that."

"Too late."

"Oh, no. Late. I'm going to be late!" Rachel jumped up and pulled her wallet out of her purse. "I hate to do this, but if I don't leave right now, Freud will never forgive me."

"Freud will…"

Rachel saw the puzzled expression on Julia's face, but she didn't have time to explain. As it was, she would have to sprint across the street to the train station. She picked up the check, which the server had stashed underneath the sugar caddy, and threw down a twenty-dollar bill. "That should cover it. I hate to eat and run, but…"

"Wait! Where are you going? I drove."

"The train station is across the street. My train should be pulling in within the next five minutes." Rachel stuffed her wallet back in the purse and took the first step toward the door.

"Wait!" Julia yelled after her. Rachel stopped in her tracks. "If I show up next Friday, do I get to ask more questions?"

"No."

"No?"

"Nope. Next Friday, it's my turn to ask the questions." Rachel winked and ran out. Out of the corner of her eye at the end of the row of windows fronting the diner, she could've sworn she saw an elderly woman's side profile that looked a lot like her grandmother's. "Now you're hallucinating." She sprinted across the street and over to the northbound platform.

CHAPTER FIFTEEN

G oldie turned her face away from the window glass and thrust up her pocketbook to obscure any view of Ida. She wasn't sure, but she didn't think Rachel saw her.

"What in the world are you doing, you crazy person? Put that thing down before you hurt someone."

"Shh, Ida."

"Shh? Why should I shh?"

Goldie pointed at Rachel's retreating form, and then at Julia, who was just exiting the diner.

"Oh," Ida said in a whisper Goldie was sure could be heard from three blocks away. Ida turned up the lapel of her fur coat and hid behind it. Several moments later she asked, "Are they gone, yet?"

"I think so," Goldie answered. She peeked out from around Ida. "The coast is clear."

"Whew! That was a close one."

"Tell me about it."

"Almost gave me another heart attack."

"Are you okay? I never should have let you talk me into this meshugenah caper," Goldie said. Ida was pale and breathing heavily.

"Are you kidding? And let you have all the fun? Never."

"We should go."

"Not so fast," Ida said. She put a restraining hand on Goldie's arm. "What did they say?"

"Who?"

"Who? The girls. Our granddaughters. What were they talking about?"

"How should I know? I was out here with you, or didn't you notice?"

"Very funny, Gold-e-lah. You were the one with your nose to the window. As bad as your hearing is, you don't read lips?"

"No, I don't read lips. Whatever gave you that idea?"

"Excuse me." A woman pushing a stroller pointed to Ida's walker, which took up the majority of the sidewalk. "Can we get by?"

"What? Oh. Sure, sure." Ida wheeled the walker closer to the building. When the woman and baby had passed, Ida said to Goldie, "We need to know what they said to each other."

"Well, it's too late for that now."

"Nonsense." Ida pointed to the server who had waited on Rachel and Julia.

"What about her?"

"Grease her palm."

"What?" Goldie asked.

Ida rubbed her thumb and two fingers together. "Pay her off. Grease her palm. Find out what she knows."

"You've lost what's left of your mind."

"Have I? You want to know what the girls talked about and why your Rachel ran off in such a hurry? She's the only one who can tell us."

Goldie bit her lip. Should she do it? It seemed so…Humphrey Bogart in "The Maltese Falcon."

"Hello? Gold-e-lah? It's cold out here. Go in there and give that girl five dollars. She'll spill the beans for sure."

Goldie wasn't so sure five dollars would do the trick. "I've got a better idea. Come on." She led Ida to the front door.

"What are we doing? If we both go in there, she might get suspicious."

"Yes, because an old lady walking up and handing her five dollars and asking a bunch of questions wouldn't be the least bit suspicious," Goldie said. "I'm afraid that blockage you had has gone to your brain. You're not thinking clearly."

Ida bristled. "And I suppose you are?"

"Watch and see." Goldie opened the door to the diner and motioned Ida to precede her inside. She stepped up to the hostess stand. "Table for two, please." She saw that Rachel and Julia's table was still open. "Can we have that one over by the window?"

"Certainly." The hostess led them to the table.

"What are you doing? I'm not hungry," Ida complained.

"Hush, for goodness sake. For once in your life, just be quiet and let me do the talking."

The server approached. "What can I get you, ladies?"

"We'll have two cups of coffee, black," Goldie said.

"Anything else?"

"I thought I saw those two girls who sat here before us get something that looked yummy. What was it?"

"I'm not hun—"

Goldie kicked Ida under the table.

"Ouch!"

Goldie batted her eyelashes at the server. "So, what did those two girls who sat here before us have?"

"Two girls?"

"You know. They were young and pretty. Looked like movie stars, if you ask me."

The server gazed back toward the kitchen, where the cook was yelling, "Order up, Zelda! Sometime today."

"I'd have to go look at their order, and I don't have time for that. It wasn't anything special, I can tell you that. Do you want more than just the coffee or not?"

"No," Ida said.

"Yes," Goldie said.

"Which is it?" the server asked.

"No," Ida repeated. She squinted to read the server's nametag. "Zelda, is it? What we really want to know—"

Goldie kicked Ida under the table again, this time harder.

Ida gave Goldie a murderous glare and turned her attention to Zelda. "Did you overhear what the young women who just left this table five minutes ago were talking about? There's five dollars in it for you if you tell us."

The server shook her head.

"Zelda! You want to keep working here? Come get this order! Food's getting cold."

Zelda glanced back over her shoulder toward the grill. "I'm coming!" She returned her attention to Goldie and Ida. "You two are crazy, you know that? Do you want the coffee or not? I've got to go get that order or I'll be fired."

"So does that mean you're not going to tell us what we want to know?" Ida persisted.

"Lady, I have no idea what it is you think I know, but whatever it is, I don't know it. Is that clear enough for you?"

"Well, you don't have to be rude about it," Ida rejoined. "Come on, Goldie, I can see this person doesn't want our business."

Ida rose in a huff and grabbed her walker. As she maneuvered in the tight space between the crowded tables, she banged into the chair of a small boy. Undeterred, she backed up the walker, angled it slightly to the side, and shoved it through the opening again, this time successfully.

Goldie lingered behind. "I'm sorry for my friend," she said to the server. "This is for your trouble." She handed her a five-dollar bill.

"Whatever, lady."

Goldie hustled to the front of the diner, where Ida was ramming her walker into the glass doors, trying to get them to open. If the two of them were lucky, they wouldn't get arrested for attempted bribery or disturbing the peace or some other charge before they could get back to the safety of Shady Acres.

Rachel changed into a pair of comfy sweats and warm socks. As she hung up the clothes she'd been wearing, she addressed Freud, who was staring dolefully at her from the closet doorway. "I'm sorry I was late. You know dinnertime is a fluid concept. We discussed this. Anytime after four o'clock means you might get fed at four, if I'm home, or at eight, like tonight, when I've got someplace I have to be."

Freud didn't blink.

"In my defense, I did pay fifty bucks for the dog walker to take you out several times."

Still, the dog didn't budge.

"Come on. Cut me some slack. This isn't a one-way street, you know. You're costing me a lot of money. You weren't exactly in my budget plans for the year. Dog beds, dog toys, dog food, a feeding station, a new collar, checkups at the vet, a dog walker..." Rachel ticked the expenses off on her fingers.

"Speaking of which, you could save me a lot of money by telling me exactly how long you can go without, well, going, if you know what I mean. Is it four hours? Five? Six? Everything I read says it depends on the dog. If I knew how long you could hold it, I could figure out whether I need to hire someone to walk you every few hours or not, depending on how long I needed to be gone."

Freud trotted off.

"Sure. Wander away when the discussion isn't to your liking. Well, not this time." Rachel followed Freud into the living room and plopped down on the sofa. "I'll have you know, I left a perfectly lovely person in the lurch in order to race home to you."

Freud grabbed a stuffed chicken in his teeth and squeaked it.

"That's right," Rachel raised her voice to be heard above the racket, "Julia and I were having a very nice conversation that I had to cut short so I could be here for you." She pointed a finger at the dog. "I've made real sacrifices."

Freud sat in front of her, the stuffed chicken dangling from his mouth.

"How am I supposed to take you seriously with a chicken hanging out of your mouth?"

Freud deposited the chicken at Rachel's feet and laid down.

"That's better." She reclined on the sofa and fluffed a pillow under her head. "Not that you haven't made sacrifices too. I'm not saying that. I mean, geez, you've had your whole life turned upside down. You lost your person..." Rachel cleared her throat. "I know I'm not any kind of substitute for Mr. Crawford, Freud, but I hope you realize I'm doing the best I can."

Freud whined and put his head on his paws.

"I know, I'm sorry you lost Mr. Crawford too. I wish I could change that for you. I do. But I can't. I even tried to get them to let me bring you for a visit. That's against policy at the nursing home. I'm afraid you're stuck with me."

Freud popped up and put his cold nose under Rachel's hand, so that her hand landed on top of his head.

"What in the world are you doing?"

Freud scooted closer so that his body was leaning against the sofa. He tilted his head so that it rested against Rachel's cheek.

If Rachel didn't know any better, she'd have thought he was trying to give her a hug. She rolled over onto her side to face Freud. "Are you trying to comfort me?" She got up off the sofa, knelt next to Freud, and wrapped her arms around him. "That's so sweet. I'm the one who should be comforting you, not the other way around."

She scratched his neck and he responded by burying his head against her chest. "I love you, you crazy beast."

Freud lifted his head and licked Rachel square in the face.

"Eww. Too much. Too much." She wiped the sleeve of her hoodie across her mouth. "There isn't enough mouthwash in the world to sanitize me after that." She got up, went into the bathroom, and washed her face and brushed her teeth. God only knew where Freud's mouth had been.

When she'd finished, she made herself a cup of hot tea, grabbed her iPad, and sat back down on the sofa.

Her home screen showed several email notifications from Tony and Claudette. Rachel swallowed hard. She knew what the emails would say even without opening them.

From Tony, the messages would be, "You're on fire. We've got to strike while the iron is hot."

From Claudette, the refrain would go something like, "Where are you? I've been trying to reach you for a week. You do remember you've got a deadline coming up soon, right? Three new wedding sentiments?"

Rachel sighed. She had responsibilities, she knew that. But ever since the YouTube debacle and the Cujo date, she hadn't been able to bring herself to go online. Worse still, she hadn't written a word, making this the longest stretch since college that she hadn't produced at least one usable sentiment. Her eyes alit on Freud, watching her intently from a few feet away.

"Stop looking at me like that. I know I can't avoid going online forever. But you'd be a little gun shy too, if the entire universe was laughing at you."

Freud stood and shook, tracked down his Nylabone, which was in the toy box, laid down again, and chewed.

"Okay. I get the point. Maybe it wouldn't bother you, but I'm not you. So it's taken me a little while to get over it. I think that's fair." She pulled the iPad toward her, used her thumbprint to unlock the home screen, and opened the Gmail app.

The first three emails from Tony were exactly as expected, each one more hysterical and urgent than the one before. It was the fourth and last email that caught Rachel's attention.

> Rachel, for the love of GOD, please respond to this email. Hallmark is rolling out a new promotional campaign. They're featuring the artists behind the sentiments. Each month, in every Hallmark store, they'll display a tastefully done poster of the featured artist. The poster will include a picture of the artist, a little bit about him or her, and a quote from them. They want to feature you in the first poster. This would be HUGE. I've got your headshot and I've pulled a snippet from your bio. You need to supply the quote. They want it directly from you. If I don't hear from you TODAY, I swear, I'll make something up and tell them I'm you. I'm desperate here.

Rachel checked her watch. It was late, but not too late for Tony, who seemed to be constantly working. She scooped up her phone and scrolled through her recent calls for the number. Tony answered on the first ring.

"Rachel! Thank God. I was beginning to wonder if you'd jumped off a bridge, or maybe you were off scaling another fire escape or something."

"That was sensitive."

"Ooh. Ouch. Sarcasm. Was that too soon?"

"Anytime in the next century would be too soon," Rachel responded.

"Right. But hey, look on the bright side. With over three million views and five thousand comments, you're practically a household face."

"Three mil...?" Rachel closed her eyes as a wave of nausea swamped her. Millions of people across the globe had seen her make a fool of herself. Thousands of them had commented. It was unfathomable.

"Focus here, Rachel. Here's what's important. You're hotter than the pavement in Phoenix on an August day. Everybody in the world wants access to you for an interview."

"That's nice. I have zero desire to be everybody's favorite punch line."

"Right. So that's why we've got to turn the attention back to your professional career. This Hallmark gig is huge. You need to get something to them by tomorrow."

"Tomorrow?"

"Yeah. Why do you think I've been trying to get hold of you?"

"Okay. What kind of thing do you think they want?"

"Give them something relatable."

"What does that even mean?" Rachel asked.

"It means tell them something personal about why you write what you write. Make it something that tugs at their heartstrings. We know it's predominantly women who are going to see these. Appeal to them."

"Okay. How long should it be?"

"Fifty to seventy-five words."

"Wow. That's not much."

"It's more than most of your sentiments."

"True." Rachel turned over a few ideas in her head. What they wanted was an elevator pitch. Well, she could do that.

"I can hear your gears turning over here. Don't get lost down that road yet. I've got something else for you—something big and unique."

"I'm listening."

"This one just came in tonight. It's a new concept from *Poetry Magazine*. They want you to submit a poem for their next issue."

"A poetry magazine wants a piece from me? Why?" Rachel asked.

"Don't ask me why. All I can tell you is that the magazine is prestigious and has a large subscription base. More ink for you. And they'll pay you for the poem. Not much, but it'll be something. And an important credit."

"When do they need it by?"

"Yesterday."

"Do they know that I'm not a poet?"

"Apparently, they think that what you do is, in a sense, poetry."

"How long should it be? Does it have to rhyme?"

"I'm sending you the parameters now. So, you'll do it?"

"Why not." It had been years since Rachel had written a poem, and then it was only for her girlfriend at the time. Could she do this? Maybe. It would be nice to stretch herself a little, anyway.

"Okay. Get to work. And for God's sake, don't drop off the face of the earth again. See you."

"See you." Rachel put down the phone and rummaged in the end table drawer for a pad of paper and a pen. The only times she ever felt the urge to write poetry were when she was in love.

Her iPad dinged, informing her of the incoming email from Tony with the instructions for the poetry submission. She read through it. *Simple enough.*

Simple enough if she were in love, that is. Rachel tapped the pen against her chin. She tried conjuring up past lovers. Those memories certainly offered inspiration—but of heartbreak, not romance. She would have to get creative and imagine falling in love again. What would that person be like? What kind of emotion would they instill in her?

She closed her eyes and let her mind wander. Her thoughts turned to her afternoon with Julia. Could she use a harmless encounter with an acquaintance as fodder for a love poem? It felt somehow intrusive. Heck, for all she knew, Julia already could have a partner or wife. On the other hand, no one but Rachel need ever know that she used someone she barely knew as inspiration for the poem.

She wrote several versions of an opening stanza and discarded them, crumpling up the pieces of paper and tossing them in the direction of the wastepaper basket.

Freud retrieved the wadded-up papers and brought them back to Rachel, setting each one on the sofa.

"I didn't throw those so that you would bring them back. I just have bad aim and missed the can."

Freud panted and thumped his tail against the floor.

"Go lie down. We don't have time to play. I've got work to do." Rachel tapped the pen against her chin again. "Come on. Imagine you saw Julia across a crowded room and it was love at first sight. And what if it had been the first time for both of you? How would that feel?"

Rachel smiled as she envisioned Julia that first time they'd been introduced outside Shady Acres, and again at the diner earlier today. She bent her head and composed.

Finding Our Way

We love in silence
We hide in fear
Heart and mind warring
Over what is
As opposed to what "should be."

So much energy
So many years
Spent in the service of perfecting the disguise
That we hardly recognize the truth anymore.

But the time is not wasted
As it has brought us to this most wondrous space.

A place where secret longings
Morph into dreams come true
And our passion becomes our present.

A reality to celebrate
A home at last.

© Rachel Wallach

When she was done, Rachel sat back, the paper and pen in her lap forgotten. It was so raw, dredged from deep within. Her soul cried out for something approximating what she'd written on the page. She felt naked and exposed. Could she release this poem to the public?

It isn't like it's about you and Julia. It's fiction—hypothetical.
She grabbed the iPad, composed a new email to the magazine, and

typed the poem, in format, in the body of the text. Her hand shook as the mouse hovered over the "send" button.

Don't think. Act. After another second's hesitation, she hit "send."

CHAPTER SIXTEEN

S orry I'm late." Rachel unwrapped the scarf from around her neck, shimmied out of her overcoat, and sank into the corner booth where Julia sat nursing a cup of coffee. "The train ran a little behind."

"No problem. I'm still on my first cup." Julia noted that today Rachel wore her hair swept back from her face. It made her look slightly more worldly and sophisticated, yet still fresh, vibrant, and beautiful.

"What's wrong? Do I have something on my face? Did my mascara run?" Rachel put her hands to her cheeks.

"No." Julia shook her head. "No," she repeated. Had she been staring? "It's nothing like that. I was just admiring your hair. It looks pretty today."

"Oh."

"Not that it doesn't look great normally," Julia rushed on. *Geez.* "I only meant that you're wearing it in a little different style today, and I like it."

"Okay. Thanks, I guess."

"It was definitely a compliment." If there was a way to dig herself out of this hole she'd created, Julia didn't know what it was.

"What can I get you?" The server, a different one today, nodded in Rachel's direction. Julia breathed a sigh of relief for the interruption.

Rachel heard the sizzle of burgers cooking on the grill and smelled the sautéed onions, but it was too close to dinnertime to indulge. "Just coffee, thanks."

"Better bring her an entire tub full of creamers and Splenda." Julia teased.

Rachel blushed an appealing shade of red. "I can't help it. I only ever drink coffee when I'm out in restaurants, and then only if it doesn't taste like coffee."

"I wasn't judging, just observing." *And your bashfulness is adorable.*

"Well, you're very observant."

"It's my job," Julia said.

"That's an excellent segue." Rachel folded her hands on the table. "You agreed that I'd get to ask the questions today. I hardly know anything about you."

"How can you say that? You know things almost nobody knows about me." Julia tried not to fidget. It was her job to observe others, not to be interrogated by them.

"Like what?"

"Here's your coffee." The server placed a cup and saucer in front of Rachel, along with two bowls of creamers and a newly refilled container of sweeteners.

"Thank you," Rachel said.

"Refill?" the server asked Julia.

"Yes, please." When the server had gone, Julia continued. "You know that my family puts the 'fun' in dysfunctional."

Rachel laughed. "You haven't met my family yet."

"I've met Goldie. She's fabulous."

Rachel's smile lit up her face. "She truly is special, isn't she?" Julia nodded.

"She's the only sane one in the family," Rachel said.

"I know that's not true," Julie disagreed. When Rachel looked puzzled, she added, "There's you."

"Me? You think I'm normal?"

Julia reflected briefly on Rachel running out of the diner, saying she was going to be late and Freud would never forgive her. That jibed with the feedback Julia received from that potential match who cancelled a second date with Rachel because she continually referenced conversations she was having with Freud. Was Rachel balanced and normal? Nothing else that Julia had seen led her to believe that she wasn't, but…

When Julia refocused, Rachel was wrapping her scarf around her neck and getting ready to leave. "Where are you going?"

"Of course you don't think I'm normal. You've seen the video, like the rest of the world. Nobody thinks I'm normal. Why would they after seeing that?"

Rachel stood up. Panic swamped Julia's senses. She half stood, and took Rachel's arm.

"Please, sit back down."

Rachel didn't move.

"Please? You're misinterpreting how I feel."

"Am I? Your silence was deafening."

"If I let go of your arm, will you promise to sit back down?" Julia heard the desperation in her own voice, but she didn't care.

In answer, Rachel pulled out of Julia's grasp and sat, but she did not remove the scarf. "I'm listening."

Julia's pulse continued to hammer in her ears. If she mentioned the Freud thing, she'd be on dangerous ground. How could any talk of Sigmund Freud not be considered to be a question about one's psychological state?

And if you take any longer to say something, she's going to misconstrue your silence again and take off.

"In general, I have a hard time with the word 'normal.' I mean, what is normal? Who decides?" Julia warmed to the topic. "Look, I see and evaluate people every day. I'm a jury consultant. I couldn't give you a definition of normal if I tried. When you ask most folks what normal is, they'll tell you 'average.' Normal equals average."

Rachel's expression was inscrutable.

"Rachel? I might say many things about you, but that you were average would never be one of them." The naked truth of the words settled in Julia's heart. *You're complicated, and sweet, and shy, and...*

"You're a jury consultant?" Rachel asked.

"What?" Of the rejoinders Julia might have expected, a question about her profession wasn't on the list.

"You said you're a jury consultant."

"Yes. You didn't know that?"

"No. We've talked about your family, but never your work life."

"Huh. Well, now you know. I spend my days evaluating which potential jurors would be most likely to convict or to acquit." It was an over-simplification, but, for now, the job description was sufficient.

"Do you work for the good guys or the bad guys?"

Julia smiled. "By 'the good guys' you mean…?"

"The good guys. The prosecutors."

"So that would make all defendants the bad guys? What happened to the presumption of innocence?"

"Do you always answer a question with a question?"

"It depends."

"On?"

"On the question, and who's asking it. For you, I'll answer anything."

"So, do you work for the good guys, or the bad guys?"

Julia gave Rachel points for persistence. "Let's put it this way—it's my job to help clients get the best possible jury and a favorable outcome."

"So, you work for the bad guys." Rachel's disappointment in the answer was unmistakable.

"That's an oversimplification. It doesn't work that way." A chill ran through her. The idea of Rachel losing respect for her… Well, she simply couldn't, that was all. How could Julia make her understand?

"No?"

"No." Julia scooted forward in her chair, her coffee forgotten. "I never take a client I don't believe in. That would be cynical, and I'm not that. I don't represent anyone who is accused of a crime against a minor, or a sex crime, or any defendant who is charged with committing violence against a woman. I just finished assisting the prosecution on a case where three teens were accused of murdering a transgendered youth they'd been bullying in school."

"The Solomon case?" Rachel's eyes grew wide.

Julia nodded. The newspapers and television stations had been saturated with details of the gruesome torture and murder of a sixteen-year-old honors student, Celeste Solomon. The story had been featured on the major networks, CNN, Fox News, and MSNBC. The trial set off a media frenzy.

"All three of those punks got tried as adults and convicted, right?"

"They did," Julia answered. More quietly, she added, "First degree murder, kidnapping, and sexual assault. Each of them got life in prison." She still held close the cherished memory of the lead prosecutor hugging her and thanking her after the verdicts came in. The voir dire and jury selection had been brutal, with both sides contesting every potential juror. Culling out those candidates with unconscious biases or prejudices against transgendered individuals required every bit of Julia's skill.

"I'm sorry if I seemed judgmental before." Rachel broke into Julia's reverie. "That was unfair."

Julia shrugged. "I'm used to it."

"Well, you shouldn't be. I hate it when people do that to me. I never want to be the one who does that to others. I'm sorry."

Julia gauged the sincerity in Rachel's expression and body language. She was an open book. "Apology accepted."

"More coffee, ladies?" the server asked.

Julia looked to Rachel. "I know you have to go see Goldie. You probably don't have time—"

"One more cup," Rachel said. "I've got more questions."

The server topped off their cups and turned her attention to the next table.

"Should that make me nervous?" Julia asked.

"That I have more questions? Only if you have something to hide. Do you? Have something to hide?"

Julia searched Rachel's eyes. There was pain hidden just beneath the surface that bespoke of past lies, hurts, and heartbreaks. Julia swallowed around the lump in her throat. *I have nothing to hide, if you don't count that your grandmother hired me at one point to send dates your way, and I did it without your knowledge or consent.*

When she thought about it now, agreeing to Goldie and Ida's scheme had been folly and the worst kind of mistake. More than anything, she wished now she could undo it. But it was too late for that.

"Julia?"

"Huh?" Julia snapped back to the moment.

"Where were you just now?"

"Me? Why?" Julia knew she was stalling for time. Rachel probably knew it too. But the last thing on earth she wanted to do was to answer any more questions from Rachel. She knew she couldn't—no, wouldn't—lie, and the truth would likely cause so much pain.

"I don't know. You just seemed—sad and far, far away."

"I'm sorry. That case was so emotionally difficult." There was a truth, even if it was designed to deflect.

"I can only imagine. So, back to my questions."

"Okay." Julia steeled herself for what was sure to come.

"How do you know if a person will be a good or a bad juror? How can you tell?"

Julia wanted to weep with relief. These kinds of questions she could handle. "The mistake most lawyers and judges make when they conduct voir dire—when they question prospective jurors to qualify or disqualify them—is asking them a filter question."

"What's a filter question?"

"You know, like, do you think you could be objective in this case? Or do you have an opinion about, dot, dot, dot?"

"That's a mistake because…?"

"Let's take the Solomon case. If the judge or one of the counsels asked a prospective juror, 'Are you prejudiced, or do you have a bias against transgender people? Nine out of ten people would say they didn't, even if they did. Why? Because most people understand that society views bigotry as wrong."

"So they might answer no, even though they might have a serious problem with it?"

"Exactly."

"But don't lawyers and judges always ask questions like that? I've had jury duty before, and I've been asked something similar every time."

Julia nodded. "That's where someone like me comes into play. I advise the attorney to ask the question like this: What are your opinions about, dot, dot, dot?"

"What's the difference?"

"Asking what your opinions are about something rather than *do you have an opinion* acknowledges that you already have a bias; we just want to know what it is. And, on a psychological level, it tells you that it's okay that you have an opinion."

"Wow. That's subtle. And tricky."

"That's me, subtle and tricky," Julia agreed with a smile.

Rachel glanced at her watch. "Oh, gosh! I've got to go." She fumbled for her wallet.

"Don't worry, I'll get it. You bought last time you ran out on me." Julia smiled. "Besides, I'm not due at Ida's for another half hour. I've got plenty of time to take care of this."

"I'm so sorry. I don't mean to keep dashing off. I was so caught up in what you were saying, I lost track of the time."

"No worries. Honestly. Go."

"We have to do this again, and next time I'll make sure I don't have such a tight schedule." Rachel shrugged into her coat. "See you soon?"

"You bet," Julia said. *You bet.*

∽᥉᠊ᡒ

"You're running late today," Goldie said, when Rachel bounded into her apartment. Her face was flushed, she was wearing a nicer outfit than her normal Friday attire, and she'd obviously given greater care than usual to her hair style. Goldie imagined she knew the answer to the next question, but she asked it anyway. "Where were you?"

"I'm sorry I'm late, Grandma. I met Ida's granddaughter, Julia, for a quick cup of coffee when I got off the train." Rachel kissed Goldie on the cheek and sat in her usual spot.

"I thought Ida told me you had coffee with her granddaughter last week."

"We did."

"Two cups of coffee in two weeks. That sounds promising."

"What? Grandma!" The flush morphed into a bright-red blush.

"What? It isn't promising?" Goldie adopted her most innocent expression.

"It isn't what you think." Rachel fussed with a button on her sleeve.

"What do you think I think?"

"I don't know what you think, but it isn't that."

"Whatever you say, bubbeleh."

Goldie couldn't ever remember seeing Rachel this flustered, except maybe for that time when she was four years old and ate an entire raw batch of her mother's chocolate chip cookie dough.

Deborah had covered the dough and thrown it in the refrigerator for a few minutes while she jumped in the shower. The temptation had been too great for little Rachel. When she realized she was going to get caught, Rachel ran to get Goldie and asked her to make a new batch so her mother wouldn't know. Then she got good and sick.

Of course, Goldie had covered for Rachel then. Should she let her off the hook now?

"It's nice spending time with someone my age. She's interesting."

"I'm sure she is," Goldie said.

"Don't say it that way."

"What way is that?"

"Like you're reading something into it."

Goldie suppressed a smile. "I'm just listening to you."

"Did you know Julia's a jury consultant?"

"She's a..." Goldie clamped her mouth shut. She'd almost given herself away and corrected Rachel. Julia was a matchmaker, not a jury consultant.

"She helped win a conviction in a huge case last year. You probably heard about it—the three teenage boys who murdered that poor transgendered classmate. Do you remember the story? It was major news."

Goldie would have to ask Ida about this jury consulting business. She was sure Ida hadn't mentioned that Julia had another job. Julia hadn't said anything about it, either. So, either Ida and Julia had omitted something significant, or...

"Grandma?"

"Mm?"

"Did you hear what I said?"

"I'm sorry?"

"You seem preoccupied," Rachel practically shouted. "Are you okay?"

"I'm fine, darling. Don't worry about me." *Except for my ruptured eardrums from your screaming.* Goldie tried to recall what Rachel had been saying. Something about a case involving transistors and teenagers. Teenagers didn't listen to transistor radios anymore, did they? So why would there be a case about them?

"Grandma? You're scaring me. Are you sure you're okay?"

"I'm fine, darling. Just fine."

"I don't have to go to Mother and Dad's. I could stay here with you a while longer if you're not feeling well."

"No. There's no reason for you to stay here. I'm just a little bit tired. I'll lie down for a while and be good as new. You go on, now."

"If you're sure."

"I'm sure." Goldie shooed Rachel toward the door. "And don't tell your mother you're worried. The last thing I need is my daughter barging in here."

"I won't."

"That's a good girl." Goldie patted Rachel's cheek and kissed her on the forehead.

"I love you, Grandma."

"I love you too, bubbeleh. See you next week."

Goldie closed the door behind Rachel, counted to ten Mississippi, and opened it a crack. The coast appeared to be clear. As quickly as she could, she hustled down to Ida's place.

She raised her hand to knock, then hesitated. What if Julia was there? Should she confront her directly with this jury business? She put an ear to the door. She didn't hear anyone talking, but...

"What are you doing?"

Ida's voice behind her nearly sent Goldie through the roof. She clutched both hands to her heart. "You want me to have a heart attack like you? How many times do I have to tell you not to sneak up on me like that?"

"Me, sneak up on you? You're the one with your ear to the door. You want I should give you a glass to hold up against it so you can hear better? What are you doing spying on me, anyway?"

Goldie straightened up. "I am not spying on you."

"No? Then why the private eye snooping?"

"I wanted to know if you were alone, or if your granddaughter was over."

"Well, you could just knock like normal people."

"If I knocked, then it would be too late if Julia was visiting."

Ida shook her head. "You're giving me a headache, already, with this mishegoss. You're crazy. And why do you care if Julia is here, anyway?"

"Is she?"

"Huh?"

"Is your granddaughter here?"

Ida pushed the walker past Goldie and unlocked the door. "No, Julia already left. Why don't you come inside instead of lurking in the hallway?"

Goldie followed Ida into the apartment and sat down on the sofa. She waited for Ida to get settled.

"Nu? Why are you here?" Ida asked. "And why do you look as though you're mad at the world?"

"I'm not mad at the world," Goldie bristled.

"Very well. Why do you look like you're loaded for bear and I'm wearing the bull's eye?"

Goldie decided to get right to the point. "Is Julia or is she not a shadchan?"

"You know she is. You hired her, remember? Then you fired her, or have you forgotten that too?"

"I remember perfectly well, thank you. So then she lied to Rachel about her profession."

"My Julia does not lie." Ida crossed her arms.

"No? Then explain to me how she didn't lie when she told Rachel that she was a jury consultant."

Ida eyes grew wide.

"Aha! Like I said."

"No. Not like you said, Gold-e-lah." Ida sighed heavily. "Julia told the truth. She is a hoity-toity jury consultant. A very good one too."

"Then she lied to me, and you lied too."

"No, my friend. We weren't lying."

"You can't have it both ways, Ida."

Ida took a deep breath. "The truth is, she's both."

"Come again?"

"Julia has two jobs. By day, she's a successful jury consultant. In her spare time, she's a shadchan."

Goldie absorbed this new information. "Why didn't either of you tell me this?"

"What difference does it make?"

"What difference does it make? You lied to me."

"No, we didn't. I told you Julia was a matchmaker, and so she is."

"Okay, you want to split hairs, do you? You lied by omission."

"Have you been watching 'Law and Order' again? Lied by omission," Ida scoffed. "I did no such thing. I simply left out an unimportant detail."

"Unimportant detail? The fact that Julia has a whole other job? That's not exactly a minor detail." Goldie's nostrils flared. She'd been betrayed—again—and she wasn't going to sit here and take it.

"That's one person's opinion," Ida said, ceding no ground. "Anyway, you're missing the big picture."

"I am, am I?"

"You are. Our girls are sweet on each other. Listen, I may be old, but I still know love when I see it. These girls are falling in love. Ain't it grand?"

Goldie sat back and swallowed her hurt. As much as she hated to admit it, Ida was right. Rachel's face lit up when she spoke of Julia. The joy reached her eyes, which were alive and bright in a way they hadn't been for...well...forever.

"Rachel practically floated into my apartment earlier. I quizzed her about it, but she insisted it was nothing."

Ida nodded. "Julia did the same thing."

"For two smart kids, they're clueless." Goldie chuckled.

"They are. Can't see the forest for the trees," Ida agreed. "It's a shame."

"My Rachel got very defensive when I even suggested there might be something more than friendship going on."

"My Julia was the same way. For someone who makes matches for a living, you'd think she'd figure it out."

"I know what you mean."

"You know, Gold-e-lah, if we leave it to these girls, we might be dead and cold before they ever figure it out."

Goldie pursed her lips. Ida was right. "What do you think we should do?"

"I think we should maybe give them a push."

The gleam in Ida's eyes told Goldie she'd already given the matter a great deal of thought and had a plan. "I'm in."

CHAPTER SEVENTEEN

Julia stood in the middle of her grandmother's acreage, now technically her land. *Her land.* The thought was so foreign. She would always think of this tract as belonging to her grandparents.

When she was a child, her grandmother would tell her stories about how when Grandpa Bernie retired, they were going to build their dream home on this land, overlooking the mountains and the lake. But Grandpa Bernie never made it to retirement, and Ida never had the heart to build that dream place without him.

Often, she would tell Julia, "Without my Bernie, it might be a house, but it would never be a home. Julia? When you find that special someone, build yourselves that dream home right away. Don't wait for some day far in the future, because someday might never come."

Julia smiled wistfully. Wise words. Words to live by, except that Julia long ago had given up hope of finding that one special girl. A wave of sadness washed over her. When she was young and discovering her sexuality, she never could have envisioned herself growing old alone.

It doesn't pay to dwell on it. Go for a run; you'll feel better. It was a gorgeous late-fall Saturday, and there was a beautiful park about a mile up the road. Julia calculated that if she ran to the park, took a lap around it, and ran back, she could get in a good three-mile workout.

She put on a knit cap to keep her ears warm, slid her shades into place, spent a few minutes stretching, and set off at a good pace. Normally, she would've put in her ear buds and cranked some tunes, but she was afraid she wouldn't hear a car coming and didn't want to chance it.

In a little over fifteen minutes, Julia arrived at the entrance to the park and checked her fitness tracker. She'd made good time. The park was busy with other joggers, walkers, dogs and their owners, and the occasional cyclist. She spent a minute jogging in place, scoping out her best route through the park.

The path to the left wove past a pond. Benches dotted the route, and, in the distance, Julia could see a woman sitting on one of them, having an animated discussion with her dog. The dog, for his part, was sitting in front of his owner, paying rapt attention, his head tilted to the side, as if listening and weighing the woman's words. It was an adorable tableau.

Julia started off in that direction. Several times she had to dodge parents with strollers, and once she sidestepped an errant soccer ball. As she did, she barely looked up in time to see the dog in front of the bench. Quickly, she hopped to her right.

"Whoa, big guy. I'm sorry. I nearly ran into you." The dog woofed and wagged his tail. Julia stopped running and bent down to pet him. "You're a handsome one. What's your name?"

"That's Freud. And he apologizes for impeding your forward progress."

Julia's head snapped up and, for the first time, she took a good look at the woman on the bench. It couldn't be... "Rachel?"

"Please don't tell me you saw me on YouTube."

Julia removed her sunglasses and cap. "It's me, Julia."

"Oh, my God, Julia. Hi! What are you doing here?"

Julia's eyes tracked from Rachel to the dog, who continued to nuzzle her hand. "This is your dog? His name is Freud?" Suddenly, a lot of things made more sense.

"He's not actually my dog, but he is." Rachel shook her head. "It's complicated."

"Are you complicated?" Julia asked Freud. In response, he gave her his paw. "He's charming."

"He's a chick magnet."

Julia's legs went weak and she knelt on the sidewalk. Somehow, she doubted the dog was the main attraction. She tried to gauge Rachel's expression, but the sun was in her eyes. "I imagine he is."

"The only problem is, the girls look at the dog, and never bother to see who's attached to the leash."

Their loss. Julia pointed to the empty space next to Rachel. "Mind if I sit for a minute?"

"I'd love that. But aren't we interrupting your run?"

"Not at all. Seeing you two just made my day." And Julia meant it. She laid her cap on the bench and sat on it, then hooked her sunglasses onto her hoodie. Freud insinuated himself between her knees and laid his chin on her lap.

"Freud!" Rachel reprimanded.

"No. He's fine. I love dogs." Julia smiled warmly at Freud and scratched behind his ears. "Tell me the complicated story of Freud, not that simply being Freud wouldn't be complicated enough."

Rachel laughed. "I didn't come up with the name, although I have to say it suits him. Honestly, I'm terrified of dogs. I had a bad experience when I was little, and ever since, they've freaked me out."

Freud was such a gentle boy, with a sweet, attentive demeanor, Julia had a hard time imagining how anyone could be afraid of him. Still, trauma, particularly childhood trauma, could leave deep, difficult-to-heal scars. "He sure seems to love you."

"I don't know about that. I think it's more that he tolerates me."

"No, Rachel. I've been around enough dogs to know this big guy adores you."

Rachel shrugged off the comment. "I'm all he has in the world now, so both of us will have to make it work," Rachel said. She blinked away the tears that had formed in the corners of her eyes.

"What happened?" Julia asked softly.

"My next-door neighbor, Mr. Crawford, had a pretty serious stroke a couple of months ago. After a short stint in the hospital, they sent him to a skilled nursing facility."

"That's awful."

"I know. He doesn't have anyone. Freud was his best friend, companion, and reason for living. As the paramedics were wheeling him away, Mr. Crawford begged me to take care of Freud. How in the world could I say no?" Rachel shook her head. "It's been a learning curve, I can tell you that."

"I bet. So, when Mr. Crawford recovers, he and Freud will be reunited again?" Surely this story would soon have a happy ending?

"I wish. I've been visiting Mr. Crawford once a week since this happened. I bring him homemade cookies, I read him his mail, which the mail person has been nice enough to deliver to my house, and I am his power of attorney, so I have my accountant handle his finances."

"I bet he's so grateful, Rachel. What an extraordinarily kind thing to do."

"It's the human thing to do. How could I do otherwise?"

"I'm guessing most people in your shoes wouldn't go to the trouble."

Rachel looked horrified. "You think so?"

"Sadly, I do. Everyone is so busy these days—caught up in their own little worlds. I doubt they would make the time or space in their lives to do what you're doing."

"Well then, I guess I'm not most people."

"I'm glad."

"I show Mr. Crawford pictures of Freud, and that seems to brighten him up, but the doctors say he'll never recover enough to come home. His speech is incomprehensible, he can't walk without assistance, and he can't take care of his daily needs. I promised I would keep Freud and give him the best home I can."

Julia lifted Freud's head and scratched under his chin. "You're a lucky man."

"I don't know about that. I have no idea what he wants from me."

"Love. Dogs give us unconditional love. That's what they want in return. That and to be fed and walked. Looks like you've got it covered."

Rachel patted Freud on the head. "I wish I believed that. I'm not the right person to take care of a dog. He knows how unnatural it is for me. He knows I'm afraid."

Freud moved over in front of Rachel, sat, and licked her. Then he burrowed his nose so that her hand rested on top of his head.

Julia was thoroughly charmed. "He'll train you. Don't worry."

"I simply can't imagine what Mr. Crawford was thinking. He knew I was petrified of his dog."

"He was thinking that he knew your capacity for love and kindness. I agree with him. He knew exactly what he was doing. Freud couldn't be in a better place."

"You think so?"

Julia wanted to weep for Rachel's uncertainty and vulnerability. "I know so." Unable to stand it any longer, she reached out and squeezed Rachel's free hand. Warmth spread through her and she quickly stood up. Whatever she felt, this couldn't happen. She'd spied on Rachel and worse, she reminded herself. It was unconscionable. "I've got to get going."

"Wait! Will I see you next Friday?"

"I don't know." Julia bent down and cradled Freud's face in her hands. She whispered in his ear, "Take good care of Rachel, buddy. You need each other." She kissed the dog on the top of the head, waved, and sprinted away.

Rachel watched Julia disappear down the path. Freud tracked her progress, as well. Rachel imagined the expression on her face mirrored that of the dog. She searched for the right word to identify what she was feeling. Forlorn... That was it. She missed Julia even before she was out of sight.

Belatedly, she realized that Julia hadn't answered her question about what she was doing in this area. Did she live nearby? Rachel didn't think so, but how much did she know about her new friend? *Not nearly enough.*

Why had Julia bolted so quickly? And why did she brush Rachel off when she asked if she would see her again? Was it something she said? Was it Freud? No, Julia had seemed genuinely fond of the dog. So what could it be?

"If you keep wrinkling your brow, your face will freeze that way." Rachel heard her mother's admonition in her head, drummed into her over the years. She rubbed the spot above the bridge of her nose. Whatever had spooked Julia, Rachel wasn't going to figure it out by sitting here speculating.

"Come on, Freud. We need to get home. I've got work to do." She rose and the dog stood in expectation. "Let's go."

Obediently, Freud trotted beside her. Maybe Julia was right—she could do this dog-parent thing. But could she love Freud? Did she already? She glanced down at him. He was watching her, his manner attentive, as if the only thing in the world he wanted was to please her. Of course she could love him, she just needed to open her heart and let love in and give it in return. They both deserved that. Everyone did.

⋘⋙

"I tell you, Gold-e-lah, I'm worried." Ida reached for the bowl on her end table and cracked open another pistachio nut with her teeth, and Goldie winced.

"If you keep doing that, you'll need a new bridge."

"Bah." Ida waved her off. "I only do this when I'm stressed."

Judging by the number of times Goldie had witnessed this behavior, Ida was stressed often. "She'll come around, you'll see."

"It's not like Julia to miss two weeks in a row. She's a responsible girl."

"What does she say about it?"

"When I can get her to answer the phone, which isn't often, she just says she's busy on some new case. Then she apologizes and hangs up before I can ask when I'll see her again." Ida scooped up another handful of nuts and got to work on them.

Unable to stand it anymore, Goldie snatched the bowl away.

"Hey!"

"They'll give you a tummy ache."

"What are you, my mother?"

Goldie ignored Ida's grouchiness. "No. Your mother wouldn't have let you have the nuts in the first place."

"Eh. You make a valid point." Ida made a grab for the bowl, but Goldie moved it out of her reach. "Anyway, back to my Julia. This is so unlike her. I know there's something wrong. I can tell. She's being evasive."

"Have you asked her point blank?"

"What do I look like, an amateur Jewish grandmother? Of course I asked her what's bothering her. Several times."

"What does she say?"

"She says it's just the job getting to her, and that this too shall pass."

"But you don't believe her."

"Not for a second." Ida made one more lunge for the nuts, nearly unbalancing herself and falling off the sofa.

"Stop it. They're a crutch."

"And you're a pain in the tush."

"Sticks and stones," Goldie said. "You'll thank me later."

"As God is my witness, Goldie Horowitz, you're a cruel woman."

"God forgives me for keeping you healthy."

"What should we do?" Ida wrung her hands.

"What can we do?" Goldie rejoined. "Julia is a big girl. If she's says she's fine, then she is."

"Nonsense." Ida slapped her hand on her walker for emphasis. "You'd be singing a different tune if this was your Rachel we were talking about."

Goldie had to agree with that. "What do you want from me?"

"I was thinking maybe we could take that car of yours and pay her a visit. If Mohammed won't come to the mountain, then the mountain will go to Mohammed."

"You've lost your mind." Goldie searched for signs that Ida was kidding. She found none.

"Why not?"

"You can't be serious. Didn't you say Julia lived upstate? As in two hours from here?"

"A little more than that," Ida said, "but why quibble?"

"Absolutely not." Goldie folded her arms.

"Don't be such a fuddy-duddy."

"I'm not being a fuddy-duddy. I'm being realistic. First of all, I can't drive that far, and you can't drive, period. Second, we'd get caught before you could say, 'We're innocent.' And third… I don't know, but I'll think of a third."

"You're a chicken liver, Gold-e-lah."

"Name calling will get you nowhere."

"All this worrying is bad for my heart, you know this."

Goldie recognized the change in tactics. "Playing to my sympathies doesn't change a thing. We can't take a road trip, and that's final."

Ida sighed heavily. "Well, we simply must do something."

Goldie could see that Ida truly was concerned for Julia's welfare. In all fairness, she was a little worried too. "Rachel will be here in a little while. I could ask her when the last time was she saw Julia."

Ida brightened. "I could come over and we could grill her."

"No." Goldie could just imagine Rachel's reaction to that. "It needs to be subtle."

"I can be subtle," Ida bristled.

As a freight train. "Let me have a go at it. If that doesn't work, we can get more creative."

Ida checked the time. "What time did you say she'd be here?"

"Soon."

"And you'll come see me straightaway and tell me what she said?"

Goldie crossed her heart.

"I still think taking a drive and confronting Julia is the way to go."

"Ida..." Goldie drew her friend's name out.

"Oh, all right, already. Do it your way. But if that doesn't work..."

Goldie took her leave, the threat still hanging in the air between them.

Rachel peeked around the corner of the hallway where Ida lived. There was no sign of either Ida or Julia. She knew she could knock on the door, but what would she say?

"Hi, there. Julia ran away after we had a chance meeting in a park and I'm wondering if I said or did something to scare her away?"

No. That would never work. Dejectedly, Rachel continued on to Goldie's apartment. She knocked three times.

"Come!"

"It's me, Grandma." Rachel stepped inside, walked over to Goldie, and gave her a kiss on the cheek.

"What's the matter, bubbeleh? You're not your usual, perky self."

"Hmm?" Rachel chided herself. Of course her grandmother would know something was amiss.

"You're a million miles away. What's wrong?"

Wrong? Nothing was wrong, except that Julia had disappeared without a trace. "Have you seen Ida's granddaughter, Julia?"

"Why? When was the last time you saw her?" Goldie crossed her left ankle over her right, then reversed and crossed the right over the left. Her gaze darted around the room, alighting on everything except Rachel.

Curious. If Rachel didn't know any better, she might've thought Goldie was hiding something. But what would she have to hide where Julia was concerned?

Out loud, Rachel said, "A couple of weeks ago. We ran into each other in a park. I figured maybe she was coming to see Ida on weekends, or another day of the week other than Friday, and that's why I haven't seen her."

"I don't keep track of her comings and goings," Goldie said, "but I don't think she's been to see Ida in a while."

What if Julia was hurt, or sick? Rachel's heart rate sped up. "Is there something you're not telling me? Did something happen to Julia? Did Ida tell you something about her? Has she heard from her?"

"Why would you ask me those things? It's not like we sit around talking about you and Julia."

"Geez. No need to get defensive about it," Rachel mumbled under her breath. It wasn't like Goldie to be short with her. "I'm sorry. I'm worried."

"I just left Ida a little while ago. Julia wasn't there. I'm sure they've been talking on the phone, though. I don't know what else I can tell you, darling." Goldie folded her hands in her lap.

Rachel shook her head. Most likely she was misinterpreting things. She'd been on edge ever since Julia zoomed off. Rachel had gone over the details of their conversation so many times she could recite the interchanges verbatim. And still, she had no idea what she'd done to upset her friend. If she even *had* upset her.

Several times, she'd picked up the phone to call Julia. Each time, she'd balked at the last second. Julia knew where to find her. Rachel was certain that she'd made it clear that she enjoyed their get-togethers and was looking forward to another visit. Maybe the hard truth was that Julia simply didn't want a friendship with her. Her shoulders slumped.

"Bubbeleh?"

"Yes."

"I hate to see you so sad."

Rachel simply nodded. What else was there to say?

⤜⤝

"Nu? So? What did Rachel say? How did it go? Tell me everything."

"Slow down, Ida." Goldie came the rest of the way into her old friend's apartment and sat down heavily on the sofa.

Ida was practically vibrating, standing across from her. "Oy. I can't stand the suspense. Tell me, already."

"Something's definitely happened. Rachel hasn't seen Julia in some time, and she looks exactly the way she did when she got passed over for the school play in the sixth grade. She insisted her life was over then, and she's even more of a sad sack now."

"Then it's worse than I thought," Ida said, tapping her chin. "Gold-e-lah, we have to do something."

"You're right."

"My original plan won't work if they're not seeing each other."

Goldie thought for a minute. "What if we forced the issue?"

"How?"

Goldie turned the idea over in her head. If she said it out loud, there'd be no going back. "What if...?"

"What if?" Ida leaned forward in anticipation.

"What if I called Julia and told her I wanted to rehire her to find Rachel a match?"

Ida recoiled. "Why would you want to do such a thing? We can see that our two girls are in love. Why push Rachel into the arms of another?"

"That's just the thing," Goldie said. "Julia would realize she was in love with Rachel and she couldn't go through with making a match for her. She would have to admit the truth to herself."

"Hmm. That's tricky." Ida drummed her fingers on her walker in thought. "Very, very tricky. What if Julia agrees to make the match?"

200

"You think she would?"

Ida pursed her lips. "I don't know…"

"I can't envision it," Goldie said. She hoped she sounded more certain than she felt.

"Well, we have to try something," Ida reasoned. "I suppose we could see how she reacts. And that would only require a phone call, not a drive."

"Exactly," Goldie agreed.

"Let's do it."

CHAPTER EIGHTEEN

Julia stared out her office window. She didn't need to work late. In fact, she'd turned in her research for the Lawson case hours ago. It was Friday evening, and the rest of her team was out celebrating a major victory in a long-running case that returned a huge civil verdict for their client.

She spun her chair around and came face-to-face with Rachel—more precisely one of the glossy photos of Rachel from the *People* magazine article, which lay open on the otherwise empty desk. Therein lay the problem. Julia couldn't concentrate on anything but Rachel, and it was making her positively miserable.

Right now, Rachel probably was leaving Goldie's to drive to her parents' house for Sabbath dinner with the family. Julia wanted to beg her not to go.

Everything Rachel told her about them made it plain that they didn't understand or value Rachel enough. Why they couldn't recognize that she was sensitive, accomplished, talented, and successful, Julia had no idea. If she were there, she'd make sure they knew how lucky they were to have a relative like Rachel.

Julia turned the page and stared at the rest of the photo spread. Rachel's smiling face gazed back at her, warm, open, and welcoming. If she closed her eyes, Julia could remember that feeling as she took hold of Rachel's hand in the park. Warmth spread through her and she squirmed in her seat.

Just as quickly, and as had been the case ever since their encounter in the park, Julia's imagination conjured a snapshot of how Rachel's smile would falter and morph into a pained expression when she learned of Julia's betrayal. It was that one-two punch that made her run from Rachel that day, and why she was avoiding her still.

Pain blossomed in the middle of Julia's chest. She snapped up the bottle of Tums she kept in her bottom drawer. A fortune from a Chinese fortune cookie, stuck to the bottom of the bottle, floated to the carpet, and she bent over and picked it up.

"Honesty makes the heart grow fonder."

Julia banged her head on the desk. Even a Chinese fortune cookie mocked her. She downed a handful of multi-colored Tums.

The cell phone rang, intruding on her moment of self-pity. According to the display, it was Goldie. The Tums lodged in Julia's throat, and she struggled to swallow them. This couldn't be good. She swiped to accept the call.

"This is Julia."

"Hello, darling. This is Goldie, your grandmother's friend."

"Hi, Goldie." Julia cleared her throat. "What a surprise. Is Grandma Ida okay?"

"Oh, yes. She's fine, just fine."

"Thank goodness." Another terrifying possibility struck Julia. "Is it Rachel?"

"As a matter of fact…"

Oh, my God. Something's happened to Rachel, and I'll never get to tell her how I feel about her. Julia's hand trembled so badly she bobbled the phone. When she put it back to her ear, Goldie still was talking.

"I'm sorry. Can you repeat that? I didn't catch what you said."

"That's usually my problem," Goldie quipped. "I was saying that Rachel has been so depressed lately, and I feel like it's at least partially my fault."

No, it's probably my fault. "How so?"

"She's lonely, and I let my squabble with your grandmother get in the way of doing the right thing for her."

"I'm not following you." *Please, don't let this be about finding dates for Rachel. Please don't let this be about finding dates for Rachel. Please don't…*

"I shouldn't have fired you."

There it was. "I don't know, Goldie. From what I've seen, Rachel is perfectly capable of finding her own dates. She doesn't need my help." *Please accept this answer and let it go. Please accept this answer and let it go. Please accept...*

"I want to rehire you."

In the silence that ensued, Julia considered and discarded dozens of excuses why she couldn't play matchmaker for Rachel. Goldie wouldn't have bought any of them, she knew.

"Julia? Are you still there? This damned phone..."

"I'm here."

"Did you hear what I said? I want to rehire you. Rachel needs companionship. She needs to find that certain someone."

I'm that certain someone, Julia wanted to scream.

"She's too special to spend her time alone, writing love notes for other people."

You're not wrong about that. Julia paused to compose herself. "My calendar is full. I wish I could help you, but—"

"Poppycock."

"I'm sorry?"

"Nonsense. Surely you can make the time to help Rachel. I know you can see what a lovely girl she is. She's miserable. We have to do something."

"Like I said—"

"I'm not taking no for an answer, so you can stop right now. I'll give Ida a check for you, or you can stop by and pick it up yourself. When will you be here next?"

"I don't have any plans in the near—"

"You know your grandmother's frail, yes? That heart of hers could give out any second. She tells me you haven't been to see her in weeks. That's unacceptable. You need to take advantage of the time you have with her."

Julia wanted to object. "I—"

"Next Friday. I'll tell her to expect you. 'Bye, now."

Goldie disconnected the call. Julia held the phone out and stared at it. What had just happened? *You got played, that's what happened.*

Julia pulled up her recent calls. She would call Goldie back and tell her, firmly, that she couldn't do it. Her finger hovered over Goldie's number. This was the right thing to do—the moral thing to do.

Certainly, she couldn't go through with getting Rachel dates—that would only compound an already indefensible mistake. Besides, how could she stand by and watch other women woo Rachel when she was in love with her?

The reality crept out from its hiding place deep in Julia's subconscious. She was in love with Rachel. Julia's hand fell away from the phone and she slumped back into the chair. She was in love with Rachel, and there was no future in that. Heck, there wasn't even a present in it. How could there be?

What she'd done in procuring prospects for Rachel was, at best, underhanded and dishonest. It would take only one slip-up from Goldie or Ida and Rachel would learn the ugly truth and kick her to the curb.

"As if you'd ever consider asking Rachel out before disclosing the facts yourself. Let's just imagine how that would go. 'So, Rachel, here's the thing... I'm in love with you and I want to spend the rest of my life making you happy. There's just one catch—your grandmother has been paying me to set you up with dates. That's not a problem for you, is it?'" Julia rolled her eyes.

"Julia? Are you okay?"

Julia's hand clutched her chest as she spotted her executive assistant standing in the doorway. "What are you still doing here?"

"I came back for my phone. I forgot I left it charging in my drawer. Who were you talking to?"

"No one. What did you hear?"

"Nothing. Just you mumbling." The assistant stood staring a second longer, openly assessing her. "You know that talking to yourself is the first sign of mental instability, right?"

"Good to know."

"Okay, then. I'm out of here. Goodnight."

"Have a good weekend," Julia called after her.

How embarrassing was that? Julia shook her head. She should go home. The open magazine caught her attention again. It should have been a clue to her how she felt about Rachel when she'd gone out of her way to get not just the online subscription of *People*, but also a physical copy of the magazine. She caressed Rachel's two-dimensional cheek and ran her fingers over Rachel's lips. Then she carefully closed the magazine and slid it into her briefcase.

It was no good to dream like this. A relationship between them was out of the question. Rachel deserved so much better than what Julia had given her, even as a friend.

Goldie was right about one thing—Rachel was too extraordinary to spend her life alone. Julia knew what it felt like to be that lonely; that was not the life Rachel should have.

What should she do? Goldie expected her to show up at Shady Acres next Friday and resume her matchmaking duties.

It wasn't as if she hadn't already crossed the moral Rubicon. If Julia couldn't be the great love of Rachel's life, maybe she could facilitate the perfect match. Maybe, just maybe, she could play a small part in securing Rachel's happiness. And she shouldn't wait until next Friday to start. She should find her the match now, before she changed her mind.

The thought made Julia's stomach roil. She reached back into the bottom drawer for the bottle of Tums, although she was pretty sure there weren't enough antacids in the world to alleviate this situation.

Rachel clutched her stomach. The way she felt right now reminded her of the trip to Disney World when her brother had insisted they ride Space Mountain for the fourth time. Why she agreed to this date was beyond her, except that sitting around, pining for a phone call from Julia that obviously was never going to come, was both demoralizing and depressing.

"You said yes, so suck it up and make the best of it." Rachel squared her shoulders and pulled open the door to the Château des Reines. At least her date had excellent taste in restaurants.

"May I help you, Mademoiselle?" The maitre d' asked.

"I'm meeting someone. The reservation is under Heather."

The maitre d' perused the reservation list. "Ah, yes. I believe your date has already been seated." He snapped his fingers and a young man in a tuxedo stepped forward. "Please show Mademoiselle to table ten."

"Right this way."

Rachel followed along to a banquette in a quiet corner of the restaurant. When they approached, a tall, elegantly attired, attractive brunette stood to greet her.

"You must be Rachel. I'm Heather. What a pleasure to meet you in person."

Her handshake was warm and firm, and her smile reached her eyes, like Julia's did. Except that Heather wasn't Julia.

"Nice to meet you too."

"Please, have a seat. Is that side okay for you? Or are you someone who can't stand having her back to the door?"

Rachel shook her head. "This is fine. It's not my night to worry about getting whacked by the mob."

Heather laughed, a full, rich sound that was not unpleasant, and the tension in Rachel's stomach eased ever so slightly.

"Good thing. And, in any case, I promise to give you a heads-up if it looks like you're in danger."

"I feel safer already." Rachel unfolded her napkin and placed it in her lap. "Were you here long before I got here? Do you know what you want?"

Heather shook her head. "I only arrived a minute or five before you, and that was only because I'm habitually early. You, on the other hand, were exactly on time."

"Which is a minor miracle, I assure you. I have the best of intentions, but something always seems to crop up at the last minute and put me behind schedule."

The two women opened their menus and spent several minutes making their selections before the server came and took their orders.

"You write romantic greeting cards for a living, correct?"

"Yes."

"That sounds fascinating, especially to an attorney like me whose days are filled with facts, research, and the law. I do have a question, though, while I'm thinking about it."

"Sure." Rachel braced herself for the usual inquisition about where she got her ideas or inspirations.

"How could a suitor ever possibly find the right romantic sentiments card to give *you*? I mean, it would have to be one that you hadn't written, because, well, that would be embarrassing.

And if the sentiment was composed by someone else, that would be insulting. I just don't see a way to win there."

Rachel burst out laughing, and it felt wonderful.

"What? I'm serious."

"I guess it's never come up, so I've never had to deal with it."

"No one has ever showered you with cards and flowers? As beautiful and charming as you are, I can't believe that."

"Smooth. Very smooth."

The conversation flowed easily over salad, chateaubriand for two, mousse au chocolat, and demitasse. Remarkably, not a thing had gone wrong. *Yet*, Rachel reminded herself. Nothing had gone wrong, yet.

Heather, as it turned out, was intelligent, pretty, good company, and easy to talk to. The only problem was, she wasn't Julia. Still, compared to the dates Rachel had been on lately, Heather was like manna from heaven.

"I had a great time tonight," Heather said as she walked Rachel to her car.

"Me too. I'm glad you asked me."

"I'm glad you said yes."

Rachel stopped walking. "This is it. This is my car."

Heather's face was lit by the glow of a street lamp. "I can't believe someone as wonderful is you isn't already taken. Why is that?"

Rachel shrugged. "Just never worked out for me." An image flashed through her mind of Julia's hand resting on hers on the park bench, her eyes so bright and compassionate. And then Julia's retreating form as she ran away. Rachel willed the hurt and disappointment away.

"Well, it's the rest of the world's loss," Heather said. She leaned in and Rachel realized with a shock that she was about to be kissed.

It was short, and soft enough not to be too forward, but firm enough to suggest that Heather wanted more. Guilt flooded Rachel, and she battled through it. Here was a perfectly lovely woman, standing right in front of her. Yes, she'd been thinking about Julia, but it wasn't as if she was cheating on her. After all, Rachel was single and eligible, and Julia hadn't so much as sent her a text message in the past two weeks.

"Julia was so right about what a catch you are."

Rachel's heart banged against her ribs. "What did you say?"

"I said, Julia was right about you. I'm so glad she suggested I look you up."

"J-Julia? Spielman?"

"Yep. One and the same. We work together on lots of cases."

"Julia Spielman gave you my name? Why didn't you mention that in the first place?"

"I guess I should have. I'm sorry. She thinks highly of you. I can see why. I'll be sure to send her a thank you note."

Rachel leaned heavily against her car.

"Are you all right?"

"Yes. Just a little tired, I guess." Rachel forced the words to come.

"Of course. It's late. I'm sorry." Heather took her hand. "Can I see you again? I'd really like to. Maybe next Saturday night?"

"I don't know. I need to check my schedule."

"If you didn't have a nice time…"

"No," Rachel said quickly. "No. It isn't that. I had a marvelous time." And she had, hadn't she? Clearly Julia had no interest in her. If she had, she wouldn't have sent someone else to ask her for a date. Rachel rubbed the sore spot in her chest.

"If the kiss was too forward…"

"No. You were fine. Yes." Rachel made a snap decision. "Yes. Next Saturday will be fine. I'll call you."

"I'll look forward to it. Good night, Rachel. Thanks for a perfect evening."

"Good night, Heather." Rachel unlocked her car door, folded herself into the driver's seat, locked herself in, waited until Heather was a safe distance away, and cried.

Rachel buried her face in a mascara-stained pillow. She was pajama-clad and lying face-down on the couch, a Kleenex clutched in her hand, a blanket thrown over her.

Freud trotted over and laid his favorite stuffed groundhog under Rachel's chin, then sat at attention.

"I know what you're going to say." Rachel dabbed at her eyes. "I did this to myself. I made unfounded assumptions that Julia enjoyed our time together as much as I did and that we were developing a beautiful friendship that might turn into something more."

Freud blinked.

"Go ahead, say 'I told you so.' I deserve it, I know. I let my imagination overtake my logical brain. What could I have been thinking? I wasn't thinking. So what else is new?"

Freud leaned forward and licked her cheek, then returned to his attentive position.

"Yes, everyone makes mistakes. But you'd think with the number and breadth of the ones I've made, I'd have learned by now that happily ever after just isn't in the cards for me."

Rachel choked on a sob. Freud scooted forward to nuzzle her cheek as the sob morphed, yet again, into a shower of tears. "I don't want to spend the rest of my life alone." She buried her head in his fur. "Except for you, I mean." Rachel kissed Freud's nose. "I'm not trying to say you're nothing and that you don't count, so please don't take it that way."

She fumbled around for the Kleenex box, which somehow had wound up behind her butt, and yanked out a handful of tissues.

She blew her nose noisily, belatedly realizing that her nose was level with Freud's ear.

"I'm sorry. That was rude."

If Freud minded, it wasn't apparent, since he rested his chin on the sofa inches from Rachel's face, his big eyes filled with compassion and worry.

"For the record, I wasn't referring to pet companions. I was talking about the human species, in particular lesbian women."

Freud whined.

"You're right. That was redundant. If they're lesbian, by definition they're women. Good thing I don't write for a living. Oh, wait. I do."

Rachel sat up, sniffled, dried her eyes, and drew in a ragged breath. "Now that we got that cleared up... I'm just going to have to face it, Freud. Julia isn't who I thought she was. She pawned me off on a colleague like I was a commodity for sale."

She stumbled on the last word, and fresh tears rolled down her cheeks. "Who does that?"

Freud cried with her.

"Are you crying in agreement? Or do you have to go potty?"

Freud slid down until he was prone, his head resting on his paws.

"I guess that answers that question." Rachel remembered Julia telling her that Freud loved her and that he wanted only unconditional love in return. Julia was so at ease with Freud, and he genuinely seemed taken with her. Rachel had read somewhere that dogs were great judges of people.

"She had us both fooled, Freud." Rachel threw off the blanket and struggled to her feet. Freud followed behind as she rummaged in the linen closet for a washcloth. He continued to trail her into the kitchen, where she filled the cloth with ice cubes.

Together, they returned to the living room. Rachel lowered herself to the floor, leaned her back against the sofa, pulled the dog's head into her lap, and stroked his fur with one hand as she applied the compress to her swollen eyes.

Julia lifted Doris Kearns Goodwin's *Team of Rivals* off her chest, inserted a bookmark, and placed the book on the coffee table. She rubbed the sleep from her eyes and squinted to see the time on her iPad. 1:37 a.m. She stretched and sat up on the sofa. The last time she remembered checking, it was a little after ten o'clock.

She swiped the screen to wake the iPad and used her thumbprint to unlock it. A text notification popped up on the screen and disappeared just as quickly. She clicked on the messages app.

I can't thank you enough for this one, my friend. Rachel did not disappoint. She's hot, and cute, and sexy, funny, and kind, all rolled up into one intelligent human being. Oh, and she's a great kisser. I owe you. Drinks on me next time we do a case together. XOXO, H.

Julia gripped the edge of the coffee table for support as the room spun. She closed her eyes and slid off the sofa onto her knees. Her teeth chattered and her hands shook. She wrapped her arms around herself to keep her hands still and rocked back and forth. Nothing in her life had ever hurt like this.

This is the best thing for Rachel. This is the best thing for Rachel. If Julia could hold onto this knowledge, maybe she could survive this.

CHAPTER NINETEEN

T he phone rang, and Julia ignored it. Daylight streamed in through the bedroom window. In her distress, she'd neglected to pull down the shade. She rolled over and pulled the covers over her head. For the first time in years, she'd called in sick, which she reasoned, was the truth. She was sick to her stomach. Guilt intruded about missing a Monday morning client meeting, but Julia knew she wouldn't have been of any use today, anyway. She would reschedule the meeting for tomorrow. Maybe tomorrow she'd feel halfway human again.

The phone rang again. Again, Julia let it go to voicemail. She didn't want to talk to anyone, didn't want to see anyone, didn't want to deal with anyone. If the whole world stopped spinning right now, it would be fine with her.

When the phone rang a third time, Julia threw the covers off, snapped it up, and checked caller ID. It was Grandma Ida, all three times. She didn't have the strength to deal with her grandmother now. The display indicated a third voicemail.

"Your grandmother is frail, you know," Goldie had said. What if something had happened?

Julia played the first voicemail. "Julia? This is your grandmother. I'm worried sick about you. I haven't seen you in weeks, and your office tells me you called in sick today. Please call me. Okay? 'Bye."

Grandma Ida never called her at the office. Julia listened to the second message. "Julia? I'm sorry to bother you. Obviously, for whatever reason, you don't want to talk to me. But I thought you'd like to know that I have to go to the doctor later this afternoon. These over-eager nurses are worried about my blood pressure.

Some mumbo-jumbo about whether or not the stent is working properly. I'm sure it's nothing, but they suggested I have a family member go with me. Now that I've kicked that no-account son and daughter-in-law of mine out on their ears, I'm afraid you're all I've got. But, I'm sure you're busy doing important things. Not to worry. I'll take a cab."

Julia's heart lurched. How could she be so self-absorbed? She listened to the voicemail a second time. Ida hadn't said what time the appointment was. Julia pushed the play button for the third message.

"I can't believe I forgot to say I love you. I love you, my favorite granddaughter. There, now I feel better."

Julia checked the time on her phone. Eleven o'clock. If the appointment was at two or after, she could be there in time. She called Ida back.

"Hello?"

"Grandma? It's Julia."

"Oh, Julia. I'm so glad you called me back. I've been worried about you. That nice woman at your office said you were out sick today. Do you have that nasty flu that's going around?"

"No, I don't have the flu. Are you okay, Grandma? What's going on with your heart?"

"Are you sure you don't have the flu? You sound stuffy."

Julia closed her eyes. *I sound stuffy because I've been crying for two days.*

"Julia? Are you still there? Hello?"

"I'm here. What time is your doctor's appointment?"

"Two forty-five. But as I said, I can take a cab. Especially if you're sick. I don't want you to make the trip if you're not well. I'll be fine."

"How long does it take to get from your place to the doctor's office?"

"I don't know, dear. Probably half an hour. Everything around here takes about half an hour."

"Okay. I'll be there no later than two o'clock to take you."

"But you're not well."

"I'm fine. I have to hang up now so I can get ready. I'll see you soon. I love you, Grandma."

"I love you too, sweetheart."

∽⒢⒭∾

"You look horrible. Come here and let me feel your forehead. Did you take your temperature?"

The last thing Julia wanted was Ida fussing over her. She'd done her best with makeup, but no amount of makeup in the world could completely eradicate the black circles and puffiness under her eyes.

"I don't have a temperature, Grandma. Let's get you ready. Do you have an address for the doctor's office?"

"It's right here, dear, in my appointment book."

Julia plugged the address into Google Maps. "It'll take us twenty-three minutes. We should leave soon."

"In a minute." Ida was staring at her. "There's something you're not telling me. What is it?"

Julia fiddled with the address book, straightening it so that it was square with the counter.

"Julia Ann Spielman. I have known you your entire life. I held you when you were less than an hour old. I know when you're hiding something. Spill the beans. Now."

Julia fought off the tears that sprang to her eyes. She turned away and looked out the window. She'd never been good at hiding her emotions from Ida. It was no surprise that Ida was calling her out now.

"Do you remember when you were little and something upset you? You'd come running to me, and I'd pull you into my lap, and you'd tell me about whatever it was that was bothering you. We'd have a good talk about it. You always ended up feeling better. Do you remember?"

Of course Julia remembered. Her grandmother had been her best friend and confidant throughout her childhood and young adult years—until her parents threatened her about revealing her sexuality to Ida. The need to keep that secret created distance. But there were no secrets now, and Ida was all she had too.

"Grandma?" Still, she couldn't face her. "Did you ever…" Her voice faltered, and Julia needed a second to gather herself. She wrapped her arms around herself. "Did you ever make a match, and then regret it as soon as you made it?" Tears leaked out the side of Julia's eyes, and she shook her head to clear them.

Ida wrapped her arms around Julia from behind. "Oh, bubbeleh, what's this about? Hmm?"

"Nothing. It's nothing." Julia wiped her eyes on her sleeve. "Look at the time. We've got to get going or you'll be late. You know it takes time to get your walker in the car. In fact, I'll go get the car and bring it around front. Meet me out there in five minutes."

Julia broke free, nearly unbalancing Ida, and headed for the door. She never looked back. Hopefully, by the time she got the car and loaded Ida into the passenger seat, she would have control of her emotions again.

"Goldie? Goldie, are you in there?"

Goldie hit the mute button on the television and extracted herself from the recliner, where she'd been napping. "Coming. I'm coming. Stop breaking the door down."

Goldie opened the door, and Ida practically ran her over with the walker.

"Where's the fire?"

"Goldie, we've got big trouble." Ida banged into the wall, redirected herself, banged into the arm of the recliner, and finally came to a stop in front of the sofa.

"Sit, why don't you, before you destroy any more of my property."

"This is no time for levity, Gold-e-lah."

"I can see that."

Ida looked windblown and as though her hair was on fire. "Where have you been?"

"The doctor."

"Are you all right? Is it your heart?"

"Yes, yes. I'm fine. The doctor says I'll live another hundred years." Ida waved away Goldie's concerns. "That's not why I'm here."

"Sit, already. You're making me nervous."

"I'm too worked up to sit."

218

"What is it?"

"Did you put the plan in play?"

"What?"

"Did you call Julia when we talked about it and tell her you wanted her to go ahead with the matchmaking for your Rachel?"

"I did. I told you I would."

"Oy, Gold-e-lah." Ida leaned heavily on her walker.

"What is it? That's what we decided to do. To make them wake up and realize they were sweet on each other."

"I think it backfired."

"What are you talking about?"

"It backfired," Ida yelled. More quietly, she said, "It backfired. Oy, gevalt, did it backfire." She put her hand to her head.

"Explain, and for God's sake sit, before you fall down."

Finally, Ida sat on the edge of the sofa. "I called Julia this morning. Finally, after three calls, she called me back. She was out sick from work today, but she came down to take me to my doctor's appointment. She looked horrible—like death warmed over, only worse."

"You said she was sick, how did you expect her to look?"

"My Julia has never called in sick a day in her life. And I don't think she was sick, sick. You know what I mean?"

"Get to the point, Ida. I'm not getting any younger."

"I'm getting, I'm getting, already. So I said to her, 'Nu? Julia, what's wrong? Are you running a fever?' And she says she's not."

"Ida…"

"I'm getting, I'm getting. Are you going to let me tell the story, or what?"

"Then tell the story, already."

"I'm not going to get there any faster if you keep interrupting me."

Goldie took a deep breath and begged for patience. She gestured for Ida to continue.

"Okay, then. So I can tell something's desperately wrong. I know my Julia. I ask her again, 'What's wrong, bubbeleh?' At this point, she can't even look me in the eye. She turns away."

Ida demonstrated, and Goldie began counting to ten in her head. *Patience is a virtue.*

"Finally, she says to me, in this little girl voice, 'Grandma? Did you ever make a match and then immediately regret it?' Gold-e-lah, she said, and I quote, 'Did you ever make a match and then immediately regret it?' And she was crying!"

"What did you say?"

"I didn't get a chance to say anything; she ran out the door to get the car."

"She didn't say another word about it?"

"Not a single one."

"She didn't say anything on the ride there or back?"

"Gold-e-lah? I just told you, she said nothing, nada, zip."

When Goldie didn't say anything, Ida said, "Don't you see? She made a match for Rachel and it worked, and she's sick about it!"

Goldie's brow furrowed. "You don't know that."

"How can you say that? Of course, I know it. I know it in my bones. You should've seen the way she looked. The bags under her eyes had baggage. She was sick, all right—lovesick." Ida finally sat back into the sofa.

"All she did was ask you a question."

"What's your point? Whose side are you on? You don't believe me?"

Goldie was afraid Ida would begin foaming at the mouth at any second. "I didn't say that."

"You might as well have."

"Ida Pinsky, you are insufferable. I'm just trying to be sure you're not jumping to conclusions."

"Well, if you'd seen her, you'd agree."

Goldie lowered herself into her recliner. "Let's say you're right—"

"I am right."

"Let's say you're right," Goldie began again, "what do you think we should do?"

"I don't know, but we have to do something. Think, Gold-e-lah. What did Julia say when you called her?"

Goldie thought back. Julia certainly had been reluctant; it was Goldie who pushed the issue. Was it possible that Julia went ahead and made a match so quickly? It was possible, sure. But why the hurry? Nothing made sense. "We need to know more."

"What?" Ida asked.

"We don't have enough information. We need proof. We need Julia to tell us, in her own words, what she did."

"You don't believe me."

"It isn't that. Let me ask you this. Why would Julia go ahead and make a match so quickly if she was in love with Rachel? What was in it for her?"

"How should I know? She just mumbled something about closure, or disclosure, ethics, and some other nonsense. Honestly, I don't know what she was talking about."

"So she did say something else!"

"I would hardly call that something else. It didn't even make sense."

"Think, Ida. What, precisely, did Julia say about it?"

"I am thinking! I couldn't hear well, between the engine and the traffic…" After several seconds, Ida said, "I know what it was. She said she had committed a fatal error and violated her principles by failing to disclose something, something, something, I couldn't hear… And that ethically, she felt she had no choice but to go ahead with the match."

"Oh, no."

"Oh, no, what?" Ida asked.

Goldie shook her head. "This is my fault."

"Gold-e-lah, I don't want to say anything, but I think you've lost it."

"No, I haven't. Do you remember, back when this started and I hired Julia, she wasn't so sure it was the right thing to do?"

"No."

Goldie sighed in frustration. "Ida, Julia stood right here in this apartment and told us she had reservations."

"She did?"

"She did. She said she wasn't so sure it was kosher to find dates and send them to Rachel without Rachel knowing about it."

"She did?"

"Where were you when we were having the discussion, outer space?"

"There's no need to get nasty about it."

"We talked her into it. This is my fault. I have to fix this." Goldie could see that Ida didn't get it. "If Julia did go ahead and make this match for Rachel, it must be because she thinks there's a real reason she and Rachel can't be together. If you heard her correctly in the car—"

"I'm not the one with the hearing problem," Ida bristled.

"Like I said, if you heard Julia correctly, she thinks what she did was wrong. That's why she won't allow herself to be with Rachel."

"Huh?"

Goldie was losing patience. She remembered Ida's excitement at the idea of playing private eye at the restaurant. "We need to get Julia to spill the beans."

Ida stared at her blankly.

"We need to get Julia to talk so that I can incriminate myself—you know—take the blame."

Ida's eyes lit up. "You mean like on *Perry Mason* when he gets someone to take the stand and confess?"

"Exactly."

"What does that have to do with Julia and the matchmaking?"

Goldie pursed her lips in thought. This could work. "We could record what Julia says to us when I formally rehire her on Friday."

"Why would we do that?" Ida asked.

"If she's in love with Rachel—"

"She is."

"If she's in love with Rachel and she made a different match for her, we have to get her to admit it so that I can rightfully take the blame."

"I'm not following you."

"Ida, if Julia is in love with Rachel, why would she make a good match for her with someone else?"

"Beats me." Ida shrugged.

"If you heard her right—"

"I did."

"If you heard her right, she feels like she can't be with Rachel because she did something wrong. We need to get her to talk about that out loud so that we have it on tape. Then we play the tape for Rachel. When she hears it, she'll know the truth, and, if she feels the same way—"

"Of course she does."

"If she feels the same way, she'll realize she doesn't want to be with this other person, she wants to be with Julia. End of problem." *Unless Rachel can't forgive Julia, but we'll cross that bridge if we come to it.*

"I'm still not following you. But if you think it will work…"

"Trust me, it will work." *I hope.* "All we need is a cassette recorder."

"I saw an ad for all kinds of electronic gizmos at Walmart. There's one not too far from here."

"I'll get my car keys. You look out for nosy Evan."

Rachel sat staring at a blank Word document, her fingers poised over the keyboard in much the same way they'd been for the past three hours. Her hair stuck up at odd angles from where she'd run her fingers through it in frustration. Wadded up Kleenexes littered the desk, and an empty bottle of Diet Coke rested on a coaster next to the computer monitor. Freud dozed on his bed, a well-chewed Nylabone wedged between his paws.

All Rachel wanted to do was to go back to lying on the sofa, curled up in a fetal ball. Alas, she'd used up every excuse she could muster and Claudette was lurking out there, waiting for two more submissions to complete the package due to American Greetings by close of business today.

This, she reminded herself, was the reason only happily married, or happily single people should write romantic sentiments. How was she supposed to write about love when her heart had been put through a shredder?

"Self-pity will get you nowhere." Rachel sat up straighter. Malinda had suggested journaling. Long-form writing wasn't her style, though, and Rachel found herself coming up with more and more inventive ways to avoid her diary.

"Then do what you're good at," her therapist said. "Just do something to get your feelings out of that stuck place inside you."

Rachel excelled at short and sweet—that was why she was at the top of her field. Greeting card companies craved short and sweet. It was one of the first things she'd learned as a young, unseasoned writer. Customers perusing the racks and spinners spent an average of one and a half seconds reading a sentiment before they moved onto the next. Too much text was a killer.

Rachel had no idea if it would help, but one thing was certain—she needed to get unstuck in a hurry. She typed:

"Your smile lit up my world. Your betrayal left behind scorched earth. How will I ever learn to trust again?"

That should've felt good. Instead, Rachel blinked back tears. Surely, three days later, she should be done crying. Julia certainly wasn't moping around. Most likely, Rachel was nothing more to her than a name in her recent calls list. She typed again:

"With you, all my cares melted away, leaving a future filled with promise. With you, I thought I'd found home. Instead, you sold me like chattel."

Rachel sat back. Spelling out her feelings didn't improve her mood, nor heal her heart, but at least she'd bled out some of the toxicity. Now she could focus on the task at hand.

She closed the document and opened a fresh one, named it, and sat again, fingers poised over the keys. *I am successful. I am accomplished. I am enough. I am successful. I am accomplished. I am enough.* She typed:

"In your eyes I see reflected the joy of a life lived together, the promise of a lifetime of shared love, and all the happiness the universe has to offer. Happy anniversary, darling."

Rachel spaced down three lines. "Of all the women in the world, you chose me. I loved you from the start. Now I find that as we grow old together and the years unfold, I love you even more. Happy anniversary, my love. I am now and forever yours."

Rachel shoved back her chair and covered her mouth to stifle yet another sob. These were the things she longed for, and the things that she knew now she would never have with Julia.

Freud, sensing Rachel's distress, snatched up his groundhog and once again laid it on her lap. He sat in front of her, soulful eyes willing her to feel better. She ruffled his ears. How had she ever been afraid of this sensitive soul?

"You want a treat?" Freud wagged his tail and woofed softly. "Okay. Give me a second to send this to my editor and I'll go get you one."

Rachel saved and closed the file, opened her email, drafted a short note to Claudette and attached the file. She congratulated herself on beating the editor's deadline by a full half hour.

"Let's go, buddy." She and Freud adjourned to the kitchen, where she sliced an apple for him.

When he was finished, the two of them returned the office. "I don't have anything else for you, you mooch." When Freud licked his lips in expectation, she held out her empty hands for him to see.

Her computer chimed with an incoming email, and Rachel sat down to see what it was. Her brow furrowed. Claudette normally was quick, but this was a record. She clicked to open the email.

> Rachel, you and I have known each other a long time. As a result, I'm going to chalk this up to a prank or an error. At least that's my hope. If I don't have the REAL file in my inbox in the next fifteen minutes, I'll be forced to tell American Greetings that you failed to deliver and they should move on to the next writer.

Rachel gasped. What had happened? Admittedly, the sentiments she sent might not have been her best, but still, they didn't warrant such a vicious response.

She read the email again. The second reading only amplified her agitation. It made no sense. It had to be a misunderstanding. She reached blindly for the mouse and it fell on the floor. She dropped to her hands and knees and crawled under the desk to retrieve it. What was going on? She lifted up, and slammed her head into the bottom of the desk.

"Ouch! Damn it, damn it, damn it." She rubbed the sore spot, checked for clearance, and managed to get back into her chair without further incident. Her hands were shaking so hard it took her several attempts to highlight her outgoing email. She opened it and clicked on the attachment. Her breath stalled somewhere north of her lungs and south of her brain.

"Your smile lit up my world. Your betrayal left behind scorched earth. How will I ever learn to trust again?"

"With you, all my cares melted away, leaving a future filled with promise. With you, I thought I'd found home. Instead, you sold me like chattel."

She double-checked the file name and dropped her head into her hands. What a colossal cluster!

She hit reply to answer Claudette's email.

> Holy, Hannah! Please accept my deepest apologies. No, that was NOT the correct file. Attached please find the sentiments you requested for American Greetings. I hope you will find this work up to the high standard I hold for myself and consistent with the quality I have been delivering to you and your clients over these many years. Again, my deepest apologies. I promise you that will NEVER happen again.

Rachel triple-checked the file attachment and hit send. It was three minutes to the deadline. She clenched her fists to stop the shaking and waited.

It didn't take long. The email notification chimed and she squeezed the mouse so hard that her fingers turned white. *Please let this be good news.*

> Rachel,
> I understand that sometimes things happen. Hence the second chance. As I said, you and I have worked together for a long time. I know the level of your professionalism and the quality of your work. That's why I was so surprised to get the first file. I thought perhaps a rebellious teenager had gotten into your computer and was pulling a prank.
> I am much heartened to see the second file. That's more like it! Good work. The most recent verses have great bones. I'll firm these up and get them off to American Greetings posthaste. All the best...

Rachel threw her head back and pumped a fist in the air. *I am successful. I am accomplished. I am enough. I am successful. I am accomplished. I am enough.*

CHAPTER TWENTY

Julia gripped the steering wheel so hard she half expected it to bend. It was only one o'clock in the afternoon on Friday, which should be early enough, but still, how could she be sure Rachel wasn't here visiting Goldie? There was no way she could hide her feelings now. If she ran into Rachel...

No, it would be better for everyone concerned if they never saw each other again. Rachel could be with Heather and Julia could go on about her life. Misery crept up her spine, nearly paralyzing her. What kind of life would it be?

Until recently, Julia had thought herself satisfied with focusing on her career and making love matches on the side for others. Rachel had changed that forever. Now she craved what she could not have.

A loud rap on the window nearly sent Julia into the stratosphere. Grandma Ida stood there, waiting for her to open the car door.

"Are you planning to sit out here all day, or are you coming inside? I'm tired of watching you out the window. It gives me a crick in my neck."

"I love you too, Grandma." Julia got out of the car. "Why are you spying on me?"

"Me? I'm not spying on you. I just happened to be watching out the window and poof, there you were. I expected you'd be inside any second, but no. You were busy contemplating your navel, or in this case, your steering wheel. What exactly were you doing, anyway?"

"Nothing."

"Well, that was a whole lot of nothing. You were there for at least fifteen minutes. I probably accumulated three more gray hairs in the time you were sitting there."

"You already were fully gray, Grandma."

"Don't quibble with me."

The automatic doors opened and Julia led the way inside. She turned left and Ida bumped her with her walker from behind.

"Not that way."

"What do you mean, not that way? Your apartment is that way."

"I know. I'm not so demented that I don't know where I live. We're going directly to Goldie's place."

"G-Goldie's place?" Julia's nostrils flared. "Why?"

"Because she asked to see you, that's why." Ida sped up with the walker, so much so that Julia was afraid she would stumble.

"Slow down. What's your hurry?" Certainly Julia was in no rush to get there.

"Hurry? Who said anything about a hurry?" But Ida did not slow down.

"You'll fall. You need to be more careful."

"Oh, psshaww. And anyway, we're here." Ida banged on the door with the walker. "Gold-e-lah? We're here, my granddaughter Julia and me. Are you ready? I mean, are you decent? We're coming in now."

Julia quirked an eyebrow. Ida's tone was overly loud, and she seemed nervous. If Julia didn't know any better...

Goldie opened the door with such force it almost hit her in the face. "Come in, come in." She motioned for them to step inside. "Julia, what a surprise." Goldie was practically shouting.

"A surprise? You summoned me."

"Summoned? Now that's an exaggeration." Goldie held her jacket pocket practically in front of her face. "Come over here and sit right next to me." Goldie sat on the sofa and patted the spot next to her. She arranged her jacket on her lap oddly, as if trying to prop up the front pocket. Ida trailed behind and settled in the recliner where Goldie usually sat.

Julia's gaze swiveled from Goldie to Ida and back again. Why were they both acting so squirrelly?

"So, just to be clear…" Goldie said, still fondling her jacket strangely, "…I called you here because several months ago I, Goldie Horowitz, took it upon myself to ask you, Julia, to make a match for my granddaughter, Rachel. You didn't want to do it. I was the one who pushed you into it."

"I could have, and should have, refused," Julia said. "Why are we rehashing this now? It doesn't matter anymore."

"Of course it matters," Ida interjected. She leaned forward so far toward Goldie that she nearly fell out of the recliner. "The *circumstances* matter. They were extenuating."

Julia had no idea what was going on, but the one thing she knew for certain was that she wasn't going to sit here and talk about what she'd done. Her stomach already was rebelling at the thought of it.

"I pushed you into it," Goldie insisted. "You said you thought it was a bad idea from the start, didn't you?" She pointed her pocket at Julia.

"I told you I felt as though it was an ethical and moral violation without Rachel's consent, yes—"

"Aha!" Goldie declared triumphantly. "Like I said, you didn't do this because you wanted to."

Julia couldn't stand it anymore. "No, I didn't want to do it. I wouldn't have done it except that you wanted so badly for Rachel to be happy. I could see that… And I convinced myself that what I was doing was okay, because you had the best of intentions."

Goldie moved closer to her. "Go on," Goldie prodded.

Julia felt as though she was in the middle of a Kafka story, but she didn't care. She didn't care about any of it. What was done was done. "But it wasn't okay. As soon as I met Rachel, I knew that she didn't need my help getting dates. Heck, she didn't, and doesn't, need anyone's help. She's beautiful, kind, loving, warm, smart, and anybody would be lucky if she looked their way." Julia's voice cracked, and she cleared her throat.

"I kept convincing myself that I wasn't doing anything wrong. After all, I was just pointing potential matches toward her public Facebook profile. Whatever happened after that was between Rachel and the prospective match. I wasn't violating her privacy— matches could only see what Rachel let the world see. I made an ethical equivocation." Julia paused for a breath.

"The truth is, I was kidding myself. What I did was wrong, unequivocally wrong. Rachel had no idea how these women were finding her. I violated every code I live by. I knew better, and I did it anyway. Shame on me. Never in the course of running my dating service have I made, or attempted to make, a match that wasn't initiated by the person for whom the match would be made. Never." Julia dropped her head in her hands. "Until now."

"What was that?" Goldie asked. She moved closer still. "Can you pick your head up? I can't hear you clearly."

Julia lifted her head, not caring that Goldie and Ida could see the tears on her cheeks. "I said, until now. And it's ruined everything. Well, not for Rachel, because I hope she's going to get the happily ever after you wanted for her, Goldie."

"What are you saying?" Ida interjected. "What have you done, darling?"

Julia laughed mirthlessly. "I did exactly what Goldie wanted me to do. I made a match for Rachel with someone I pray will love her the way I do, and will give her the life she deserves."

"Why would you do that?" Ida exploded off the recliner and had to grab onto her walker to keep from falling.

"I did it because I'm in love with Rachel! There, I said it out loud." Julia lowered her voice. "I did it because I'm in love with your granddaughter, Goldie." Tears dripped off Julia's chin, and Goldie handed her a tissue. Then she handed her the whole box.

"I don't understand," Goldie said. "If you're so in love with my Rachel, why would you make her a match with someone else?"

"What I did was unforgivable. By making matches for her without her knowledge and consent, I was lying to Rachel."

"That wasn't a lie, darling. It wasn't yours to tell. It was Goldie's. Right, Goldie?" Ida gave her friend a pointed look.

"Exactly," Goldie answered.

"It was dishonest and disingenuous, and I'm ashamed of myself." Julia blew her nose.

"You have nothing to be ashamed of, dear girl." Goldie stroked Julia's cheek. "You only did what I asked of you because you're a kind-hearted soul—a good woman with a big heart."

"Don't you see? It doesn't matter why I did it. No good relationship can be built on the foundation of a lie. Trustworthiness, honesty, respect, and integrity." Julia ticked the

230

qualities off on her fingers. "These are the cornerstones of any good relationship. Someone as extraordinary as Rachel deserves a partner who loves her, cherishes her, respects her, and is trustworthy. I violated her trust before I even knew who she was, and I can't change that. What I did was unconscionable and unforgivable."

"I think you're being a little hard on yourself, darling."

"No, I'm not, Grandma. I'm not being hard enough on myself. It's too late, anyway. I made Rachel a match with a friend of mine—an attorney I work with who is a lovely, wonderful person, who is worthy of Rachel and will treat her well. I know Heather will do right by Rachel."

"You shouldn't have done that, Julia," Goldie said.

"What are you talking about? It's precisely what you wanted for Rachel."

Goldie shook her head. "What I wanted for Rachel was for her to fall in love with the perfect woman for her. That's not whoever this other woman is. That's you."

Julia dabbed at her eyes with a tissue. "I doubt it. And even if you were right, it's no good."

"I know love, Julia. Rachel is in love with you. And I can see that you're in love with her. Love is the most powerful thing in the universe. Love forgives. Love finds a way."

"I can never face Rachel again without telling her the truth. If I did, she'd be done with me for good, as she should be.

"It's just best for everyone if I never see her again. She can move forward with Heather and be happy. Besides, I imagine Heather told her who pointed her in Rachel's direction. If she didn't on the first date, she will soon enough. That will be the end of any hope I might harbor."

"Don't give up on Rachel, darling. You two are the perfect match." Now Ida was crying too.

Julia shook her head. Her heart felt like a lead cannonball. "Rachel deserves the very best. I let her down. She deserves better. If you love someone, set them free, right?"

"The heck with that old line. If you love someone, go after her!"

"I love you both. You, Goldie, and you, Grandma. I know you mean well, but I've finally done the right thing. And now, if you don't mind, I'd like to go home. I'm tired, and I'd like to be alone." Julie rose, kissed first Goldie and then Ida on the cheek, and walked out, closing the door quietly behind her.

∽✍✎∼

Goldie and Ida sat in stunned silence as the door clicked closed behind Julia.

Eventually, Ida said, "It's worse than I imagined. I've seen this before, yes, of course. Someone in my line of work is well acquainted with heartache. But my Julia? I've never seen her so distraught. This is not good, Gold-e-lah. I'm afraid for her."

"I know," Goldie said. "Do you want a can of Ensure?"

"What? How could you ask me that at a time like this?"

"I always think better after I've had a little pick-me-up."

"Eh. It can't hurt. What flavor?"

Goldie toddled over to the refrigerator and peered in. "I've got milk chocolate, vanilla, strawberry, and butter pecan."

"That's quite a selection. What? Are you opening a store?"

"What flavor do you want? I don't want to keep the door open, it's a waste of energy."

"I'll take a strawberry, please, and thank you."

Goldie came back with two glasses, one filled with strawberry Ensure, and the other with chocolate.

"To love," Ida said, raising her glass.

"To love," Goldie clinked glasses with Ida.

"So, first, did that contraption work, or not? You looked like you were trying to knit a sweater out of it."

Goldie pulled the candy-bar-sized device from her pocket. "Oh, my God. I forgot to turn the darned thing off." She pushed the red stop button.

"Never mind off. I'm more concerned about on," Ida said. "Please tell me you remembered to turn it on before Julia and I came in. I gave you plenty of warning."

Goldie held the recorder under the light so she could see better. "Of course I turned it on." She pushed play.

"Testing, one, two, three. Testing. Is this thing on?" Goldie's voice sounded tinny through the speakers.

"Well? Where's the rest?" Ida asked.

"Hold on, will you? In the meantime…" Goldie pointed to Ida's upper lip. "You've got a little mustache going on there." She handed Ida a napkin.

"How can you be so calm? Did you record the whole thing, or not? Because if all you've got is testing, we've got a big problem."

Goldie turned the recorder first this way, and then that.

"Well?"

"Stop pushing me, Ida. You're not helping." Goldie struggled to calm her nerves. She was certain the man at the store had said to push the orange button to record. She'd done that, hadn't she? Then, he said, just push play to listen to the recording. Simple enough.

She pushed play again. "Testing, one, two, three. Testing. Is this thing on?"

"You're kidding me with this, right? Because right now, we're finished," Ida said. She polished off her Ensure.

"The man said something about folders. Do you remember?"

"I was supposed to remember? You were the one making the purchase." Ida stood up, grabbed her walker, and paced with it, back and forth, back and forth. "I told you not to go for the cheap one, but no. You didn't want to spend the money."

"Genug! Stop it. You're driving me crazy. I'm trying to think here." Goldie's arthritic hands fumbled with the tiny device. She hunched over it under the light of the nearby lamp. On the screen in tiny letters she could make out the word, "Folders." She found a menu button. That looked promising. She clicked on that. Then she clicked on the folders button. Two folders flashed on the screen. Folder one was highlighted. She clicked on that.

"Testing, one, two…" As quickly as she could, she pushed the off button. Maybe what she wanted was folder two. But how could she get to it?

A knock on the door nearly scared her out of her disposable underwear.

"What if it's Rachel?" Ida whispered.

"That's not Rachel's knock," Goldie answered in a stage whisper.

"Mrs. Horowitz? Are you in there?"

"It's Evan," Goldie said. "What should I do?"

"Let him in. He's a young guy. He probably understands gizmos like these. Maybe he can help."

"Come!" Goldie yelled.

Evan, the certified nurse's assistant, entered carrying two small clear plastic cups, one with pills in it, and the other with water. "It's time for your afternoon pills, Mrs. Horowitz."

"Hello, Evan," Ida said.

"Hi, Mrs. Pinsky. Nice to see you again. If I'd known you were here, I'd have brought your medications too."

"No rush," Ida said.

Goldie put down the recorder and held out her hand for the pills. She took the cup of water and swallowed all of the pills at once.

"I don't know how you do that, Gold-e-lah. I can barely choke down one at a time."

Evan turned to leave.

"Wait!" Goldie picked up the recorder. "I wonder if you could help out two old ladies." She thought about batting her eyelashes for good measure, but nixed the idea.

"We have this gizmo," Ida said.

"What Ida is trying to say is, do you know how to work this thing?"

"I don't know," Evan said. "Let me have a look."

Goldie handed him the recorder. "It says it has folders. I think what we want must be in folder number two."

Goldie stood right next to Evan so she could see what he was doing. He pushed the menu button, then the folders. Folder one was highlighted.

"You're sure you don't want this one?"

"I'm almost positive," Goldie answered. "How do we get to that other folder?"

"I'm guessing we do this." Evan pushed an arrow key, and folder two blinked.

"Now what?"

"I guess we push play and see what happens," Evan said.

"Come in, come in." Goldie's voice boomed through the speaker. "Julia, what a surprise."

"A surprise? You summoned me."

"Summoned? Now that's an exaggeration. Come over here and sit right next to me."

There was rustling on the tape. "So, just to be clear…I called you here because several months ago I, Goldie Horowitz, took it upon myself to ask you, Julia, to make a match for my granddaughter, Rachel. You didn't want to do it. I was the one who pushed you into it."

"That's enough," Goldie said. She grabbed for the recorder and it fell to the carpet.

The recording continued to play. "I could have, and should have refused. Why are we rehashing this now? It doesn't matter anymore."

"Of course it matters." Ida's voice came through loud and clear. "The circumstances matter."

"I pushed you into it," Goldie was saying. "You said you thought it was a bad idea from the start, didn't you?"

"I told you I felt as though it was an ethical and moral violation without Rachel's consent, yes—"

Ida lunged for the recorder and her walker tipped over. Evan caught her just before she fell and set her upright, and the walker too.

"Let me get that," he said. He picked up the recorder, pushed the stop button, and carefully placed the item on the table as if it were something toxic. His eyes resembled a toad's—protruding and prominent.

The apartment went silent, but for the loud ticking of Goldie's kitchen clock.

"I'd better get going," Evan said, as he bolted for the door.

"Wait." Goldie trundled after him. "Can you please put it back to the beginning so that all I have to do is press play?" She asked it as sweetly as she could, then handed the recorder back to him.

"Sure thing, Mrs. Horowitz." He made short work of it and slipped out the door without another word.

When he was gone, Goldie and Ida burst out laughing. "Did you see the look on his face?" Ida asked, holding her belly. "I thought he was going to plotz right there on your living room rug."

"He couldn't get out of here fast enough," Goldie said. She was laughing so hard, tears leaked out the corners of her eyes.

When their laughter subsided, Ida said, "You know, I haven't had this much fun since I watched Moses get lost in the desert and refuse to stop to ask for directions. A woman would've stopped and asked directions, but not stubborn Moses."

"You were there, Ida?"

"Eh. Most days I feel old enough to have been a witness."

"In the good news department, we know the recording worked," Goldie said.

"Right. That's the important thing. How long before Rachel gets here?"

Goldie checked the clock. "Any second now."

"Okay. I'll make myself scarce." Ida squeezed Goldie's arm. "Good luck, Gold-e-lah. Remember, love conquers all."

Goldie nodded. This really, really needed to work.

CHAPTER TWENTY-ONE

Rachel stared at the pavement in the Shady Acres parking lot and forced her feet to move forward. She didn't want to see anyone, not even Grandma Goldie. If she could crawl into a cave and stay there for the rest of her life, and have some nearby shepherd leave bread crusts and water for her every day—that would suit her just fine.

Her phone erupted with the theme from "Jaws." Well, that was just perfect. She stopped walking in the middle of the parking lot. "Hello, Mother."

"Don't you 'hello, Mother,' me, young lady."

"What do you want?"

"What kind of way is that to talk to your mother? You call here at a time you know you're going to get my answering machine—"

"Voicemail."

"Don't interrupt me. You call here at an inconvenient time, hours before dinner, to cancel."

"Would you rather I hadn't called at all?"

"Don't sass me, Rachel. I'd rather you stopped making excuses and came to Shabbat dinner."

"I'm sorry, Mother. I'm simply not feeling up to it." That was certainly the truth.

"Are you running a fever? Throwing up? What?"

"I'll be fine, Mother. Listen, I've got to go."

"Why? Are you running for the john?"

"Goodbye, Mother."

"Don't hang—"

Rachel disconnected the call. "Up," she said. She walked the rest of the way to the entrance and paused at the automatic doors to collect herself. Goldie always knew when something was wrong. How was she going to be able to hide something this big from her?

She stepped through the doors and ran headlong into Ida, the last person—correction, the second-to-last person—she wanted to see.

"Hi, Ida."

"What?" Ida squinted at her as if she didn't know her. "Oh, is that you, Rachel? Are you going to see Goldie? Good. She'll be so happy to see you. Well, ta-ta! Have fun." Ida waved and revved her walker into high gear.

Rachel watched after her. Where was the fire? She turned the corner and passed one of the CNAs. What was his name? Evan. She waved and he averted his gaze.

Was today a full moon or something? Rachel continued to Goldie's apartment without further encounters of the strange kind.

"Hi, Grandma." She kissed Goldie's cheek.

"Hello, bubbeleh." Goldie wrapped her fingers around Rachel's upper arms. "Let me look at you." Rachel squirmed. "If you don't mind my saying, you look like yesterday's fish."

"Grandma!"

"I'm sorry, darling, but it's true. Come. Sit down. I'll make us some tea and you can tell me your troubles."

When Goldie was done fussing in the kitchenette, she carried the tea mugs into the living room. Rachel helped her set them on coasters on the end table.

"What's the matter, my Rachel?" Goldie smoothed Rachel's hair back, as she'd done when Rachel was a little girl sitting on her lap telling her the day's troubles.

Rachel swallowed hard, her resolve to say nothing crumbling. Her lower lip trembled and she bit it.

"Come here." Goldie pulled Rachel to her and held her. "Everything's going to be all right."

"No, it's not." Rachel's voice was muffled against Goldie's chest. "It never will be again."

"Nonsense. You'll see."

"You don't know, Grandma."

"I bet I know more than you think I do."

Rachel pulled back. "What does that mean?"

238

"Does this have to do with Ida's granddaughter, Julia?"

At the sound of that name, Rachel shivered. "N-no."

"Lying doesn't suit you, bubbeleh."

"Yes." Rachel sighed.

"Right. Well, I want to talk to you about that."

"You do?"

"I do." Goldie nodded. "Let me tell you a story."

"Please tell me it starts with, 'Once upon a time,' and ends with, 'Happily ever after,'" Rachel joked feebly.

"I'm hoping for that." Goldie took a sip of tea. "Sit back, darling. This may take a while."

Rachel made herself more comfortable, or at least as comfortable as she was going to be. What could Goldie possibly know, or have to tell her, about Julia?

"Do you remember the first time you met Julia?"

Did she remember? Of course. How could she forget? "It was the night I came to pick you up and take you to Yom Kippur break-fast."

"That's right. Julia arrived to pick up Ida at the same time you did."

"Why are you asking me this?"

"Be patient, bubbeleh. In time, everything will become clear." Goldie took another sip of tea. "You weren't supposed to meet her that night."

"What does that mean?"

"It means, you were never supposed to meet Julia."

"Why on earth not?" Indignation rose up inside Rachel's chest.

"Please don't be mad when I tell you this," Goldie began.

How could she be mad at Goldie about Julia? Rachel hoped this would start to make sense soon.

"This is my fault." Goldie's voice faltered and Rachel reached out for her.

"I love you, Grandma. I don't have a clue what you're talking about, but nothing is your fault."

"Oh, darling. It most definitely is. You see, some time before that night I asked Ida for help. You were so unhappy, and I thought that if you had love in your life—someone to share your life with—you would be so much happier."

"Oh, Grandma."

"I love you so much, Rachel."

"I love you too, Grandma, but why did you think Ida could help?"

"Back in the day, Ida was a shadchan."

"A…what?"

"A shadchan. A matchmaker. I thought maybe she could help me find you a match."

"Like they did in 'Fiddler on the Roof?'"

Goldie nodded. "Drink your tea, darling, before it gets cold."

Rachel had no desire to drink the tea, but she took a sip anyway.

"Ida said she was long retired, but her granddaughter was carrying on the tradition."

"Wait. Julia is a matchmaker?"

"Yes."

Had Julia lied to her? "I'm confused. She told me she was a jury consultant."

"Apparently, that's her main job. She runs some kind of computerized matchmaking company on the side."

Rachel tried to wrap her mind around the information.

"I asked Ida to introduce me to Julia for the purposes of hiring her, and she did, and I did."

"You asked Julia to find me dates?" Heat raced through Rachel's blood. "Without even asking me first if that's what I wanted?"

Goldie hung her head. "Yes."

"How could you do that to me? When was this?"

Goldie kept her head down. "Sometime late in the summer, I think."

Rachel did some quick calculating in her head. That was around the time random women started sending her private Facebook messages asking her on dates. She'd thought those had come her way as a result of Facebook changing its algorithms. Had all of those been generated by Julia? Mortification warred with anger until Rachel wasn't sure whether she wanted to run, to scream, or to let the ground swallow her whole.

"Rachel. I've known you since the day you were born, and I know that look. I can see now that maybe I made a mistake, but please understand that I only wanted for you to be happy."

"And you thought that would make me happy? Going on dates with random strangers selected by someone who didn't even know me?"

"I can see that you're angry. I understand why. But, bubbeleh, every week you would come here and tell me how miserable you were and how awful your dates were. I thought, if we could find you the right girl, your troubles would melt away."

"First of all, that's the most convoluted, wrong-headed strategy I've ever heard."

"I—"

Rachel held up a hand. "I'm not finished. Second of all, speaking of hearing, I thought you couldn't hear most of what I said. Grandma? Have you been faking deafness this whole time?"

Goldie blushed. "Not completely. I don't hear nearly as well as I used to…"

"Grandma! Why would you do that?"

"Have you met your mother? Living over there was making me nuts. I had to get sprung. In order to qualify for assisted living, you must need assistance with at least two areas of daily living. You remember that time I confused the stool softener with my blood pressure pills? Needing help with taking medications is strike one."

"Let me guess, deafness was strike two?"

"Exactly. Well, that and the time I forgot I left the gas on for the stove and nearly burned down the neighborhood."

"So then you didn't need to feign deafness, after all."

"Insurance, darling. Insurance. I wanted to make sure I got in."

"I can't believe you've been lying to me this whole time. I feel like an idiot."

"No, no, no. I wanted to tell you, but then you would've had to lie on my behalf, and I couldn't have you do that."

"So why tell me now?"

Goldie shrugged. "It's true confessions day. Which brings me back to the matter at hand."

"What more is there to talk about?" Rachel jumped up, stalked to the door, and whirled back around to face Goldie. "You hired Julia to meddle in my life, let her believe that I was so inept that I couldn't get a date unless someone else arranged it for me, and she steered likely candidates my way. Does that about sum it up? I can't begin to tell you how disappointed I am in you. You played me, Grandma! I feel like I don't even know you. I trusted you!" Rachel covered her face with her hands. "I trusted you."

"I know, bubbeleh. Please, come back and sit down. There's more to the story."

Rachel scrubbed her face and crossed her arms. How much more could there be? And how could it change anything?

Goldie pulled something from her jacket pocket. "I want you to listen to what's on this recording. It's important."

Before she could answer, Goldie pushed play.

When the recording finished playing, Goldie patted the spot next to her on the sofa. "Come closer, bubbeleh. I can't speak to you when you're so far away."

Rachel wasn't ready to let go of the very last shreds of her hurt and disappointment, but she did as Goldie asked.

"I can only imagine how hard this is for you. You feel like everyone you love has let you down. I let you down, Julia let you down..." Rachel started to say something, and Goldie put a hand on her arm. "Let me finish, please. But I'm still your bubbe, I've lived a long, long time, and I have some advice I hope you'll heed."

Goldie turned fully so that she and Rachel were practically nose to nose. "Great love only comes along once in a lifetime. Trust me, this I know for sure. Please don't pass up a chance for that one great love because Julia made a mistake."

"This wasn't like accidentally ruining a dress you borrowed, Grandma."

"No. No, it wasn't. You heard Julia on the gizmo. She knows how she feels. I ask you, who among us hasn't made a mistake in our lives? Who among us hasn't done something of which they were ashamed? Something they wish they could take back? Something they would do differently if they had a chance to do it over again?"

Goldie's blue eyes were filled with remorse and regret, and Rachel realized with a shock that she was speaking not only of Julia, but of herself, as well.

"I can't tell you what to do, bubbeleh. You're a grown woman. I know that now. You need to make up your own mind, and nobody knows your heart like you do. I ask only that you look—

really look—inside your heart, and ask yourself, what would you have done in Julia's position? And who would you be punishing by turning your back on her? Her? Or yourself?"

"Are you done?"

"One more thing. I know you could hear the words, but you didn't see her face. Julia is completely devastated by this. She's tearing herself apart. If you can't find it within your heart to love her and trust her with your heart, maybe you could at least forgive her. You think?"

Rachel closed her eyes and took a deep breath. "Is she really in love with me, Grandma? Are you positive?"

"I know this like I know my own face, darling. She is."

"Do you think I can trust her? How can I? She deceived me in the worst way."

"Was she trying to deceive you? Or was she trying to do the best she could to fulfill an old woman's honest wish for her granddaughter's happiness without violating that young woman's privacy?"

Rachel thought back to what Julia said. She only sent women to look at Rachel's public Facebook profile. She didn't in any way violate Rachel's choice to accept or reject overtures. Was what she did unforgivable? Should it be?

"Love like what Julia feels for you is rare, bubbeleh. If you feel as she does, go to her and tell her. Have a frank discussion. Work it out. Don't let your pride stand in the way."

"I love you, Grandma, but you're not off the hook yet."

"I love you too, bubbeleh. I've got big shoulders. I can take it. But, I'm tired. I think I'll take a rest if you don't mind."

"Are you okay?"

"I am. Just old and worn out."

Goldie rose and headed toward her bedroom. Rachel jumped up and took her by the elbow. She looked older and more frail than Rachel ever had seen her. This was her Grandma Goldie, her favorite person in the whole world. She wasn't going to be here forever. If something happened to her now and the last words she'd said to her were in anger…

She helped Goldie lie down on the bed and sat next to her. "I forgive you, Grandma. I know that what you did, you did out of concern and love for me. You didn't mean any harm."

"Certainly not, darling. If I'd been thinking more clearly, I would've realized how embarrassed you'd be. More importantly, I would've remembered what I've known all along—you don't need your bubbe meddling. You just needed to find your own confidence. Love shows up when you least expect it, and unfolds in ways you can't imagine." Goldie closed her eyes and drifted off to sleep.

Rachel sat for a few minutes, holding her hand. What harm had Goldie done? She'd wanted what any loving parent or grandparent should want for their child—love and happiness. Perhaps she'd gone about it the wrong way, but her heart? Her heart was unquestionably in the right place.

Rachel leaned over and kissed Goldie on the forehead. "I'll see you next week, Grandma. I love you."

"I love you too," Goldie mumbled. "Just in case you should want it, Julia's street address is on the counter in the kitchen."

Rachel chuckled. "Thank you, Grandma." She kissed Goldie once more for good measure and slipped out of the apartment.

As she walked through the parking lot, Rachel glanced at the piece of paper in her hand, surprised to know that Julia lived so close to where she lived. Rachel would have to stop and pick up Freud along the way. She had no dog walker scheduled, couldn't get one at this late hour, and there was no way he could hold it that long. If she hurried, she could get to Julia's before full dark.

CHAPTER TWENTY-TWO

Julia heard a strange commotion outside her living room window. She lay on the sofa in front of the window, a blanket pulled up to her chin. Her eyes were still puffy and swollen from crying, and her nose was red and sore from being blown too many times.

It sounded like a woman's voice. Then a dog barked—a deep, rich bass. Big dog, she decided.

The dog continued to bark, and the woman—Julia was certain now that it was a woman—sounded increasingly frantic. The noise was close enough that it might have been in her own driveway.

One more round of barking, and Julia scrambled to her knees. She pulled back the shade just enough to get a look outside.

"Holy sh—" Julia ducked down and pulled the shade tighter against her face so that she couldn't be seen. "You've got to be kidding me!"

Rachel stood in the middle of her driveway, staring into a Subaru Forester. She was exhorting the dog to do something. Carefully, Julia opened the window a crack so that she could hear more clearly.

"Freud, please. Just, step on that button there with your paw." Rachel mimed the motion. Freud barked, his breath steaming up the driver's side window.

"No." Rachel agitatedly ran her hand through her hair. "Okay. Just use your mouth. Use...your teeth...to pick up...the key fob...and bite...on that tiny button." Rachel demonstrated as she talked, her hair wild in the blustery wind. Freud barked again.

It was almost more than Julia could stand, except that it was a hilariously funny tableau, and Rachel was adorable.

245

"Please," Rachel whined. "Freud, you've got to help me out. I look like a dolt. Please, open the door and let me in."

Rachel slumped against the car in defeat, and Julia couldn't bear it. She ran into the bathroom, brushed her hair, threw off her sweats, jumped into a pair of jeans and a sweater, slipped into her loafers, and ran toward the front door.

She knew her makeup was a mess. She paused with her hand halfway to the door knob. Why was Rachel here? Had she found out that Julia had set up the date with Heather? Was she here to ream her out? Why else would she be here? Well, she wasn't going to find out standing on the inside of this door speculating, and clearly Rachel did need assistance. Julia pulled open the door and stepped out onto her front porch. She took a deep breath and tried to settle her heart.

"Hi." Julia approached slowly, her hands in her jeans pockets. "I don't want to intrude, but, well, you are in my driveway…" Up close, Rachel looked stunning, if distraught.

"Um… Hi." Rachel pointed to the car and Freud. She threw her hands up. "I locked my keys in the car and Freud's in there. Well, you can see that, obviously. And I can't get him to open the door. I've tried everything I can think of. I just put the keys down on the seat for a second so that I could get the leash from the back. Before I could get to the back door, the wind blew my door shut, and then Freud was excited and bumping around, and he must've stepped on the fob and…"

Rachel's lower lip trembled.

"Slow down. Breathe. It's okay." Julia cupped her hands to the window and peered in. "Hi, Freud! Remember me? Of course you don't. Don't worry. We'll get you out of there in a jiff, buddy. Just relax and stay calm."

Freud barked and wagged his tail.

"Right," Julia said. "Listen. Everything's going to be fine. The car's not running, and it's cool out. Freud's not in any danger. We'll just get someone over here to unlock the car and voilà, problem solved."

"You must think I'm a complete idiot," Rachel said.

"I think no such thing. These things happen. Do you have roadside assistance?"

"No."

"Right. Me, either. Don't worry about it, we've got other options. Why don't you come inside, I'll get you something to drink, and we can decide whether to call the police for help, or a locksmith."

"The police?"

"Yes. They regularly get these types of calls. Most of them carry around jimmies for just such occasions."

"This has never happened to me before."

"Really? I thought you looked like a seasoned pro out there." Julia did her best to sound cool and collected. *Keep it light and easy.* She led the way into the house.

"Do you think Freud will be okay? I left the back window cracked a smidge so that he could get some air while we were driving. I didn't want to open it too far in case he got the bright idea to jump out."

"Excellent thinking. He'll be fine, I promise. Besides, it won't take too long to get this sorted out." Julia took a critical look around. Apart from the blanket and pillow on the sofa and a half-empty box of Kleenex on the coffee table, the place was in good order.

She snapped up the blanket and pillow and threw them in the hall closet. "Have a seat. I'm sorry for the mess."

"Mess? This place is immaculate." Rachel sat on the sofa.

"Give me a second and I'll find what I'm looking for." Julia grabbed her phone from the end table and went through her list of contacts. She selected one and placed a call.

"Hey, Amy. I need your help. Are you on duty or off?"

"On."

"Anywhere close to my place?"

"Not too far. What's up?"

"My friend locked her keys in her car and her dog's in there. Can you please swing by and unlock it for us?"

"What make and model?"

"Subaru Forester."

"Roger that. I'll be there in a few."

"Thanks, pal." Julia put her phone down. "My friend will be here soon to help."

"You have a friend who's a cop?"

"I have a lot of friends who are cops."

"Oh."

They sat in awkward silence for a minute. "Can I get you something to drink?"

"No, thank you."

"Rachel?"

"Hmm?"

Time to face the gallows. "If it's not too forward, what are you doing here?"

"Oh!" Rachel sat up straighter.

There it was. Julia thrust her hands in her front pockets to hide the fact that they were shaking. She didn't trust her voice, so she said nothing.

"She played me the tape."

"What tape?" Julia asked.

"I forgot, you don't know." Rachel smiled at her apologetically. "Goldie recorded your conversation this morning."

"She…" It made sense now… The stilted speech, the weird fiddling with the jacket. How could she have missed it? Julie grabbed blindly for something to steady her. The end table was closest, so she leaned on that.

"I'm sorry. She didn't mean to invade your privacy," Rachel rushed on, "or do anything illegal or underhanded."

Goldie had recorded their conversation. Julia sifted through the things she had said—all of it damning, embarrassing, and incriminating. She closed her eyes and pinched her fingers on the bridge of her nose, where a headache was blooming.

"So, now you know," Julia said.

"Now I know."

"I-I'm so sorry, Rachel. For all of it. You didn't deserve any of it. I never meant to…" Julia let the sentence die on her lips. There was no justification for what she'd done. "I was wrong, and I'm sorry. I recognize that that doesn't cut the mustard or take away the hurt and anguish you must feel. I can't ever take it back, or undo it, although I wish with all my heart I could.

"I know it's unlikely that you'll forgive me or what I did, and I don't blame you. I hope you'll accept my apology, at least, and rest assured that, other than Goldie and Ida, nobody knows anything about it. Not even the women I sent to your profile. I told

248

them only that I saw someone I thought they might find interesting. That's all."

"Julia?"

"Yes?"

"Will you stop talking for a second?"

Julia swallowed hard and finally looked over at Rachel, who was watching her intently. Her expression was inscrutable.

"I'll admit," Rachel began, "I was stunned the other night when Heather told me you were the one who'd suggested she call me. It hurt. A lot. I enjoyed your company. I wanted to spend more time with you. It stung when you ran away from me and Freud in the park and never called or answered my calls after that. I missed you terribly; your absence left a huge void in my life." Rachel's voice shook, and she paused.

"When Heather said that, it felt like the worst slap in the face... Like you thought so little of me that you pawned me off on your friend like I was a commodity to trade or barter."

"No!" Julia shook her head. "No, no, no."

"Let me finish. I heard what you said on the tape. I heard your rationale for giving Heather my name. Let me say, that is the most bone-headed, misguidedly chivalrous, lousy thing anyone's ever tried to do for me."

"I'm sorry."

"I've got the floor," Rachel said.

"Right." Julia let go of the end table and stuffed her hands back in her pockets.

"Still. After listening to everything you told Goldie and Ida, I think I get it. I think I understand why you did what you did, how you tried to make it right, and why, in your twisted logic—and it was twisted—you thought simply coming clean with me was impossible."

"I—"

"I'm not done," Rachel said. "Goldie said something to me after playing me the tape, which, by the way, I begged her not to do because I felt that it violated your privacy. Then again, when has Goldie ever listened and not done exactly what she wanted to do?"

"Just like my grandmother," Julia said.

"Goldie said to me, and I'll probably mangle the quote, 'Great love only comes around once in a lifetime, if we're lucky. Don't pass up the opportunity because someone makes a mistake. We all make mistakes. Love is about forgiveness.' Well, that's more or less what her message was."

"Wise words."

"I'm still not done."

Julia clicked her jaw shut.

"I have a question for you, and I want you to think very carefully before you answer me."

"Okay."

"Did you mean what you said on the tape? Are you in love with me?"

Rachel looked up at Julia from underneath long lashes, her expression hopeful, vulnerable, and unsure. Julia's heart skipped a beat.

"I don't need to think about it, Rachel. I know. I know with all my heart and my very being that I am in love with you. I have been from the moment I saw you from across the street. I followed you into the Hallmark store near Shady Acres and pretended not to pay attention as you watched someone reading your greeting cards."

"You were spying on me?"

Julia shrugged. "Just the once, when Goldie first asked me to help you. I needed to have some sense of who you were, so that I could make sure that the women I sent your way would be people you were interested in, and people who might be right for you."

"Is there anything else you'd like to disclose?"

"Yes. That day, I bought twelve cards with your sentiments. They were the most beautiful, most tender words I'd ever read. I couldn't imagine that someone with such an obviously loving heart would need anybody's help with romance. I was correct, and I should've trusted my instincts right then. If I had, none of this would've happened."

"That's true. Then again, if you had, I might never have met you."

Julia shrugged. "Our grandmothers are best friends. We probably would've run into each other sooner or later."

"Don't ruin the moment, smart girl."

Julia smiled for the first time in what seemed like years. "Right. We might never have met. Gotcha."

"Let me ask you one more time, is there anything else you've kept from me?"

"No. Nothing. And I promise you, I would never, ever, keep anything from you again."

"Good. And you stand by the statement that you're in love with me? You're sure?"

"Rachel, I have never been surer of anything in my life."

"Good." Rachel nodded. "One more thing."

"Okay."

"Who did you give those cards to?"

"What?"

"The twelve greeting cards with my sentiments. Who did you give them to?"

Julia laughed. Then she looked at Rachel's face. "You're serious?"

"Of course."

"Nobody. They're right here." Julia reached in the end table drawer and pulled out the cards. "Satisfied?"

"Yes."

"Now can I ask you a question?"

"Sure."

"Grandma Ida says that she's certain that you're in love with me. Goldie agrees with her. I don't know how they can know that, but love was Grandma's business for longer than you and I have been alive. She reads love and romance the way I read potential jurors."

"That reminds me. You are a jury consultant, right? That was true?"

"Yes. Of course. My integrity is my bond." The doubt and uncertainty in Rachel's eyes was nearly Julia's undoing. "I never lied to you, Rachel. You never asked certain questions, and I didn't offer information freely, but I didn't lie. I would never do that."

"You omitted critical information. That's the same thing."

Julia nodded. She had to admit the truth of that. "Noted. And I promise never to do that again, either."

"Good."

"So, back to my question," Julia said. "Are Goldie and Ida right? Are you in love with me, Rachel?" Julia bowed her head. She didn't want to see what was in Rachel's eyes. She braced herself for the rejection she feared and hoped against.

"Yes."

Julia thought she must've misheard. "What did you say?"

"I said yes. Yes, I'm in love with you, Julia. If I weren't, I wouldn't be here, and Freud wouldn't be sitting out there barking his fool head off, locked in my car."

"I thought maybe you came to tell me off—to have your say."

"I came to see for myself what was in your heart. I came to see if I had it in my heart to forgive you, and if I could learn to trust you again."

"And?" Julia asked quietly.

For long seconds, Rachel didn't answer. Finally, she shrugged. "And, God help me, I can and I do."

"You do, what? Just to be clear."

"I forgive you. I trust that you'll never keep anything from me again, that you'll act in integrity, that you'll respect me enough to communicate clearly, openly, and honestly, and that you'll never make a colossal mistake like that again."

"So, where does that leave us?" Julia asked.

"You tell me."

Julia reached out for Rachel's hands and pulled her up to stand in front of her. "Rachel Wallach? I'd like to start over, if you'll let me."

"I'd love that." Rachel was smiling, and Julia felt her confidence rising by the second.

"Would you consider going on a date with me?"

"When?" Rachel asked.

"How about right now?"

"I'd like that very much."

Warmth spread through Julia. She said yes. Rachel said yes! She wanted to leap for joy. "I have an idea. But I'm going to need some help to execute it."

They both turned with a start as a police siren sounded briefly outside. Julia let go of Rachel's hands and they hustled outside.

The police officer was standing outside her vehicle, a slim jim in her hand.

"Hey, you." Julia hugged the woman and stood back. "Amy, this is my friend, Rachel. The car and the dog are hers."

"Your friend, huh? Looks like more than that from where I'm standing." Amy winked at Julia, and Julia blushed. "Aha! I'm right. I didn't think anyone would ever land this one. Congratulations," she said to Rachel.

"We're not—"

"Uh-huh. Save it. Let's get your pooch out of there, shall we?" Amy shoved the slim jim in between the door and the door frame, felt around, and after several tries, the lock popped open. "Is he friendly?"

"Yes," Rachel and Julia answered at the same time.

"Hi there, guy." Amy opened the car door and Freud came bounding out. He wagged his tail and licked her hand. "What's his name?"

"Freud," Rachel said.

"Froid? As in French for cold?"

"No," said Rachel, "Freud as in German for the famous father of psychoanalysis."

"Oh, that's awesome. I think."

"Hey, are you in a rush?" Julia asked. "Busy night?"

"Deathly slow for a Friday night, actually."

"I've got an idea, but we need your help."

"What do you have in mind?"

Julia glanced at Rachel. "We have a situation… Freud needs to visit an old friend—his person—who is in a skilled nursing facility. The problem is—"

"No pets allowed," Amy finished for her.

"Right." Julia looked to Rachel. She had a look of awed appreciation on her face, and Julia winked at her. "This guy, the dog's owner, is too sick and old ever to get out of that place. Rachel is taking care of the dog for him. But it just seems so wrong that Freud and Mr. Crawford will never get to say a proper goodbye."

"You want me to come with you to the nursing facility with Freud and make that happen?"

"Can you do that?" Julia asked.

Amy cocked her head to the side. "Why the heck not? It's the right thing to do."

"Really?" Rachel asked.

"Sure."

"How about right now?" Julia asked.

"Unless a call comes in. Where is this place?"

Julia glanced inquiringly at Rachel. She gave Amy the address.

"I know that one. Sure. It's not too far. Why don't you three follow me over there?"

"This is our first date?" Rachel mouthed to Julia.

Julia nodded.

❧

Rachel snapped Freud's leash on him. "I can't believe this is happening. I can't believe you're doing this for me."

"Technically, I'm doing it for Freud and Mr. Crawford, and even more technically, Amy's the one doing the heavy lifting."

Amy knocked on Rachel's window, and Rachel opened the door.

"Let's go." Amy took Freud's leash from Rachel.

"You think they'll give us any trouble?" Rachel said to Julia.

"I doubt it. Amy can be very persuasive."

"Were you two ever…?"

"Me and Amy? No! She's so not my type."

"What is your type, exactly?" Rachel asked.

"You."

"Smooth answer. Quick too."

They were at the front desk.

"Officer McGrath to see Mr. Crawford, ma'am."

The front desk attendant leaned over the desk. "We don't allow animals—"

"This is a special circumstance, ma'am. We won't be but a minute. Please point us in the right direction."

"I-We—"

"Ma'am? We're wasting valuable time. I promise you won't get in any trouble. Now, can you please direct us to Mr. Crawford's room?"

Rachel spoke up. "I know the way."

"Excellent," Amy said. "Thank you for your help, ma'am. As I said, we won't be but a minute."

Amy indicated that Rachel should lead the way. Freud, naturally, wanted to walk alongside Rachel, so Amy flanked them on the other side. Julia trailed behind.

When they got to Mr. Crawford's room, Rachel gently tapped on the door. It was partially open, so she pushed it to make the opening wider and peered around the door. Mr. Crawford was asleep in his chair.

"Let me go first," she whispered to Amy and Julia.

"Mr. Crawford?" Rachel approached the chair. "Mr. Crawford? It's Rachel." Blearily, Mr. Crawford opened his eyes. "Hi, Mr. Crawford. It's Rachel."

"Ray-shul."

"Right, that's it. I've got someone here who wants to see you. He's missed you." Rachel beckoned for Amy to bring Freud.

"You do it. I'll cry," Amy said to Julia.

Julia took Freud's leash and led him into the room. As soon as he saw Mr. Crawford, he bounded forward. "Whoa!"

Freud skidded to a stop in front of the chair, his whole body vibrating, his tail wagging wildly to and fro.

"Hey, bud!" Mr. Crawford's eyes lit up and he smiled lopsidedly. "Hey, bud," he slurred.

Freud moved forward until he was in between Mr. Crawford's legs. He leaned forward and licked him in the face.

"Easy, Freud." Rachel feared that he would hurt him.

"Hey, bud," Mr. Crawford continued to say. He patted Freud's fur.

"He sure misses you, Mr. Crawford." Rachel sniffed. "He sure misses you."

Mr. Crawford looked from the dog to Rachel and back. A smile split his face. It was grotesquely crooked, but it melted Rachel's heart. It was the first time she'd seen his face light up since before his stroke.

"We can't stay long," Amy said from the doorway.

"I know," Rachel said.

Freud seemed to understand. Gently, he slid his head under Mr. Crawford's hand. He nuzzled Mr. Crawford's side, and then reached up one more time and licked him on the cheek.

"Ove you too, bud."

It was the most Rachel had heard Mr. Crawford say since his stroke.

Freud blinked, stood up, backed away, and came to sit next to Rachel. He gazed up at her and Rachel could've sworn he winked. Surely, she was seeing things. Freud picked up the leash in his mouth from where it was lying slack on the floor and handed it to Rachel. Then he turned and led her toward the door.

He looked back one last time—they both did. Mr. Crawford smiled that lopsided smile and waved. "Think us," he said.

Julia looked at Rachel inquiringly.

"That was thank you," Rachel said. She squeezed Julia's arm. "Thank you," she said. "That was the most incredible thing you just did."

"I didn't do it," Julia reminded her, as Amy escorted them out of the facility. "Amy made it happen."

"It never would've been possible if you hadn't set it up." Rachel snuggled into Julia's side.

"Date's not over, you know."

"So this is our first official date?" Rachel asked. "I thought you were kidding."

"Can you think of a better way to spend it?"

Rachel thought for a second. "No, I can't."

They reached Rachel's car, and said goodbye to Amy.

"Thank you so much," Rachel said.

"You're very welcome." Amy leaned over and whispered in Rachel's ear. "Anybody who is that special to Julia is that special to me. She's a good egg. Hold onto her. And, for the record, I've never seen her look at anyone the way she looks at you, and I've known her most of her life."

"When you two are done conspiring, can we get going?" Julia asked.

Amy punched her in the arm. "See you around, Jules."

Rachel loaded Freud in the car and got behind the wheel. "Where to?"

"Not far," Julia replied. "Start driving."

Rachel followed the directions Julia gave her. When Julia had them turn up a gravel road, she got a little nervous. "Are you sure this is right?"

"Positive."

"It's not paved."

"Not yet."

"Are we trespassing?"

"Absolutely not." They drove a little farther. "Stop here."

"Here?" Rachel asked.

"Yep."

Rachel glanced around. "We're in the middle of nowhere."

"Not exactly nowhere," Julia corrected. The lights of the city glimmered in the near distance. She opened her window. An owl hooted. The scent of pine resin permeated the air, and the trees creaked in the wind.

"Okay, I'll bite. Where are we? You know all of my dates go horribly wrong, right?"

"Rachel?"

"Yes?"

"I'm going to give you a piece of advice I learned a long time ago from my grandmother."

"What's that?"

"When love doesn't happen for someone as wonderful as you are, it's because you're too busy trying to be whatever it is you think your date wants you to be."

"Is that right?"

"Mm-hmm. Rachel?"

"Yes?"

"All you ever need to do is be yourself. That's who I fell in love with. You're at your best when you're just—you."

"Even when I lock the keys in the car with the dog inside?"

Julia laughed. "Especially then." Julia closed the window, opened her door, and got out. "Come on, and don't forget the keys this time."

"Should I bring Freud?" Rachel peered into the back seat, where the dog was happily curled up on a blanket.

"Let him nap."

Rachel turned off the ignition, stowed the keys in her pocket, and exited the Subaru. She watched Julia in profile as Julia gazed at the view.

"Want to tell me where we are now?"

Julia turned to face Rachel fully. "Home."

"Pardon me?"

Julia took Rachel's hands and stared into her eyes. Rachel tried not to squirm. Julia's gaze was intense, as if she could see within.

"Say something," Rachel said.

"I've stood in this spot many times," Julia began, "always by myself. It felt so lonely. I told myself it would be okay. I just wasn't meant to have love in my life."

"Oh, Julia."

"Let me finish." She held a finger fleetingly to Rachel's lips, and then resumed holding Rachel's hand. "Someday, I plan to build a beautiful house on this plot of land. That's what Grandma Ida and my Grandpa Bernie meant to do. This was supposed to be the place where they lived out their lives, together and in love. But Grandpa Bernie died before they could realize the dream."

"That's so sad," Rachel said. "This is the land Ida signed over to you."

"Yes, it is. And when she did, she told me one thing. 'Julia, don't wait until it's too late. Make your dreams come true now. Life is too short to put things off.'" Julia smiled and squeezed Rachel's hands.

"I know it's too early, and we have a lot of issues to work through, but standing here with you like this, Rachel, this place finally feels like home."

Rachel nodded. "In the greeting card business, when a sentiment has a good foundation, the editor says it has great bones. That's what I think our relationship has—great bones."

"I like that," Julia said.

"Yes, by the way." Rachel said.

"I haven't asked a question."

"If I leave it to you, we might never get there. Yes, I want to build a life with you, Julia. Yes, I want this to work. Yes, I want true love and all of the things I write in cards for other people to experience. And, yes, I want those things with you. Yes, yes, yes."

"Rachel?"

"Yes?"

"Stop talking."

Julia's lips claimed hers, and Rachel melted into her embrace. So this was what all those sentiments felt like. She deepened the kiss.

THE END

About the Author

Lynn Ames is the best-selling author of The Kate & Jay series, *One ~ Love*, *Heartsong*, *Eyes on the Stars*, The Mission: Classified series, *All That Lies Within*, *Bright Lights of Summer*, *Great Bones*, and one of five authors of the collection *Outsiders*. She also is the writer/director/producer of the history-making documentary, "Extra Innings: The Real Story Behind the Bright Lights of Summer." This historically important documentary chronicles, for the first time ever in her own words, the real-life story of Hall-of-Famer Dot Wilkinson and the heyday of women's softball.

Lynn's fiction has garnered her a multitude of awards and honors, including five Goldie awards, the coveted Ann Bannon Popular Fiction Award (for *All That Lies Within*), and the Arizona Book Award for Best Gay/Lesbian book. Lynn is a two-time Lambda Literary Award (Lammy) Finalist and winner of a Rainbow Award for Lesbian Romance. *All That Lies Within* was additionally honored as one of the top ten lesbian books overall of 2013.

Ms. Ames is the founder of Phoenix Rising Press. She is also a former press secretary to the New York state senate minority leader and spokesperson for the nation's third-largest prison system. For more than half a decade, she was an award-winning broadcast journalist. She has been editor of a critically acclaimed national magazine and a nationally recognized speaker and public relations professional with a particular expertise in image, crisis communications planning, and crisis management.

More about the author, including contact information, news about sequels and other original upcoming works, video clips, author interviews, book excerpts, and purchasing assistance can be found at www.lynnames.com. You can also email Lynn at lynnames@lynnames.com, friend Lynn on Facebook and follow her on Twitter and YouTube.

Other Books in Print by Lynn Ames

Stand-Alone Romances
Bright Lights of Summer
ISBN: 978-1-936429-10-3

It's March, 1941. Captain America appears in a comic book for the very first time. New York City receives 18.1 inches of snow, its 3rd largest snowfall in history. In Holland, the Nazi occupiers forbid Jews to own businesses. In Poland, Heinrich Himmler inspects Auschwitz. World War II is raging in Europe, but America has yet to enter the fray.

And in Phoenix, Arizona, a 16-year-old scrap of a girl named Theodora "Dizzy" Hosler, takes the field to try out for the World Champion P.B.S.W. Ramblers softball team.

Set against the backdrop of perhaps the most dramatic time in US history, comes the story of Diz and Frannie, two women fueled by an unquenchable passion for the game of softball and feelings for each other that go far beyond the bounds of friendship. Will their love for the game bring them closer together or tear them apart?

All That Lies Within
ISBN: 978-1-936429-06-6

How far would you go to hide who you really are inside? And what do you do when you find the one person from whom hiding your true self isn't an option?

Glamorous movie star Dara Thomas has it all—an Oscar nomination, dozens of magazine covers proclaiming her the sexiest woman alive, and people of both sexes clamoring for her attention. She also has a carefully guarded secret life. As Constance Darrow, Dara writes Pulitzer Prize-winning fiction, an outlet that allows her to be so much more than just a pretty face.

Rebecca Minton is a professor of American Literature in love with the work of the mysterious, reclusive author Constance Darrow, with whom she strikes up a correspondence. A chance phrase in a letter leads her to a startling conclusion about the author.

What happens next will change the course of both of their lives forever.

Eyes on the Stars
ISBN: 978-1-936429-00-4

Jessie Keaton and Claudia Sherwood were as different as night and day. But when their nation needed experienced female pilots, their reactions were identical: heed the call. In early 1943, the two women joined the Women Airforce Service Pilots—WASP—and reported to Avenger Field in Sweetwater, Texas, where they promptly fell head-over-heels in love.

The life of a WASP was often perilous by definition. Being two women in love added another layer of complication entirely, leading to ostracism and worse. Like many others, Jessie and Claudia hid their relationship, going on dates with men to avert suspicion. The ruse worked well until one seemingly innocent afternoon ruined everything.

Two lives tragically altered. Two hearts ripped apart. And a second chance more than fifty years in the making.

From the airfields of World War II, to the East Room of the Obama White House, follow the lives of two extraordinary women whose love transcends time and place.

Heartsong
ISBN: 978-0-9840521-3-4

After three years spent mourning the death of her partner in a tragic climbing accident, Danica Warren has re-emerged in the public eye. With a best-selling memoir, a blockbuster movie about her heroic efforts to save three other climbers, and a successful career on the motivational speaking circuit, Danica has convinced herself that her life can be full without love.

When Chase Crosley walks into Danica's field of vision everything changes. Danica is suddenly faced with questions she's never pondered.

Is there really one love that transcends all concepts of space and time? One great love that joins two hearts so that they beat as one? One moment of recognition when twin flames join and burn together?

Will Danica and Chase be able to overcome the barriers standing between them and find forever? And can that love be sustained, even in the face of cruel circumstances and fate?

One ~ Love, *(formerly The Flip Side of Desire)*
ISBN: 978-0-9840521-2-7
Trystan Lightfoot allowed herself to love once in her life; the experience broke her heart and strengthened her resolve never to fall in love again. At forty, however, she still longs for the comfort of a woman's arms. She finds temporary solace in meaningless, albeit adventuresome encounters, burying her pain and her emotions deep inside where no one can reach. No one, that is, until she meets C.J. Winslow.

C.J. Winslow is the model-pretty-but-aging professional tennis star the Women's Tennis Federation is counting on to dispel the image that all great female tennis players are lesbians. And her lesbianism isn't the only secret she's hiding. A traumatic event from her childhood is taking its toll both on and off the court.

Together Trystan and C.J. must find a way beyond their pasts to discover lasting love.

The Kate and Jay Series
The Price of Fame
ISBN: 978-0-9840521-4-1
When local television news anchor Katherine Kyle is thrust into the national spotlight, it sets in motion a chain of events that will change her life forever. Jamison "Jay" Parker is an intensely career-driven Time magazine reporter. The first time she saw Kate, she fell in love. The last time she saw her, Kate was rescuing her. That was five years ago, and she never expected to see her again. Then circumstances and an assignment bring them back together.

Kate and Jay's lives intertwine, leading them on a journey to love and happiness, until fate and fame threaten to tear them apart. What is the price of fame? For Kate, the cost just might be everything. For Jay, it could be the other half of her soul.

The Cost of Commitment
ISBN: 978-0-9840521-5-8

Kate and Jay want nothing more than to focus on their love. But as Kate settles into a new profession, she and Jay are caught in the middle of a deadly scheme and find themselves pawns in a larger game in which the stakes are nothing less than control of the country.

In her novel of corruption, greed, romance, and danger, Lynn Ames takes us on an unforgettable journey of harrowing conspiracy—and establishes herself as a mistress of suspense.

The Cost of Commitment—it could be everything...

The Value of Valor
ISBN: 978-0-9840521-6-5

Katherine Kyle is the press secretary to the president of the United States. Her lover, Jamison Parker, is a respected writer for Time magazine. Separated by unthinkable tragedy, the two must struggle to survive against impossible odds...

A powerful, shadowy organization wants to advance its own global agenda. To succeed, the president must be eliminated. Only one person knows the truth and can put a stop to the scheme.

It will take every ounce of courage and strength Kate possesses to stay alive long enough to expose the plot. Meanwhile, Jay must cheat death and race across continents to be by her lover's side...

This hair-raising thriller will grip you from the start and won't let you go until the ride is over.

The Value of Valor—it's priceless.

Final Cut
ISBN: 978-1-936429-12-7
Nearly three decades ago, Katherine Kyle and Jamison Parker saved the life of the President of the United States, in the process exposing an exceedingly dangerous, powerful shadow organization. The entire episode came at great personal cost and forever changed the trajectory of the couple's lives.

Now at the peak of her career as one of the preeminent novelists of the day, Jay is finally ready to put the past to rest in a fictional treatment...until powerful government forces intervene.

Oscar-winning actress Dara Thomas and her new wife, screenwriter Rebecca Minton, may hold the key to disseminating the truth.

Two of the most visible, formidable power couples in the country stand against the might of a government hell-bent on keeping secrets.

From the hallowed halls of the White House to the glittering streets of Hollywood, this is one adventure for the books.

The Mission: Classified Series
Beyond Instinct – Book One in the Mission: Classified Series
ISBN: 978-1-936429-02-8

Vaughn Elliott is a member of the State Department's Diplomatic Security Force. Someone high up in the United States government has pulled rank, hand-selecting her to oversee security for a visit by congressional VIPs to the West African nation of Mali. The question is, who picked her for the job and why?

Sage McNally, a career diplomat, is the political officer at the US Embassy in Mali. As control officer for the congressional visit, she is tasked to brief Vaughn regarding the political climate in the region.

The two women are instantly attracted to each other and share a wild night of passion. The next morning, Sage disappears while running, leaving behind signs of a scuffle. Why was Sage taken and by whom? Where is she being held?

Vaughn's attempts to get answers are thwarted at every turn. Even Sage does not know why she's been targeted.

Independently, Sage and Vaughn struggle to make sense of the seemingly senseless. By the time each of them figures it out, it could be too late for Sage.

As the clock ticks inexorably toward the congressional visit, the stakes get even higher, and Vaughn is faced with unspeakable choices. Her decisions will make the difference between life and death. Will she choose duty or her own code of honor?

Above Reproach – Book Two in the Mission: Classified Series

ISBN: 978-1-936429-04-2

Sedona Ramos is a dedicated public servant. Fluent in three languages, with looks that allow her to pass for Hispanic, Native American, or Middle Eastern, she is a valuable asset to the super-secret National Security Agency. When she accidentally stumbles upon a mysterious series of satellite images revealing activity at a shuttered nuclear facility in war-torn Iraq, somebody wants her dead.

With danger lurking at every turn and not knowing who among her colleagues might be involved, Sedona risks her life to get the information to the one person she can trust—the president.

The implications of Sedona's discovery are clear and quite possibly catastrophic. Potential suspects include foreign terrorists, high-ranking Cabinet members, and assorted others. Whomever the president picks for this mission must be above reproach.

Vaughn Elliott is enjoying her self-imposed isolation on a remote island, content to live in quiet anonymity. But when old friend Katherine Kyle brings an urgent SOS from the president of the United States, duty trumps comfort.

Time is of the essence. Vaughn, Sedona, and a hand-picked team of ex-operatives and specialists must figure out what's really going on outside Baghdad, stop it, and unmask the forces behind the plot. If they fail at any point along the way, it could mean the loss of millions of lives.

Will Vaughn and company unravel the mysteries in time? The trail of clues stretches from the Middle East to Washington. The list of people who want to kill them is long. And the stakes have never been higher...

Anthology Collections
Outsiders
ISBN: 978-0-979-92545-0

What happens when you take five beloved, powerhouse authors, each with a unique voice and style, give them one word to work with, and put them between the sheets together, no holds barred?

Magic!!

Brisk Press presents Lynn Ames, Georgia Beers, JD Glass, Susan X. Meagher and Susan Smith, all together under the same cover with the aim to satisfy your every literary taste. This incredible combination offers something for everyone—a smorgasbord of fiction unlike anything you'll find anywhere else.

A Native American raised on the Reservation ventures outside the comfort and familiarity of her own world to help a lost soul embrace the gifts that set her apart. * A reluctantly wealthy woman uses all of her resources anonymously to help those who cannot help themselves. * Three individuals, three aspects of the self, combine to create balance and harmony at last for a popular trio of characters. * Two nomadic women from very different walks of life discover common ground—and a lot more—during a blackout in New York City. * A traditional, old school butch must confront her community and her own belief system when she falls for a much younger transman.

Five authors—five novellas. Outsiders—one remarkable book.

Specialty Books - Humor
Digging For Home, By Parker & Dixie Ames (discoverable under Lynn Ames because these canine kids are too young to cash a royalty check)
ISBN: 978-1-936429-08-0

We've all done it—sat there and wondered what our canine companions were thinking while staring at the television with us during a ball game. Ponder no more! Irrepressible golden retrievers Parker and Dixie Ames have made it their mission to take you inside the dugout for a dog's-eye view of the innings and outings of the great game of softball. Assisted by their Siberian husky pal Lucy McMan-West, an obliging cast of canine cohorts, a chicken, a turtle, and a llama named LaRue, the dynamic duo reminds us that softball is not about winning or losing—it's about finding the shortest route to the concession stand.

Filled with quirky explanations and colorful photo illustrations, *Digging for Home* is a tasty ballpark treat that's packed with heart, hilarity, and plenty of doggone good fun.

All Lynn Ames books are available through www.lynnames.com, from your favorite local bookstore, or through other online venues.

You can purchase other Phoenix Rising Press books
online at www.lynnames.com or at your local bookstore.

Published by
Phoenix Rising Press
Phoenix, AZ

Visit us on the Web: www.lynnames.com

Here at Phoenix Rising Press, our goal is to provide you, the reader, with top quality, entertaining, well-written, well-edited works that leave you wanting more.

Whether you crave romances, mysteries, historical fiction, short stories, thrillers, or something else, when you pick up a Phoenix Rising Press book, you know you've found a good read. So sit back, relax, get comfortable, and enjoy!

Phoenix Rising Press
Phoenix, AZ